REST ASSURED

Recent Titles by J.M. Gregson from Severn House

Lambert and Hook Mysteries

AN ACADEMIC DEATH
CLOSE CALL
DARKNESS VISIBLE
DEATH ON THE ELEVENTH HOLE
DIE HAPPY
GIRL GONE MISSING
A GOOD WALK SPOILED
IN VINO VERITAS
JUST DESSERTS
MORE THAN MEETS THE EYE
MORTAL TASTE
SOMETHING IS ROTTEN
TOO MUCH OF WATER
AN UNSUITABLE DEATH
MORE THAN MEETS THE EYE
CRY OF THE CHILDREN
REST ASSURED

Detective Inspector Peach Mysteries

DUSTY DEATH
TO KILL A WIFE
THE LANCASHIRE LEOPARD
A LITTLE LEARNING
LEAST OF EVILS
MERELY PLAYERS
MISSING, PRESUMED DEAD
MURDER AT THE LODGE
ONLY A GAME
PASTURES NEW
REMAINS TO BE SEEN
A TURBULENT PRIEST
THE WAGES OF SIN
WHO SAW HIM DIE?
WITCH'S SABBATH
WILD JUSTICE
LEAST OF EVILS
BROTHERS' TEARS

REST ASSURED

J.M. Gregson

Severn House

This first world edition published 2014
in Great Britain and in the USA by
SEVERN HOUSE PUBLISHERS LTD of
19 Cedar Road, Sutton, Surrey, England, SM2 5DA.
Trade paperback edition first published
in Great Britain and the USA 2014 by
SEVERN HOUSE PUBLISHERS LTD.

British Library Cataloguing in Publication Data

Gregson, J.M. author.
  Rest Assured.
  1. Lambert, John (Fictitious character)–Fiction. 2. Hook,
  Bert (Fictitious character)–Fiction. 3. Murder–
  Investigation–Fiction. 4. Tourist camps, hostels, etc.–
  Fiction. 5. Police–England–Gloucestershire–Fiction.
  6. Detective and mystery stories.
  I. Title
  823.9'14-dc23

ISBN-13: 978-07278-8377-3 (cased)
ISBN-13: 978-1-84751-510-0 (trade paper)

All Severn House titles are printed on acid-free paper.

Severn House Publishers support the Forest Stewardship Council™ [FSC™],
the leading international forest certification organisation. All our titles that
are printed on FSC certified paper carry the FSC logo.

MIX
Paper from
responsible sources
FSC
www.fsc.org   FSC® C013056

Typeset by Palimpsest Book Production Ltd.,
Falkirk, Stirlingshire, Scotland.
Printed and bound in Great Britain by
TJ International, Padstow, Cornwall.

To Paula and Fred Soutter,
long-time fans and experts on all manner of things

ONE

Detective Sergeant Bert Hook was surprised to see the woman looking so anxious when he answered his front door. For a moment, he didn't even recognize her. That wasn't good for a policeman. You needed a good memory for people you'd seen before. Bert usually prided himself on his memory for faces.

He was off duty when he was at home; perhaps that's why he'd switched off. He stirred his mind into reluctant action. He'd been working until nine in CID last night and then they'd had a couple of swift pints to unwind. He didn't seem to be able to shrug pints off as easily as he once had, in his cricketing days. They'd had five or six pints sometimes, after Herefordshire had enjoyed a good day. It had never been a problem the next morning, not in those days. It shouldn't be a problem now: he was forty-three, not seventy-three, for God's sake. But as Chief Superintendent Lambert was wont to remind him, God seemed to have very little connection with the doings of policemen nowadays.

He knew who this woman was now, but that only made him feel more guilty. A neighbour – next door but one, he was almost sure. He said hastily, 'I'll go and find Eleanor for you.'

'No. No, it's you I want to see.' The woman moved her weight from right foot to left foot and then back again, like an embarrassed adolescent. 'It's you I need to see, Sergeant Hook.'

She was upset. It had taken her a big effort to come here. Hook, who was a sensitive man beneath his gruff exterior, divined that and wanted to help her. He forced a smile, cast his Saturday-morning lethargy aside and said with all the grace he could muster, 'You'd better come in, Mrs Ramsbottom.'

He'd remembered her name now, as well as her face: that was better. That was a little more professional. But it was easier when the name was slightly ridiculous, like this one.

He studiously avoided any suggestion of a smile and led her into the deserted front room. They called it the dining room, but it was the boys' homework room, really. Some of their books were still open on the table from last night's efforts. He swept them quickly into a pile and put them on the sideboard, then drew back one of the dining chairs at the table and invited his visitor to sit.

She sat on the very edge of the hard chair, as if recognizing that she was here on sufferance. Bert didn't think she'd ever been in his house before, unless she had enjoyed some private tryst with Eleanor in his absence. But he and Eleanor didn't have secrets: she'd have told him about it. He listened to the boys shouting at each other upstairs and wished that they would shut up. Mrs Ramsbottom had screwed up her resources to come here. She deserved at least a respectful hearing – not that you could expect boys to think like that, even if they'd realized that she was here.

She had a good bust, he thought suddenly, as she leaned forward a little and stared at the table in front of her. You somehow didn't expect women to have good figures, when they were housewives and had names like Ramsbottom. That was both sexist and stupid; he must really be relaxing at the weekend.

He said with a rather desperate seriousness, 'What can I do to help you, Mrs Ramsbottom?'

'It's probably nothing, really. It's probably just me being stupid.'

'If I had a fiver for every time I've heard someone say that, I'd be a rich man, Mrs Ramsbottom.'

She gave her first little smile, appreciating his encouragement. 'It's Lisa. You should call me Lisa. We're neighbours, after all. That's why I'm here, isn't it? I hope this isn't an imposition.'

'It's not an imposition, Lisa. I'm happy to give you whatever help I can. But I should warn you that people often think people like me can do far more than we actually can. I usually end up telling them to go into their local police station and follow the standard procedures.'

Her hand flew suddenly to her lips. 'I couldn't do that, Sergeant Hook. They'd laugh at me, I'm sure.' She looked at him anxiously. 'It's all right to call you Sergeant, isn't it?'

He smiled at her, trying to relax the tautness which was evident even though she was now seated. 'Strictly speaking, it's Detective Sergeant Hook. But that's when I'm at the station and on duty. Here, it's Bert. We're neighbours, as you said.'

A wider smile now. Her gratitude was out of proportion to what he had offered, but he sensed that she was relieved that she hadn't been rebuffed. He said, 'It's much better that you tell me about what's worrying you. I see a lot of life at Oldford police station. It's not all good, but at least it helps to put things in proportion. Perhaps my experience can help you now.'

She looked round, seeing first his wedding photograph, with a younger Hook looking shy and uneasy beside a radiant Eleanor, then the pictures of the boys when they were small, then the one of a very serious thirteen-year-old Jack in his new cricket flannels, playing a studious forward defensive shot. She said apologetically, 'It seems silly here, where everything's so normal. But it was scary, when it happened.'

'That's often the way of things. The context alters them. Sometimes, in the full light of day, on a quiet Saturday morning like this, things seem less threatening than they do at night, or when you're left on your own with them.'

Just when Bert was into his therapy act, there was a huge crash from upstairs and a yell of protest from his younger son. His father put his head into the hall and called, 'Quiet up there! We've got a visitor down here, Luke, in case you didn't know.'

A sudden cascade of footsteps down the stairs, a precipitate arrival of two teenage boys in the hall. Jack appeared in the open doorway. 'Sorry, Mrs Ramsbottom. We didn't realize you were here. It was Luke, you see. He dropped his tennis racket.'

Bert wondered why his elder son was trying so hard to be polite to their visitor. Then he remembered belatedly that the woman sitting at his dining table had a rather pretty daughter who was in the same year as Jack at school – very likely in the same class, for all he knew. He said sternly, 'What we want is for both of you boys to be quiet. Go into the garden, if you like. Help Mum unload the food she's bought, when she gets back from the shops. Give us a little quiet and privacy in here, that's all.'

He shut the door firmly on the boisterous energy in his hall and smiled at his anxious visitor. 'Kids! Sometimes it's easier to do these things at the station. But they won't interrupt us now. They know the score.'

'They're good boys, Bert.' She forced herself to use the unfamiliar name. 'Well, Jack is, anyway. I hardly know Luke. But they're a credit to you and Eleanor.'

'Thanks. But you didn't come here to tell me that, did you?'

'No.' Lisa Ramsbottom twined her fingers on the table in front of her, inspecting the varnish on her nails. 'I came because I'm scared. Someone keeps threatening to kill me.'

TWO

The new Chief Constable looked very smart in his beautifully tailored uniform. Important to give the public the best impression, he always thought. And you never knew when you might be on show without notice. It wasn't just the press who wanted quotes; in these days of local radio and regional TV, you were likely to be cornered at any time. Usually you could only say the standard things: the police were aware of all the circumstances and the investigation was proceeding. But he thought they carried a little more conviction if you were smart.

Today Gordon Armstrong lacked the normal breezy confidence which had been such an asset in his progress to high office. This was a private meeting, where he would be judged strictly on the words he used rather than the overall impression he created. This was a policeman, a man who operated in the same world as he did. The usual clichés would be seen as exactly what they were if he used them here. The man who was being ushered into the room knew the intricacies of the police service as well as he did; indeed, he knew the workings of one particular branch of it better than his new chief constable did.

The fact that Chief Superintendent John Lambert was older than Armstrong inhibited him a little, but he had dealt with that situation quite a few times since he had been appointed Chief Constable of Gloucestershire and Herefordshire. What he had not had to deal with before was an older man of this standing. John Lambert had a local, and perhaps by now a national, reputation. He was a man better known to the public than the urbane and highly polished Armstrong was himself. Gordon Armstrong wasn't used to dealing with police celebrities, and still less with a man referred to by the tabloids as a 'super-sleuth'. He wasn't looking forward to the experience.

Armstrong had rather hoped that he wouldn't have to do this. He had expected that by now Lambert would be either retired or on the verge of retirement. In that case it wouldn't have been necessary to meet him one to one. He could have presided over the man's retirement, presented him with gifts, and offered the sort of eulogy on an illustrious career in which he was practised and fluent. But Lambert had been so successful that the Home Office had taken the initiative in offering him a three-year extension to his normal service. That meant that this ageing luminary was now very definitely a member of staff for some time to come.

Armstrong had arranged for coffee to be brought in with the man's arrival, served in the best china cups and saucers, which were usually reserved for civic dignitaries. He dismissed the minion and poured the coffee himself. He could not tell from the impassive, lined face of the very tall man sitting before him whether he recognized the honour that was thus being bestowed upon him by his Chief Constable.

He offered the biscuits, eschewed them himself after Lambert's refusal, and came and sat down in the armchair opposite the one in which he had installed the Chief Superintendent. 'I thought it would be useful if we had a little chat, John. I like to feel I know my senior staff.' He crossed his legs and relaxed his shoulders. It was always best to give people the impression you had allotted plenty of time to them, even when you knew that your next appointment was only twenty minutes away.

'It's good of you to take the time, sir.' Lambert could play these games with the best of them, though not for long: patience wasn't his strongest suit, in situations like this. He was a problem-solver, not a diplomat. The modern world and the police service within it needed people like Gordon Armstrong, he was sure, but John Lambert would never be one of them. That wasn't prissiness: he knew he simply didn't have the skills or the patience to be a modern mandarin.

Armstrong said, 'I wanted your overview of CID in the area. There is no one better qualified to offer a confidential opinion to me.'

'I'm afraid I shall be a disappointment. I try to ensure that there is minimal corruption and maximum efficiency in the CID section for which I am responsible. I don't really have an overview beyond that. I took a decision many years ago now that I was happiest and most efficient when working directly on particular crimes and that I didn't want further promotion and more general responsibilities.'

They were phrases he'd trotted out many times over the years, but not recently. Armstrong recognized them for what they were and said with a smile, 'You're saying that you might well have been sitting in my chair at this moment, had you not chosen to stay in your present post.'

'I don't think I would ever have made that chair. I would have become impatient and thus inefficient long before I became a Chief Constable.'

'You are too modest, John. You could have done it, if you'd put your mind to it. But you chose not to do that. You despise some of the skills you would have needed to exercise to reach this office.'

'No, sir. I don't despise them. I recognize them as very necessary in today's world, where you have constantly to be the public face of the police service. Forty years ago, some chief constables could blunder through the diplomatic aspects of their jobs, if they were efficient thief-takers. That isn't so today. And I don't despise the skills involved: I simply don't possess them.'

'You've got the skills, John. You've chosen not to use them, that's all.'

'Let's agree to differ. I'm happy where I am, and I'm even more happy that people like you are able to handle the things I wouldn't have been much good at.'

'You can be as modern as any of us, when it's necessary.'

Lambert took a sip of his coffee and evaluated that word 'modern'. It carried such a multitude of meanings that you needed a context for it, before you decided whether it was a compliment or an insult. Or, as he suspected it was in the mouth of this man, a studiously neutral word. 'I'm often told I'm something of a dinosaur. Not least by DI Rushton, who handles the internet for me and co-ordinates the information on major investigations. I don't reject the description.'

'You don't sit behind a desk and direct others, as most chief supers do.'

The new man had done his homework on this veteran, whom he was now treating with a kind of cautious reverence. Lambert hadn't met much reverence and he wasn't at ease with it. 'I maintain that what I do is efficient. If it ain't broken, you don't need to fix it.'

'And you produce results. As long as you do, I'm happy to go along with your methods, even if some would consider them out of date.'

The first hint of a threat. But the man had to assert his authority. Don't be so sensitive, Lambert. He can't hurt you. If the worst came to the worst, you could walk away. But there's no need to be so negative: the new CC is merely doing what you'd expect him to do. And look at the coffee and the best china: he's treating you with kid gloves.

Lambert forced a smile. 'Contrary to popular police and tabloid press opinion, I do sit behind my desk and direct others for a large proportion of my time, sir. But when there is a major investigation, I like to be what most people now call hands-on. I find I get a clear idea of the issues and the possibilities if I get out and about and speak to major suspects myself. I'm immodest enough to think that I've acquired a certain expertise over the years, and that it is better to use it directly than to expect others to produce what I'm looking for.'

'My predecessor said you're the shrewdest copper he's ever met. He said you let people talk themselves into trouble and he still doesn't know quite how you do it.'

Good old Douglas Gibson. We had our differences, but he always did his best for me, when it mattered. As it did when he was speaking to his replacement as CC. Hope he's enjoying his retirement and his painting in oils; Gibson never enjoyed his garden and his roses, as retired coppers are supposed to do. Lambert lifted his head and smiled. 'That sounds a little too kind, even a little sentimental, though I'm grateful for Mr Gibson's thoughts. I operate in the way which seems most efficient for my unit. I also enjoy myself much more operating that way, though one can't speak publicly of enjoyment when the investigation of serious crimes is one's concern.'

'You enjoy what you're good at, like most of us. In your case, that's the direct business of investigation at the crime face.'

'Fair description, sir. But I'm part of a team. I don't neglect the coordination of an investigation and the efficient filing and cross-referencing of the huge amount of information that accrues round any major crime. Inspector Rushton is far more efficient in those things than I could ever be.'

'And the doughty DS Hook is an efficient bagman for you, as you put yourself about among those involved in major crimes.'

This man really has done his homework. Treat him with due respect, Lambert. 'DS Hook is a remarkable man, sir. He has twice refused to put himself forward for Detective Inspector rank because he enjoys his present work. That is unique in my experience: a man who recognizes that he is happy and efficient in his daily work and does not wish to jeopardize that for the sake of promotion. Hook completed an Open University degree last year, after five years of part-time study – one of the very few policemen who have done that. I like to think he complements whatever skills I have in dealing with the vast cross-section of humanity we encounter.' He grinned. 'Bert Hook is far shrewder than he looks, and that in itself is an advantage.'

'Plainly, loyalty to your staff is one of your great virtues, John.'

He's determined to use my first name whenever he can. Why on earth should I be so grudging and suspicious, when it's probably well meant? But Lambert heard himself sounding priggish as he said, 'I speak as I find, sir. And I confess I've been selfish, over the last few years. I've hand-picked staff who suit my way of working and set up my own team. If I tell you that they're efficient in their roles, it's no more than the truth.'

'And I'm assuring you that I don't propose to interfere with your methods. That's one of the reasons for this morning's meeting.'

'As long as they continue to produce results, sir.'

Gordon Armstrong was not at all discomfited by this prickly reminder of what he'd said earlier. 'That would apply to any system, surely, John? If it wasn't producing results, we'd want to examine it and see what improvements we could introduce. I suppose that would be "hands-on" for a chief constable, wouldn't it?'

Lambert grinned again and felt a little easier. The man had a sense of humour. Why had he assumed that a GSOH was surgically removed once you reached the higher echelons of the police service? 'It would indeed, sir. I like to think I'd be studying my team even more intensively than you, if it came to that.'

'I'm sure you would. What would you say is the greatest problem facing the modern police service, John? Or the CID section of it, if you prefer to confine yourself to that.'

A sudden switch, this. John Lambert had come here prepared to defend his methods and to receive bland assurances that they were acceptable. Now he was being asked for more general opinions. Was he being tested, or was his opinion genuinely sought? He said abruptly, 'Corruption, sir.'

There were a couple of seconds of silence before Armstrong nodded and said quietly, 'What sort of corruption, John?'

'It's not a new problem, sir. The service generally is much more honest and less corrupt than it was thirty years ago, when I was a young copper. The Met was a disgrace in those days. Things have been cleaned up. Some very good chief constables have had much to do with that.' He smiled again; he was long past his blushing days, but offering compliments didn't come easily to him. 'But individual corruption still exists. Coppers under pressure still try to fabricate evidence, or at least shape what evidence exists to their own ends. And the press connive at what is now the easiest and most widespread of corruptions for a modern copper. Too many men and women are passing on information for money to the press and other media. The temptations are there all the time, because the rewards are good and the prospects of being detected seem smaller than they used to be.'

'I agree with you on that. I want my senior staff to pass on the message that there will be zero tolerance of anyone releasing information for payment.'

'I'll certainly do that in the CID section, sir. Every copper who's corrupt is damaging the rest of us. That's one of the reasons why police officers are afraid to admit their occupation when they're socializing nowadays. That's much more pronounced than it was in my youth.'

'I take note of what you say and endorse it. Zero tolerance:

tell anyone who will listen. No, tell even those who don't want to listen!'

Armstrong had the good sense to close their meeting when they were agreed on something they both felt strongly about. The old bugger had been neither as prickly nor as out of date as he'd feared. He watched the cups and biscuits being cleared away and prepared for his next meeting with a feeling of satisfaction which he hadn't anticipated.

It had been good to talk to a senior man who was driven by a passionate aversion to crime and all its manifestations.

Sixty miles away from the Chief Constable and the most famous member of his staff, a woman of thirty-five was struggling with quite different problems.

Elfrida was a stupid name. She'd always thought that, even when she'd been a child and little semi-circles of adults had assured her that it wasn't. 'You're so lucky to have a name that's different!' they'd cooed at her. But when you were a child, you didn't want to be different. You wanted to be just like the rest. That way, they'd accept you and you wouldn't be noticed. You could watch the rest and think whatever you liked about them, so long as you weren't being noticed.

She'd tried making the best of it during her first year at university, when it had seemed fashionable to be different. She'd tried to spread the myth that Elfrida was unusual and thus interesting, that it gave her a start on others when it came to being noticed. But her heart had never been in that. She hadn't been sure how much she wanted to be noticed, even in the ever-changing cavalcade of student life. Then, towards the end of that first year, she'd heard three of her contemporaries mocking both her pretensions and her name, whilst she was closeted in the washroom. She'd promptly abandoned forever the pretence of liking her name.

She'd tried 'Fred' for a while. It had worked fine with the people who knew her. They'd accepted it and used it, after a week or two. But it led to tiresome explanations every time you met new people, and you couldn't use it on job applications when you came to the end of your degree and your teacher training. And some of the men apparently thought she was a lesbian, because she called herself Fred. She couldn't have that, so Fred had to go.

She was sitting in the staff room at the comprehensive school, worrying about her name when she should have been marking books. She'd come here for one term as a supply teacher, but they'd made her permanent, when the woman who had been on maternity leave had finally confirmed that she didn't wish to return. The new mum had said all along that she wasn't coming back, but the crazy system didn't allow the powers that be to accept that. She had the right to change her mind until the last minute, whilst her former pupils suffered at the hands of a succession of supply teachers.

Except that in this case they hadn't suffered. They'd had Elfrida Potts, and after the normal classroom trials of strength at the beginning of term, she'd asserted her control of her classes and achieved progress. More progress than they'd been making under pregnant Mrs Grieves, as far as Elfrida was able to divine from their exercise books and the few comments they volunteered. In her view, history could be either a lively experience or 'dead boring', the description most of her classes had volunteered to her during her first week at St Wilfred's.

Elfrida was doing her very best to give class 3B a lively experience on this Monday afternoon, when the temperature was far too low for May and the clouds scudded low and threatening past the windows. Anne of Cleves, Henry VIII's fourth wife, has gone down in history as 'the mare of Flanders'. So she was no looker: Elfrida quelled lively discussion on that topic from the male section of the class. But how did it feel for a foreign lady who had only a few phrases of English to be deposited in an alien land as a mere marriage pawn in a political game she did not understand? What did Anne feel after her rejection by Henry and her consignment to affluent obscurity in this strange country? How would you feel if that happened to you?

Mrs Potts sternly diverted an attempted discussion on whether the ageing English monarch could 'still get it up' and how much his new spouse's disappointing appearance might have contributed to that. She concentrated on the relative opulence in which Anne was allowed to live after her humiliations at court. She managed to draw from her class a good twenty minutes of lively exchanges and initiate some real learning. Without realizing it, her charges discovered a good deal of what life was like in sixteenth-century England for the various levels of society below the aristocracy.

At the end of the day, the teacher was left with a feeling of modest satisfaction. She knew by now that the teaching experience will rarely be perfect and that its successes will almost invariably have limitations. But now she had other, more personal concerns to occupy her. She told herself firmly that she was thirty-five, not nineteen, and that she should control the excitement she felt coursing through her veins.

That must be literally the case, because she felt her pulses racing as she sat in the staff room, crouching dutifully over some fifth-form essays and waiting for the rest of the staff to leave. She wondered again if her name would affect her relationship with him. Elfrida was bad enough, but she'd made it much worse when she'd married George Potts. It was all right for George, stuck away for weeks on the oil rigs. Your name was the least of your problems there. No doubt you lived for the money and the good times which came between the periods of intensive work.

But Potts made the Elfrida much worse. Elfrida Potts. It sounded like a name from a kids' comic. It would sit well alongside Desperate Dan and Dennis the Menace and Pansy Potter. Hopefully Wayne wouldn't be as conscious of her name as she was. Hopefully she'd set his hormones racing so fast that he wouldn't give a bugger about names. She was pretty sure hers were racing, along with her pulse. That must be a good start. But she needed privacy, if she was really to enjoy this. Go home to your wives and your loved ones, you teachers, for God's sake. And leave those of us with hormones to get on with it.

Mercifully, most of them took their work home with them rather than lingering over it in the staff room, as she had pretended to do. There were only two other cars in the staff car park when she put her case in the boot of the small blue Peugeot at quarter past five. They belonged to two older blokes who were running after-school clubs. The men wouldn't even see her leaving – and why should they be interested if they did? No need to become paranoid; that was a guaranteed method of drawing attention to yourself and your actions.

The lane which ran past the top of the corporation park. That's where they'd arranged to meet. Beside the third big tree past the gates, rather than at the gates themselves; he'd laughed at her when she'd stressed how important it was to be discreet about this. But she had a lot more to lose than he had. She hadn't said that to him, but she hoped he realized it.

She was scared that he wouldn't be there, that she'd have to wait and be conspicuous in her bright blue car. She'd always liked the colour until now. But tonight it seemed garish and far too noticeable in this quiet place. But he was there, bless him. Waiting for her, transferring his weight from one foot to the other and pretending to stare into the park on the other side of the big oak tree.

He was in the car almost before she had slid it to the kerb beside him. She glanced behind them, saw no one on this quiet road, and drew him swiftly to her. He kissed her more expertly than she had thought he would, his tongue hard and exploratory against her teeth, his hands caressing her shoulder blades and pressing her willing torso against his. She wanted the embrace to go on and on, but she pulled away from him after a long, exquisite moment. 'That was good!' she said breathlessly, wondering if she could check for any observers without offending him.

He smiled and said, as if he couldn't believe this, 'Mrs Potts!'

'It's Freda here!'

She wanted to kiss him again, to feel the uneven, breathless intimacy of him. He'd cleaned his teeth for her. And his body was very excited. She ran her hand down the inside of his thigh, feeling the warmth of the flesh beneath the thin denim of his jeans. Then she grasped his erect and very excited member, exulting in the gasp she heard from him at the move. No need to worry about her name here. His hormones were rampant and she was in charge of them.

Hormones dictated everything, in a boy of sixteen.

* * *

It was late in the day before Bert Hook got the chance to speak with Lambert alone. 'Did you put the Chief Constable right on things?'

'On a few things. I told him DS Hook was a bloody nuisance. An egghead who refused to become a DI.'

'Do I look like an egghead?'

The burly Hook held his arms wide in mute appeal. His features had the ruddy and weather-beaten hue of an outdoor man. His powerful physique had struck fear into the hearts of many a batsman as he had turned at the end of his pace-bowler's run. He looked like the archetypal village bobby, open to all, reliable as an oak in small matters, slow-moving and slow-thinking.

'That's just it, Bert. You present yourself as a thicko and yet you're subtle as a fox underneath. Dangerous man for a CC – he might even see you as a mole in his organization, not a fox. It's only fair that I should warn him against men like you.'

'Did he say that you should be pensioned off and digging your garden?'

'Not in so many words. He gave me coffee in china cups, so I was naturally suspicious. But he seems to be prepared to let us proceed as we've done in the past. So long as we produce results.'

'They all say that. It's like a nervous tic, with the top men. They have to say that to cover themselves. It's in case they want to bollock you and change the system, when they've got their feet securely under the table.'

'There you go again, thinking for yourself, offering your opinions. I'm not sure the latest manual allows a DS to do that. It's just as well I told Gordon Armstrong all about you.'

'And it's just as well that I know that a humble DS is far beneath the vision of a CC. He'll be much more worried about the super-sleuth in his cupboard.' Hook gave his chief a wide, bland smile, knowing just how much he hated the tabloid expression.

'Have you anything of CID interest, Bert, or have you just come in here to annoy me?'

Hook's yeoman brow was suddenly furrowed. 'Probably not. I expect you'll tell me to go away and sort out my own small problems, whilst you get on with major frauds and serial killers.'

Lambert sighed elaborately. 'Let's have it, Bert.'

'A neighbour of mine came in to see me on Saturday morning. The way neighbours do, when they're worried. Eleanor says the woman's not normally an alarmist, but I scarcely know her. She's called Lisa Ramsbottom, but we can't really hold that against her.'

'And what is it that's worrying the non-alarmist Mrs Ramsbottom? I'm assuming that she's a wife; that she volunteered herself for this surname.'

'She is indeed – so she may be a masochist. She says she's received death threats. I gave her the usual guff about anonymous threats usually coming from mistaken jokers, who have cruel minds but not the courage to reveal who they are.'

'And she didn't react well to that, or you wouldn't be in my office telling me about her now.'

'She said she was still worried. There's been more than one threat, apparently. She has a daughter and a husband. She's worried about them as well as herself.'

'As we would be ourselves, in the same circumstances.'

'Yes. They have a weekend retreat in one of these leisure parks. It seems most of the threats have been delivered there.'

'Where is this?'

'Somewhere up near Leominster, I think. In the northernmost tip of our patch. On the very edge of civilization – very nearly in Wales.'

'I forgot to tell the new CC that you were a raving racist. But I do think you should investigate, Bert. Get to know the northernmost tip of our patch.'

Lisa Ramsbottom had already invited him up there for a visit. There was a lake and a bowling green and a nine-hole golf course on the complex. He wasn't going to tell Lambert that. Bert sighed deeply. 'If I have to, I have to.'

THREE

'Y ou're welcome to spend a day at Twin Lakes whenever you like. I told you that.' Lisa Ramsbottom wished she'd had time to look in the mirror before she'd invited Bert Hook from next-door-but-one into her house. She'd whipped her pinafore off when the bell had rung, but she'd had time for nothing more. She was sure that she looked a mess.

'Thank you. I'd like to have a look round there when it's quiet, rather than full of people, if that could be arranged.'

'If you can make next Friday, that would be perfect. Ellie's off on a school trip with the netball team, so Jason and I are planning a long weekend in our place at Twin Lakes. They're classed as temporary homes and you can't live in them permanently, but they're like moveable bungalows, really. You and Eleanor could stay the night, if you'd like to.'

'Oh, I don't think we could manage that, because of the boys. But thanks for the thought.' And thanks for the presence of Jason at this mobile home on Friday, Bert thought. Some women thought CID men were glamorous conquests, even when they were as stolid and uninteresting as he was. 'Friday sounds perfect. I'll clear it with my boss. And I can easily drive up and back in the day. It can't be more than fifty miles from here.'

'It's almost exactly that. Bring your golf clubs.'

'I'll do that. It's much better that I seem like a friend on a social visit, if I'm to discover anything. That way, people won't be immediately on their guard against me.'

A game of golf whilst on paid police duty: things were looking up.

He was a big man and very black. Most people found him intimidating, at first. But George Martindale was warm and friendly; his broad smile and large, very white teeth helped people to feel at ease with him.

He was a very physical man. He worked long and hard with the council road team, and he never shirked his share of physical work, even when the foreman wasn't present. He was popular with the mixed gang of people who worked with him, because he was always willing to do more than his share, always cheerful, and always willing to accept his ration of the sometimes dubious banter which passed as humour during the rough and tumble of the working day.

George took racism in his stride. He never seemed to get upset when clumsy taunts were offered to him as wit. He was from Jamaica, he said. He never revealed whether he had been born there or whether he was a first-generation immigrant of Jamaican parents. No one was quite sure about his age and he never volunteered it. Early thirties, most people thought, but it was difficult to be certain, because he had an unlined face and clear dark eyes and not a grey hair among the crinkly black ones which grew so plentifully upon his large head.

There was an incident on this warm May day which showed that George Martindale should not be treated lightly. His formidable physique in itself made people cautious, but he was so affable that sometimes they didn't even consider that he might turn aggressive. Afterwards, it seemed to most of his fellow workers characteristic of George that he should react violently not on his own behalf but on someone else's.

The latest recruit to the gang was a stringy youth who was barely seventeen and who looked two years younger. Damien Field was willing but not over-bright; his temperament, combined with his physical limitations, led to a series of gibes from his insensitive seniors. When your thin arms worked with spades and picks, when you struggled hard to control the vigorous movements of a pneumatic drill, you were an easy target for men seeking to lighten their day with cheap humour.

They were repairing the pavement and road outside the main entrance to a now derelict building. The repeated passage of heavy lorries had caused serious potholes as well as broken flags over the years. It was heavy work and young Damien endured a series of gibes about his physical weakness. They became cruder and more sexual as the day went on. The fact that Field reacted only with a weak smile and an unconvincing pretence of finding the comments amusing only incited greater insults. According to his harassers, he was now not only incapable of getting a girl but incapable of 'giving her one' if he did. Damien didn't feel strong enough or well-established enough to tell his insulters to get lost.

In this context, that only made them bolder. They would go on baiting him and get ever more obscene until they wrung some sort of violent dismissal from him. Damien vaguely realized this, but he felt that if he turned aggressive they would bludgeon him and drive him out of this job he so badly needed. His dad was out of work and his mother was an invalid, but he couldn't tell them that. It would only show further weakness.

It was when Field almost lost control of the pneumatic drill, saw it sliding out of his grasp towards the horizontal, and had to switch it off that the day's incident occurred. The worst of his tormentors, a squat man with grimy tattoos upon his brawny forearms, was delighted to see Damien defeated. 'Too strong for a raving pooftah like you, those machines! Young lad with a delicate skin like yours could do much better as a rent boy in Brum. I could put you in touch with a man who pimps for young nancies like you, if you asked me nicely.'

The tattooed man was pinned against the grimy bricks of the windowless wall before he knew what was happening. He heard the stitching at the throat of his thick cotton shirt tear as his head was forced backwards, saw the button soaring yards from him as the pressure fired it away. The words from George Martindale came hot and loud in his ear. 'Lay off him, you stupid bugger! The lad's doing his best and he needs the work. It's hard enough for him, without stupid bullies like you making his life a fucking misery! I'm warning you, Jackson, for the one and only time. You'll be no use to man or woman without your balls. And that's how you'll be, if you don't lay off the lad!'

Jackson couldn't speak: his throat was in too tight a grip for that. The bricks felt as if they were grinding the back of his skull. He nodded frantically, his eyes bulbous with panic and physical stress. Martindale relaxed his grip very slowly. That in itself was a sign of his physical strength. His huge,

straight arm supported most of the squat man's weight; he
held him hard against the wall until he gradually allowed him
to descend again on to his own feet. George kept his black,
rounded face within a foot of his victim's. Jackson tried not
to look into it, but he couldn't fail to be conscious of the dark
brown eyes which glared so closely and so contemptuously
down upon him.

Jackson wanted to say that he hadn't meant any harm, to
whine out that it had only been fun and he hadn't meant
to hurt the lad. But it wouldn't have been convincing and he
knew it. He pulled at the neck of his shirt and turned away
from Martindale without looking at either Damien Field or
any of his workmates. The boy's champion watched Jackson's
retreat, then said to Damien, 'You need to keep those drills
very upright. Once they're off the vertical, they soon go out
of control. Most of us had trouble with them, when we started.'

The young man started the machine again, carefully obeying
his mentor's instructions. George Martindale moved back to
the other end of the workings and resumed his own work. The
six other men in the gang fell silent. They did not look at each
other for quite a long time.

Twin Lakes was a pleasant place amid pleasant countryside,
with the Welsh hills rising to the west of it and the rolling
countryside of Shropshire to the north.

Twin Lakes Country Holiday Park was the full name. These
weren't permanent homes – or not officially so. They could
be moved from site to site on the complex, with the use of a
huge vehicle to carry them, though it was rarely necessary to
do anything so radical. But they were about as far from caravans
and other forms of temporary residence as you could imagine
homes to be. They had full sanitation, double glazing, and
central heating. And gas and electricity were metered to every
one of the 110 homes on the site.

Their walls were thin, as befitted their official 'holiday home'
status, but they were better equipped and more comfortable
than the houses which many British city-dwellers occupied.
You were not allowed to live at Twin Lakes for the whole year:
to maintain their 'temporary' status, all residents had to move

out during the month of January. The owners of the site used that month for serious maintenance work. One or two of their tenants who had no other residence chose to spend their single homeless month in Spain or Florida, so as to fulfil their obligations as temporary residents at Twin Lakes.

Debbie Keane was one of those few who had lived increasingly on the site over the years since the beginning of the twenty-first century. Her husband, Walter, had a reputation as a recluse which he was happy to cultivate, but he used all the facilities of the site. He hadn't played crown green bowls at all until he had come here, but after a decade and more of practice, he was the best player on the site. He had become so by playing much of the time alone, for the site was quiet during the working week and almost deserted for many of the winter months.

Walter was fifty-five now, and the opportunities afforded by Twin Lakes suited one of his age and leanings. The nine-hole golf course was only 2200 yards long, so that length was not a problem. But it was tricky, and had become more so as the trees had grown taller and wider and thus narrowed the fairways. Walter and Debbie knew every lie upon the course and every one of its tricks; they were also respectively the Chairman and the Secretary of the handicap committee, which administered the number of shots allowed to the golfers who played cheerfully round here at the weekends.

The Keanes had the golf 'sewn up', in the rueful phrase of most of the people who used the facility. But it was not a very long or a very serious course and most people enjoyed the exercise more than the winning. And the Keanes indisputably knew more about the golf here and the people who played it than anyone else in the world, so it was logical that they should be in charge. The fact that they were willing and eager to offer their services and perform the complicated work they claimed was necessary to support their judgements was also very much in their favour. When you came here to relax at the weekends or on holiday, you didn't want to be bothered with boring administrative matters.

Walter sailed the lakes alone in his dinghy, because Debbie claimed that she didn't trust water and that it was good for her husband to have a hobby which enabled them to get away from each other. For her part, she was quite happy to walk her fox terrier in the extensive woods which formed the borders of the property and ran round the edges of the lakes which gave the place its name. The dog died in 2013, but Debbie continued to walk the familiar paths alone. She enjoyed the exercise, she said, as well as meeting the other owners, whom she quizzed in the woods on her daily walks.

Debbie was insatiably curious. She knew the business and most of the activities of almost everyone on the site, and she made it her interest and occupation to discover anything she did not know. Some thought her a tiresome busybody, but most regarded her with amusement as a harmless gossip. In exchange for a little information about their own lives, she provided them effortlessly with anything they cared to know about their fellow occupants.

Walter Keane was more of a puzzle to them. He said little and seemed to regard his wife's nosiness with an amused detachment. He was above such things, his silence seemed to say. He had his own concerns, which were far more important than the tittle-tattle which seemed to be of such concern to Mrs Keane. What exactly these concerns were, beyond bowls and golf and a little sailing, was not very clear. Recluses read a lot and thought a lot, didn't they? Perhaps that was what Walter Keane did, during the long hours and long days when Twin Lakes was but thinly populated.

There were more people around in midweek, now that May and the longer days were here. People took days off to make up long weekends, and those without children of school age sometimes took their holidays at this time, when the site was at its late-spring best and ancient towns like Hereford and Ludlow were easier to explore than they were in high summer.

Debbie Keane moved among the thirty or so people on the site and gathered information. Then she went back and related it to her husband, who listened dutifully and said very little. That is what people thought happened in the holiday home in the prime position by the lake. Walter seemed to be very patient and indulgent with the garrulous Debbie.

They would have been surprised to know the reality of the situation.

On Friday 17th May, Detective Sergeant Bert Hook drove north from his home near Tewkesbury and wondered just how much of a wild goose chase the day was about to provide.

In his home, Lisa Ramsbottom had not struck him as an alarmist. She had seemed apologetic about even contacting him. But when you felt that some unknown person was threatening you and perhaps your loved ones, it was no doubt difficult to keep a due sense of proportion. He'd seen it a couple of times before in his career and he understood it. The staid and sensible Bert felt he might even panic himself, if he was threatened like that. And he would certainly feel very violent, if anyone menaced Eleanor or the boys.

It was a pleasant drive. His milometer showed him as he skirted Leominster and approached Twin Lakes that he had come forty-eight miles. It was deep in the country, not far from the Welsh border, but he found it easily enough by following Lisa's detailed instructions. She was waiting for him at the office near the entrance when he arrived, a shapely figure in sage sweater and dark green trousers. She waved cheerfully at him, brushing back her dark blonde hair as the barrier rose to permit him to drive on to the site. 'I thought I'd meet you here. People struggle to find the right unit when they're all coloured light green and all look so similar from the outside.'

She was plainly nervous. He wondered if, now that she had brought him all this way, she felt that her fears were exaggerated and ridiculous, a feeling no doubt encouraged by the warm sun and the high white clouds scudding across the clear blue heavens. He said, 'It's probably better that you don't announce me as a policeman to anyone we meet here. People tend to clam up, or at least not speak as freely as they would normally, when they know there's a copper around.' He grinned, trying to dissipate the tension he felt between them that he should be here. 'Even one as off-duty and intent upon playing golf as this one is.'

She was still on edge, despite her determination before he

came that she would not be so. 'Our little course here isn't up to the standards of Ross-on-Wye, where you usually play.'

'It will be quite good enough to test me, Lisa. I've only been playing for two or three years – since I was finally persuaded to give up cricket. I'm more energetic than effective, as John Lambert puts it. He's one of those depressing straight-down-the-middle golfers.'

She was impressed by his proximity to the great man: even Lisa had read in the local press of the doings of John Lambert. She said, 'You'll have more time to improve, now that you've finished your Open University degree.' She had thought that Hook would be flattered by her recollecting his recent graduation, but he seemed more embarrassed than pleased. She said, 'Turn left here. We're the third one along, overlooking the lake.'

'Beautiful spot.' He wasn't being merely polite. The unit really had a splendid site, looking across the widest part of the larger of the lakes. As if they had been waiting for their cue, two swans with five week-old cygnets moved across the water beneath them, scarcely twenty yards away.

'There were six last week. We think the pike's taken one. Nature red in tooth and claw, eh?' A man with curly hair which matched exactly the dark blonde hue of his wife's came forward with outstretched hand. 'Jason Ramsbottom. Pleased to meet you, DS Hook.'

'Bert, please. I'm here on pleasure bent. And hopefully also to allay your wife's fears and assure you that you are not in danger.'

Jason glanced for a moment at his wife. 'To allay both our fears, Bert. You tell yourself not to be stupid, that it's just some crank up to mischief, but when someone sends you threatening notes, there's still a nagging fear when you're trying to get to sleep at nights.'

'You've had notes?' Bert's interest quickened. There were possibilities with notes. People gave things away when they committed themselves to paper.

Jason Ramsbottom went into the kitchen, opened one of the top drawers in the row of compact cabinets, lifted out a cutlery tray, and extracted two sheets from beneath it, using a pair of salad tongs to avoid contact with his fingers.

Bert said admiringly, 'You know all about fingerprints, then. You're familiar with our procedures.'

Jason grinned ruefully. 'I read detective novels. I watch crime series on TV. It's hard to avoid them, nowadays, but I also enjoy them. You'll find these things have got my prints and Lisa's prints on them, though. We handled both of these before we knew what they were. You don't expect that this sort of thing will ever happen to you.'

'Of course you don't. And it never does happen to most people, despite today's more violent society.' Bert took the salad tongs and handled the two significant items with the same care Ramsbottom had shown, laying them down carefully on the table by the window, where the light was brightest.

'That was the first one.' Jason pointed to the thin white card nearest to the window. The message said simply: YOU ARE LINING YOURSELF UP FOR DEATH. The letters were all capitals and had been cut from newspapers or magazines.

Bert glanced up into the two anxious, expectant faces. 'Where and when did you receive this?'

'It was delivered here on the sixth of April. It was there when I got up at seven twenty in the morning. We reckon it could have been delivered at any time after seven thirty on the previous evening. We hadn't been to the door since then. My first thought was that it was a belated April fool joke. It seemed so outlandish, and we simply weren't prepared for it.'

Jason poured out his information quickly. It was plainly a relief to speak about something which he had hugged to himself for weeks. Hook checked the date in his mind. 'That was a Saturday.'

Lisa nodded. 'The Saturday after Easter. The site was crowded. We reckon there were certainly well over a hundred people here. It could have been anyone.'

'Which may have been why the sender chose that day. If it was a he, that is.' Bert looked carefully at the second message. The method was almost identical, with letters cut from printed material and stuck to what seemed to be an identical thin white card. HEED YOUR WARNINGS. THE TIME IS NEAR.

'That was behind the door when we arrived here on the fourth of May. It could have been dropped there at any time in the previous five days. Or it might have been only there for an hour or two. It was a Saturday once more, so the site was crowded with people again.'

Bert shook his head sadly. 'Which could imply that the person who delivered this is normally only here at weekends, or that someone who is here much more frequently merely chooses to make himself more anonymous by sheltering within the crowd. I'm sorry if I'm stating the obvious: you've probably worked these things out for yourselves.'

Lisa said quickly, 'But it's good to have some sort of official confirmation. You've seen this sort of thing before, but it's totally new and merely shocking for me and for Jason. Jenny, our daughter, hasn't seen them and we'd prefer that she doesn't get to know about them.'

'Do you think these might be in any way connected with Jenny? Moonstruck teenagers and even young men can become quite unbalanced by pretty girls. It usually passes mercifully quickly.'

Lisa glanced at her husband. They exchanged quick, nervous smiles. 'We think it's highly unlikely that these have any connection with Jenny. She hasn't been here very much. She has her own circle of friends from school and we have difficulty getting her to come here with us.'

'Then you're probably right to keep this from her. The fewer people who know about it, the better. It's almost certainly a crank, and cranks thrive on publicity. If he gets no reaction at all, he's likely to get bored and either cease his activities altogether or go away and torment someone else. I presume you're willing to let me take these things away?'

Lisa shuddered. 'Very willing indeed. I hope I never see them again.'

Bert Hook smiled as reassuringly as he could. 'And I hope they don't become exhibits A and B in a court case. I think that is very unlikely.'

Jason Ramsbottom looked at the two items which had caused them so much dismay and discussion. 'I don't expect you'll get much from them. He's covered his tracks pretty well, hasn't he?'

Bert looked down at the messages again. 'The newspaper technique is quite common now – you aren't the only one who watches crime series. People think it makes them anonymous, but sometimes they reveal more about themselves than they think they are doing. The sources they use for their letters can be revealing. Even the glues they use have sometimes given pointers.' He was clutching at straws: it wasn't easy to identify anonymous letter-writers until you could question suspects, and there were at present far too many candidates. 'Have you any thoughts yourselves about who might have done this?'

The couple glanced at each other again before Lisa said, 'We've thought about it, obviously, but we haven't come up with anyone. We've only had this place for two years. We hardly know many of the people who are around when Twin Lakes is busy at weekends.'

'Has anyone shown a particular interest in you? Tried to find things out about you and the way you live your lives?'

Jason shook his head. 'No. People ask you what you do for a living when you're on the golf course or in the bar at weekends, but that's natural enough – it's no more than a means of getting a conversation going, most of the time.'

Lisa said, 'There's Debbie Keane, of course. She wants to know everyone's business, not just ours. But that's because she lives here almost all the time and hasn't enough to occupy her. She's a nosey parker, but there's nothing vicious about her. I couldn't see her being responsible for this.'

'But if she pries into people's lives, she might have some idea about who would be vicious enough to go to the trouble of devising notes like these. Because there's quite a lot of care and labour gone into those notes. And you might not be the only victims. Have you heard of anyone else who's been badgered with the same sort of threats?'

'No. But we haven't enquired. Jason thought we should keep our own troubles to ourselves. I've chatted to other women on the site, half-hoping to hear that they've had letters like ours. But no one has seemed even slightly alarmed or disturbed.'

Bert sighed. 'I now have to ask you the most embarrassing question. Is there anything in either of your lives which could make you the subject of threats like this? Nothing excuses these notes, but it might help us to identify the culprit if you could give us some clue to their resentment. Have you offended anyone in the recent past? It might not be anything very serious – the person who has compiled these notes isn't likely to be rational or balanced.'

Again they looked at each other for a couple of seconds before Jason turned to Hook and said firmly, 'No. We discussed this, seeking some sort of reason for these notes. But we haven't come up with anything.'

'I need hardly say that anything you tell me here will be treated as strictly confidential. It would be simply a pointer towards the identity of someone choosing to threaten you.'

Jason said tersely, 'No. There's nothing.'

Bert knew that he really needed to question them separately. Wives and husbands had their own secrets, even from each other. Affairs, outbursts of violence, debts incurred, incidents from a previous life. People would confess things when questioned alone which they would never reveal in the presence of a partner or spouse, however cosy and intimate they seemed together.

Hook grinned, closing his questioning, wondering where he went from here even as he said, 'I think it's time we had a knock round your little golf course, Jason. Help to maintain my status as a bona fide visitor, and tune me up for a no-quarter-given game with John Lambert on Sunday.'

It was a pleasant course, and tricky enough to lure the energetic but rather erratic golfer that was Bert Hook into a couple of high-scoring situations. But he played well enough on the other holes to beat his host two and one and trouser the modest pound which was their stake. He was introduced to seven of the residents as they played twice round the nine-hole course. That helped to justify his presence here and allay his slight feelings of guilt about using a wild goose chase to be out here playing golf on a Friday. None of the people he met seemed a possible writer of poison-pen letters – but you never knew, at this stage.

He locked his clubs in the boot of the car and walked round the lake with a couple they had seen on the course and a highly friendly Labrador. They gazed across the tranquil lake, where a solitary dinghy drifted with a fisherman sitting motionless beside his rod. The Labrador owner identified the dinghy occupant for him. 'That's Wally Keane. Decent golfer and highly skilled bowls player. Knows every yard of this site and probably just how deep that lake is at every point. Bit of a recluse. We think he sails to get away from his wife. Debbie's into everyone's business and spends most of her time chattering incessantly about it. But she's quite harmless really, and even useful, at times – if you want to know anything about Twin Lakes, Debbie's your woman.'

It was almost as if they'd been preparing Hook for what was to follow. When he arrived back at the Ramsbottoms' holiday home, a cheerful, grey-haired woman was in earnest conversation with Lisa, who introduced him. 'This is Debbie Keane. Lives here for eleven months of the year and knows every blade of grass and every bit of scandal.'

'Oh, go on with you!' said Debbie, who was obviously delighted with the description. 'Are you thinking of coming to join us here, Mr Hook?'

'Oh, Bert's just a visitor of ours for the day,' said Lisa hastily. 'He's been knocking a ball around the golf course with Jason.'

'And what do you do for a living, Bert?' asked Debbie imperturbably.

Hook took the plunge. 'I'm a police officer, Mrs Keane. Detective Sergeant in the CID, actually.'

'Oo-er! Better watch my Ps and Qs now, hadn't I, Lisa?' Debbie, who looked to be in her middle fifties, vibrated with the same giggle that had animated her thirty years earlier.

'As a matter of fact, Mrs Keane, there are a few questions I'd like to ask you, when you've finished your cup of tea. It won't take long, but I think it would be best if we spoke in private.'

FOUR

Geoffrey Tiler took his time selecting the plants. There wasn't a lot of ground available, so you wanted to be sure you made the most of it. His partner thought Geoffrey knew all about gardening. Even though he declared repeatedly that he didn't, his new companion saw that only as a becoming modesty in him. It was good to have someone who saw only the best in you.

Geoff decided on begonias and pelargoniums, in the end. The nursery had them labelled as geraniums, but you couldn't blame them for that: it was the name most people still used for them. They flowered all through the summer and on into the autumn, until the first frosts cut them down; they'd be ideal for the bed in full sun which he had prepared for them. He stowed the trays carefully in the boot of his car and shut the lid on them firmly. The little plants needed the light, but they'd have to exist in the dark for a few hours. It was warm today, but if he left the boxes of plants on the back shelf, they might roast in the sun in the airless car. There had been steady rain only a couple of days ago, so that the soil would be warm and receptive. He'd enjoy planting these annuals out over the weekend.

The lunch break was over. Tiler drove the short distance back to the factory and slipped his jacket on before he left the car, preparing himself for his different and more sober working life. He tightened the tie at his neck, threw back his shoulders and marched purposefully back through the reception area and the anteroom to his office.

'Come through in five minutes, please, Laura. I've three or four letters to answer from this morning's post. We'll decide whether they're snail mail or email when you come in.' He spoke breezily to his PA, as if it was important to establish his return from gardening to small-time tycoonery. Or to conceal his horticultural expertise and his purchase of plants, he thought ruefully. Why it should be important to him to conceal that, as if it were some sort of moral weakness, he couldn't imagine. Role-playing, he supposed; they said almost everyone did that, whatever their station in life. It was only a small factory, but he was the owner and it seemed to him as well as to his staff that he had to play the man in charge. And that apparently excluded harmless hobbies like gardening.

He smiled at the heading on his notepaper as he studied the morning's post and planned his replies: You Need It. We Make It. He still didn't like dictating anything but standard letters without a little forethought. You could annoy people if you used the wrong phrases, or even if you used the standard clichés; they made some people feel they were being fobbed off rather than receiving the individual consideration they merited. He made the odd note for each letter on the pad in front of him, then agreed with Laura that each of the four messages should be conveyed in a formal letter. Heads of firms tended to be older people, and for most of them letters still had more standing than emails.

His small plastics firm was doing well, considering the recession which had seen off many concerns of this size. Prices were keen, but orders were still coming in and one or two competitors had gone. You Need It. We Make It was the mantra he had set at the top of his stationery when it had been redesigned two years ago. It wasn't strictly true, but they would have a go at most things that offered a lucrative market and they knew where to locate larger suppliers when designs occasionally proved too complex or expensive for them.

Laura went away to prepare the letters for his signature and he called in the sales rep he had arranged to see earlier in the day. This was a man of thirty-three who had come here on a slightly reduced salary when his previous firm had folded. He was professionally affable and confident as a rule, but the prospect of this meeting with Geoffrey Tiler had obviously made him nervous.

He wasn't able to conceal his anxiety as he came in and sat down on the chair in front of the boss's desk. Not a good thing in a salesman, Geoffrey reflected; you should exude self-assurance, even when you did not feel it, if you were to convince prospective customers of the excellence of what you had to offer. But that was unfair. This was an interview with your employer, not a selling exercise, and he didn't want false bonhomie or feigned aplomb from the man.

Tiler looked at him steadily for a moment. 'We've lost the Brownlee account, Frank. Would you say that is any way down to you?'

'No, sir. I think they were determined to go. They'd made up their minds before they saw me.'

'Did you try to win them back?' He didn't make suggestions as to how Frank might have done that. He wanted those to come from the man sitting uncomfortably on the other side of the desk and having to account for himself. It was tough, but it was part of the job. He'd sat in that position himself, many years ago now. It was that experience which had made him determined to get out of sales as quickly as he could: you were always at the mercy of other people, in sales.

'I offered him the lowest price on our goods that I could, sir. The one we'd agreed I could go down to, if the customer was important enough to us.'

'But he wouldn't bite?'

'No. He seemed determined to go. I got the impression that one of our competitors had made him an offer he couldn't refuse. Probably taken a loss, just to get that order.'

'I see. Have you any evidence to support that view?'

'No, sir. It was an impression I got from speaking to Griffiths. As I said, he seemed to have decided before I got there that he was placing his order elsewhere.'

'And you hadn't seen this coming before you spoke to him on Tuesday? You hadn't had any hints at your previous meeting with him that he was considering switching his suppliers?'

The salesman shifted a little on his seat. 'No, sir. He'd seemed perfectly friendly. He'd given me the feeling that he was satisfied with the quality of what we were offering and with the prices we were charging him for it.'

'How long ago was this previous meeting, Frank?'

The man folded his arms. 'About two months ago, I think.'

Tiler glanced down at the notes in front of him, though he knew perfectly well what he was going to say. 'Three and a half months, according to my records. You haven't given him a phone call during that time?'

'No, sir, I don't believe I have. I've been pretty busy during the last few weeks, trying to work up new business.'

'And you've had a certain amount of success, Frank, on which I congratulated you at the time. But the two new orders you secured represent about a quarter of the business we have now lost, as Brownlee take their custom elsewhere.'

'Yes, sir. I realize that. Hopefully the new orders will develop into greater quantities when the clients are satisfied with our products.'

'Hopefully they might, yes. But both of them are small firms. It will take them many years to grow to the size of Brownlee, even if they are successful. They are the kind of business we should pick up, I'm not disputing that. But not at the expense of the Brownlee custom, Frank.'

'The two things aren't connected, sir.' Belatedly, the salesman became more aggressive. 'I didn't neglect Brownlee to secure these other outlets. The cancellation of the Brownlee order hit me like a bolt from the blue on Tuesday.'

'I see. Well, I accept that, Frank. The question we have to ask is whether it should have hit you like that. Clients, especially big and long-established clients, need to be kept warm. Do you honestly think that you shouldn't have seen this coming? Are you quite sure that there was nothing you could have done to anticipate it and possibly prevent it?'

The man opposite him squirmed a little on his upright seat. He was used to enlarging on the excellence of what he could offer to people who knew nothing of his background and little about the firm he worked for. This man knew all about him, and far more about the financial health of this company than he ever would. You couldn't spin yarns here; you couldn't pull the wool over this man's eyes. Even those clichés seemed third-hand and useless here; he realized in his discomfort how heavily he dealt in clichés during his working day.

The old, well-worn phrases got you by, with people who didn't know you or whom you met only occasionally in the course of your work. But this man knew him too well to be sidetracked by the conventional bits of jargon. The trouble with being a salesman was that you presented only one side of a case for all of your working life: that was what everyone expected you to do, in order to sell your product. But it also meant that no one was disposed to believe you, even when you spoke the most heartfelt truth.

He tried to produce his usual cheerful air, but felt himself failing miserably as he looked into the round, experienced face opposite him. 'I got no warning of this, sir. The MD at Brownlee seemed perfectly happy with our goods and our service when I last saw him. I – I could perhaps have kept in touch with him a little better in the intervening period, but I don't think it would have made any difference to the decision he made last Tuesday.'

'You may well be right in that, Frank. But as you didn't contact him, we'll never know, will we? I shall be seeing the Brownlee board member who oversees most of their buying at a conference next week. I'll have a word with him there and try to see whether this switch to another supplier is irrevocable, or whether we have a chance of getting back with them in the future.'

'Thank you, sir. I'm sure that you'll find that—'

'What about the other clients on your patch? Are you happy that none of them is going to defect to the competition?'

'I don't think that is likely to happen, sir.'

Tiler let that limp statement hang in the air for a moment, allowing his man to hear and endure the flaccidity of it. 'Better make sure it doesn't, eh, Frank? Better keep the buyers warm and make sure they appreciate how good our products are and how keen our prices are. What Brownlee have done will get around, as you know, and other people will be asking themselves whether they've got the best deal possible in these cut-throat times.'

The chastened man gave his assurances and left. Geoffrey Tiler looked at his desk unseeingly for a long moment. He didn't like himself much at times like this. But these things surely had to be done. Salesmen expected it, when a major contract was lost, even when there was no omission on their part. It was part of the efficient running of a successful business: you couldn't appear slack. You had to keep people up to the mark.

And it would be the weekend in an hour or two. He would get away from this office and this factory and enjoy playing an entirely different role. No, that was wrong: he would be himself, rather than merely playing the role he played here. As near to himself as he would ever get nowadays, certainly. Sometimes he longed for those student days when everything had seemed black and white and simple. For the days when the opposition had been fascists or reactionaries and you were going to create a new and better world.

Laura brought him the letters to sign. He did that with a series of brisk flourishes, then looked up at her with a smile. 'POETS day, Laura. Piss off early, tomorrow's Saturday. Do people still use that expression?'

She was mildly shocked that he had voiced a word like that. It was common enough nowadays, but she'd never heard it from Mr Tiler before. 'I think they do, yes, sir.'

'Well, we should heed them, then. Get away by half past four, today. Even earlier, if you can. Clear your desk and bugger off.'

Another word she didn't usually get from him. 'Thank you, sir. That's very kind of you and I shall do that.' It was curious that when he made concessions, her own language seemed to become more formal than usual. 'There's just one thing, sir. I have a note in my diary. You asked me to remind you about Mrs Tiler's birthday. It's on Monday.'

Laura spoke tentatively. Her boss had been divorced for two years now, and you could never tell how people would react to former spouses. If they were feeling bitter, they might even revile you for raising the subject.

Geoffrey Tiler didn't revile her. He smiled softly – even, she thought, a little regretfully, but that might have been just her sentimental streak. 'Arrange for some flowers to be delivered to her, will you – just my name, no other message. Carnations, I think. She was always fond of carnations.'

'I'll do that, sir. I'll arrange it now, before I go.' Laura made a note she did not need and stood up. She knew his wife's first name for the flowers. It was sad that neither of them had mentioned it here. 'Thank you for letting me finish early today, sir. I'll get the supermarket shopping out of the way today and have the weekend to myself.'

Geoffrey's own working week was finished now. He made a note or two for the Monday and Tuesday and listened to the noises in the anteroom as Laura cleared her desk and prepared to leave. Only when she had gone did he lock his desk and move out to the big maroon BMW.

He was soon out of Wolverhampton and driving swiftly west. He tried to relax, not race along, so that he could enjoy the journey and the late-spring countryside. The chestnuts were at their best now, like vast candelabras with their upright white or red blossoms. They'd been scarcely in leaf when he'd passed along this road three weeks ago. How quickly nature moved at this time of the year. Changing the face of the earth almost as quickly as human life itself changed at.times.

Once he was through Bridgnorth, the route became ever more rural. He liked that; it seemed to be marking the transition from his working life to the weekend and the real Geoffrey Tiler. He felt himself relaxing, but at the same time his veins throbbed with anticipation. He was fifty now, but he hadn't felt like this since he was a young man. Was he being slightly ridiculous, or just realizing his potential? He preferred the latter verdict, even if it involved some self-deception. This was the best of himself, so why not go along with it?

He greeted the man who lifted the barrier for him at Twin Lakes cheerfully. He glanced up at the sign above his head which read 'TWIN LAKES – REST ASSURED' and thought happily that it was much more accurate than most advertising slogans.

The Ford Focus was already neatly parked near the home by the lake and his heart leapt at the sight of it. He forced himself to park carefully, then climbed out and turned quickly to the figure he knew would be waiting. He held out both hands, felt them taken firmly in the grasp of the tall, slim figure who stood smiling in the doorway of the unit. They held hands and looked at each other approvingly for a moment, then clasped each other in a long, unhurried embrace.

Geoffrey Tiler was quite breathless when he eventually stood back. He said, 'It's so good to see you, Michael!'

*   *   *

Elfrida Potts was much the more awkward of the two. Wayne Briggs seemed quite confident and perfectly at home here.

He became more confident each time they had sex. She'd had to show him the way at first, and he'd come like a steam engine inside her, before she was really ready for him. But Freda didn't mind that. She enjoyed his excitement, rejoiced in the feeling that she could have this effect on a handsome young boy like Wayne. They'd done it three times in the few hours since they'd arrived at Twin Lakes, and he'd become more assertive and more skilful each time. You could do wonderful things with youth at your disposal, she thought. It was a long time since she had been this excited. Plainly Wayne was good for her.

And she was good for Wayne, wasn't she? She was helping him to grow up, marking his transition from boy to man and helping him through it. He was lucky to have an experienced older woman to guide him through that.

Not that Freda was all that experienced. She'd tried to tell him that, to convey to him that she wasn't some slapper who went for anything in trousers; that she'd had men before, but been choosy about them. She didn't think he'd registered much of what she'd said; he'd been far too excited at the time.

'You're quite a woman, Freda.' Wayne fingered the clasp at the top of her skirt, ran his hands down over her buttocks.

He was enjoying using her first name, enjoying the free exploration of her bottom even more. He'd be wanting her naked again soon, and it wasn't long since she'd dressed. Freda wondered what he would say to his mates at school about this. Would he boast about doing it with the teacher who kept them all in such strict order? Would he tell them how he'd held her moaning and helpless in his arms? Would he quote the things she'd said to him in her passion? Would he tell them about the things she'd asked him to do to her and the pleasure they had brought?

This was madness. She had always known it was madness. If she'd wanted a toy boy, why hadn't she got someone over eighteen, someone who wasn't a pupil? Someone who wasn't jailbait. She'd heard one of the men teachers use that phrase in the staff room, when he'd been talking about one of the young minxes in the sixth form who he said had a crush on him. He hadn't been talking to her, of course. No one thought that staid Mrs Potts would get herself involved in anything like this.

And yet here she was, being rogered for fun in the mobile home she and Matthew had bought to get away from it all at the weekends. 'Rest Assured', it said at the entrance, and until now that had seemed appropriate. But there was going to be no rest for her this weekend, that was for sure. Wayne had whispered in her ear that he was going to fuck the fanny off her, and she had found his words enormously and unexpectedly exciting. Quiet Mrs Potts, thirty-five years old and the conscientious head of history, was being rogered rigid and enjoying it.

Wayne would get tired of her. She'd told herself that from the start, just as she'd told herself not to get involved. She couldn't expect him not to move on: he was only sixteen. She was his rite of passage. In ten years, five years even, he'd be looking back and saying that she'd been just that. But where would she be in five years? In deep trouble, unless this boy kept his mouth shut. She made herself think of him as a boy, to remind herself of the dangers she was inviting by being here with him. But the danger was part of the attraction, just as his youth and inexperience were part of the attraction.

She said, 'Do you play golf, Wayne?' She didn't like the name, but she made herself use it. He couldn't be just a sex object, if she kept using his name and showing her affection.

'No. It's a game for old men and ponces in daft trousers, innit?'

'Some people think so. But the people who scoff don't always know much about it. I could teach you, if you like. I'm not a good player, but I know the rudiments.'

'Rudiments, eh?' He grinned and savoured the word. 'You're good at being rude, anyway, Miss.' He giggled and ran his hand round the inside of her skirt top, stroking the soft skin of her belly below her navel.

'It's not Miss! That's for school, not here!' She spoke with a feeling of panic, realizing that he would never recognize the need for caution as clearly as she did. 'You're my nephew here, remember? I'm your Aunt Freda.'

She'd settled on that because no one was going to believe she was his sister and she certainly wasn't going to be his mother. Wayne giggled. 'I like that. Aunty Freda. Take your skirt off and your drawers down and sit on my prick, Aunty Freda.'

'Don't be silly, Wayne! We can't just make love all of the time, you know.' But a small part of her said that they could; that what he had just suggested would be a new position and very exciting. She said firmly, 'It's a lovely evening outside. If you don't want to try golf and you don't want to sail on the lake, at least we should go for a walk. We'll probably have the woods to ourselves.'

'Want to do it outside under the leaves with the birds singing above us, do you, Freda? Well, I'm game if you are. Al fresco, they call it. Didn't think I'd know that, did you? I'm not as thick as you think, you know.'

'I know you're not thick, Wayne. I always knew that. You're a bright boy who isn't making the most of himself. I want to help you to do that.'

'And you are, Miss! Sorry, you are, Freda. I've never felt such a man. You can feel it, if you like.'

He reached for her hand, but she slipped away from him. 'You're a lecherous adolescent, that's what you are! And we're going for a walk. Then we'll have something to eat. I'm not just a pretty face, you know. I can cook.'

'It wasn't your face I was planning to look at,' said Wayne dreamily. He liked this. You could say things to a grown woman that you wouldn't dare say to a girl of your own age. Say things and do things, and get gratitude rather than rejection. He let himself be pulled outside. He didn't mind fresh air and a walk in the woods. And she was going to feed him. Feed him much better than he was fed at home, by the sound of it. She was a bit of all right, Miss Potts. Freda. They were the words Grandad had used about a pretty girl, in the week before he died.

Freda's home wasn't one of the ones by the lake. They were more expensive, and she and Matthew hadn't been sure about how much they would use the place when they decided to give themselves a bolt-hole. That was what this was, thought

Freda: a glorious bolt-hole where you could bring your illicit lover and hide away for the weekend. Sex affects judgement: it made Freda, who was normally rational and practical, unrealistically optimistic.

For the first time in many hours, she thought of Matthew and their life together. He was a good husband. More distant than she would have liked, but that might have been because they had to spend so much of their lives apart. It wasn't his fault that he had to work on the oil rigs. And that work brought them plenty of money. It was Matthew's money which had bought them this place and given her this opportunity with Wayne. As Freda Potts stood beside her bright blue Peugeot and waited for Wayne to emerge from the unit, she felt a surge of dark and depressing guilt. She really was a slut, despite her attempts to convince Wayne Briggs that she was something else.

Then the toilet flushed and he stood on the step above her, adjusting his jeans and looking round for the first time at this place she had brought him to. Freda gave him a shy smile and tried not to show the fear which had beset her as she had stepped out into the clear light and cool air of the late afternoon. He tried to take her hand, but she detached herself hastily and whispered, 'Aunt and nephew, remember? They don't hold hands!'

'I'll hold more than hands if you give me half a chance!'

He seemed to be determined on sexual innuendo. It was becoming a little tiresome. She didn't want to be reminded all the time of what she did in the privacy of the bedroom, of how abandoned she had been with him. That had been a surprise to her as well as to him, and she hadn't grown accustomed to it yet.

Freda hastened towards the woods and the cover they offered. She felt very exposed out here with Wayne, who was moving unhurriedly a pace behind her, chatting inconsequentially as he walked. She was relieved when they reached the path which wound among the trees, so that she could slow her pace and move beneath the canopy of bright green spring leaves. It was pleasant here, and almost deserted. The only person they met was an older blonde woman with a small and friendly dog called Rosie. This lady knew Freda and was prepared to chat, but Freda gave her a smile and a 'Hello there!' and passed quickly on. She didn't want to introduce Wayne as her nephew; she was afraid he wouldn't be convincing in the role.

'It's nice here,' he said eventually. It was the first evidence that he was trying to please her, that he wasn't completely dominated by his sexual triumphs. It wasn't much, but it allowed her to feel that there was something more than sex between them, that he felt a little of the tenderness she felt for him. They watched the swans for a minute and he said, 'There are five of the little ones.'

'Cygnets,' said Freda, and then wanted to bite her tongue for saying the innocent word. It was the teacher in her that wanted the correct term, she supposed. She identified various birds for him. She had her illustrated guide to British birds back in the unit, but she knew he'd laugh at her if she produced it for him.

They were on their way back there when they saw in the distance a grey-haired woman with a burly man she did not recognize. They were eighty yards away and Freda slowed automatically to make sure they did not meet them and have to speak. 'That's Debbie Keane,' she said quietly to Wayne. 'She knows everything that goes on here.'

He grinned. 'She doesn't know about us.'

'No. Let's keep it that way.'

Wayne Briggs didn't reply. He seemed to be observing the camp gossip with interest, but when he spoke she realized that it was Debbie's companion he had been studying. 'I know that bloke. He lives near me. He's a police sergeant. CID, I think.'

Freda was disturbed by that. She didn't like the thought that there could be a CID sergeant here, walking around the site and talking to Debbie. Learning about her 'nephew' perhaps. She turned abruptly into one of the boathouses by the lake before they could see her.

Wayne was delighted by the move. He took it as an invitation for him to renew his sexual advances, in this strange, high place with wooden walls and the coils of rope beside the two battered rowing boats which were awaiting repair. It was in

one of these that he took the Head of History, though he remembered to breathe 'Freda' into her ear as he clumsily removed
her jeans. It was good in here, once he'd got her going and
she was urging him on again. Even the strange smells of wood
and oil and sawdust added to the strangeness and the wonder
of it all. And staid Mrs Potts forgot her caution and cried out
to him to fuck her, once he'd got her going. He was getting
quite good at sex, he decided complacently. That surely was
pretty good at sixteen.

Neither of them saw the small man in the trees as they
cautiously resumed their walk. Wally Keane went back to his
home and recorded the time and the date.

FIVE

D ebbie Keane's unit was surrounded by flowers. There was a fine crimson rhododendron in a large pot, standing high above the newly planted annuals which crowded the oblong plot beside the wooden steps leading up to a balcony and an open door.

'You have a wonderful spot here,' said Bert Hook. He was quite sincere. The plants complemented the elevated home, and the longer landscape of the lake and the distant trees behind it set the place off perfectly.

'We think so,' said Debbie. 'This is our permanent home, really, so we enjoy making the very best we can of it. We have to move out for a month of each year, of course, but we understand that. And we're always delighted to move back in here. It really feels like home to us now.'

'You must know more about what goes on at Twin Lakes than anyone else around here. More than even the owners, I expect.'

'Oh, I don't know about that!' said Debbie automatically. But she preened herself a little at the thought, settling into her armchair like a bird resuming its nest after an exhilarating fluttering of its plumage. 'I suppose we do know the whole site pretty well by now. And I know most of the people who use it. They like to chat, and you get to know a little of their lives, over the years.'

I bet you do, thought Bert. Whether they like to chat or not, you find out about them and their families and their opinions. He knew Debbie Keane's type pretty well by now. Sometimes they gathered information effortlessly; sometimes they worked much harder to do it and put people's backs up. But the important fact about the Debbie Keanes of this world is that they can be very useful to the police. He took the plunge. 'My name is Bert Hook, Mrs Keane. Detective Sergeant Hook, when I'm at work, rather than enjoying myself here.'

'My word! I hope we haven't done anything wrong! You're

not going to put the cuffs on us and take us in, are you?' Debbie giggled and gripped the arms of her chair.

Bert smiled patiently. It was a little tiresome, but you had to accept that the words were meant as friendly. People didn't realize how often he'd endured this or similar reactions, just as they didn't realize how his tall chief John Lambert had been asked whether it was cold up there by short people who seemed to think the tired joke was original. 'Nothing like that, Mrs Keane. I came here for pleasure and I've enjoyed my day on your delightful site. Something has come up, that's all. Something I felt should be investigated, just to put Mrs Ramsbottom's mind at rest. And Jason's of course. He has a right to be disturbed by this, even though he's a man!' Hook gave her a big smile to show that this was a joke and that there was no need for her to be alarmed.

Mrs Keane was plainly delighted and animated by this news. 'Goodness! What on earth can have happened on our quiet little site to excite the attention of a detective inspector?'

'Detective sergeant, Mrs Keane. And an off-duty detective sergeant at that. This is almost certainly a false alarm. Many people are stupid, but only a much smaller number among them are vicious.' He was aware from her face that he was getting this wrong, that instead of making it low-key as he had intended he was adding to her excitement with every phrase. But he couldn't see what else he could have done; you had to issue the standard cautious reminders.

And now came the most important, and in this case probably the most futile reminder of all. 'I must emphasize that what I say now must go no further. I am taking you into my confidence, Mrs Keane, and it is important that you keep this to yourself.' He spoke the words with all the solemnity he could muster, but even as he pronounced them he heard their futility. You couldn't talk to the village gossip and expect her to keep what you said to herself, however steely your warnings. Because after his day on the site, Bert realized that this is what this community was: a particular kind of village, which assembled every weekend, with a few permanent occupants like Debbie Keane who made it her business to acquire and disseminate knowledge of the inhabitants' affairs.

'Oh, you're safe with me, Detective Sergeant Hook. You can say whatever you want in here and know that it will go no further.' Debbie Keane looked round at the walls and the windows of her unit and nodded sagely. Probably at that moment she actually believed what she was saying. Busybodies had an enormous capacity for self-deception.

Bert knew what would happen, but he could see no alternative. The woman was a source of information and he needed to use her. And if news of the threatening notes the Ramsbottoms had received trickled round the site, that might be the best method of suppressing them. Nutters who wrote notes did not usually welcome publicity, and the news of police investigation might well frighten them off. Suppression wasn't as good as exposure and punishment, but it was a good second best.

'Lisa Ramsbottom contacted me because she had received unpleasant notes, Mrs Keane. This is the first of them.' He produced the polythene envelope in which he had placed the card. Debbie stared with widening eyes at the words in capitals: YOU ARE LINING YOURSELF UP FOR DEATH.

There was an extended dramatic pause before she said tremulously, 'Goodness me! Someone is threatening them. Who could have done this?'

'I'm hoping that is where you might be able to help, Debbie.' He used her first name now, partly to alleviate what seemed her genuine fear, partly to emphasize how much he was taking her into his confidence. 'Can you think of anyone on the site who might have done this?'

She shook her head slowly, as if she did not trust herself with words.

'Someone with a grievance against Lisa and Jason, perhaps. You chat to a lot of people, I know. Has anyone told you that they dislike the Ramsbottoms?'

'No. We're a friendly lot here. We get on well with each other. We don't come here to do things like that.' She dipped her head towards the note, as if she feared to use her hand to point at it.

'It's not just an isolated incident, you see. There have been other notes.' He produced his second polythene cover and his second message: HEED YOUR WARNINGS. THE TIME IS NEAR.

Debbie Keane stared at the words in horror for a moment, then turned her white, round face back to Hook. 'Someone is threatening them. Do you think he's really going to attack them?'

'No, I don't, Debbie. It might not be a he, of course. But these things are false alarms, in nineteen cases out of twenty. They are sent by silly or disturbed people who want to frighten their targets. But they have to be investigated.' It flashed across his mind that it might just be this appalled-looking grey-haired woman who had slipped these messages into the Ramsbottoms' unit. And if into theirs, perhaps into others which had yet to come to light. Everyone seemed to think that she was the person who knew most about the business of others in this constantly changing village. That would make her best placed to have the material which would embolden her to issue threats like this. He said, 'You used to have a dog, didn't you, Debbie?'

She nodded, seeming to find nothing to alarm her in this odd switch of subject. 'Fox terrier, she was. Bessie. She died not long ago.'

'You must miss her.' He was studying her closely; he had known at least two elderly ladies who had become unbalanced after the loss of a pet, though they had each been at least ten years older than Debbie Keane.

'You get over it. It's a blow when they go, but you always knew they would, eventually. I still enjoy walking in the woods – still enjoy meeting other people's dogs. There are quite a few of them come here.'

No sign of any mental disorder there; Bert felt rather ashamed of himself for even considering the possibility. 'Well, as I say, it's almost certainly a false alarm, Debbie. But if you have any further thoughts on it, or hear of anyone else being threatened, you should get in touch with me immediately at this number.' He gave her his card. She studied it with the reverence she might have accorded to a royal telegram before setting it carefully against a china dog on her mantelpiece.

He was leaving her home when Walter Keane appeared and was introduced. Hook hastened away to take his leave of the Ramsbottoms and head for home. As he left he heard Debbie saying to her husband, 'You'll never guess what's happened, Wally . . .'

So much for confidentiality.

George Martindale and his family arrived for the weekend half an hour after DS Hook had left Twin Lakes.

The Martindales were popular on the site. The whole family were very black and very cheerful. Even the people who thought you should never mention the word black when speaking of people knew that you couldn't escape it with the Martindales. George and Mary seemed to thrust it at you sometimes, with their smooth dark faces and their large and very white teeth, whilst their two young children seemed totally unconscious of their colour. More importantly, they were perpetually cheerful and polite. Well brought up, people said approvingly. That phrase represented the perfect middle-class compliment for children, and there were many middle-class people who had units at Twin Lakes.

George was Jamaican and Mary was Nigerian, but many people thought that they were from the same place. Their two delightful boys were aged eight and six. By seven o'clock on this May evening, both boys were out on the otherwise deserted golf course with their father, staring at small white balls with the intensity and single-minded concentration which only children of their age can summon. Mum was preparing food. It was an arrangement which feminists would have deplored but which Mary seemed happy to accept. The boys – and the much bigger boy who had sired them – were out from under her feet whilst she got on with preparing a meal in the rather constricted kitchen of her holiday home.

The boys had cut-down clubs and were showing promise. That at any rate was the verdict of their cheerfully biased father. Tommy, the six-year-old, grew increasingly frustrated as he perpetrated two air shots, then a series of frantic swings which sent his ball scuttling along the ground. He said a rude word, was admonished by his father, and maintained sturdily that he had learned the word from him. Then, wonder of wonders, he dropped the face of his iron club on the ball correctly and it soared high and straight in front of him, to noisy acclaim from his father and more muted recognition from his elder brother.

This wonder stroke immediately became to Tommy his natural game and his usual shot. His previous efforts were forgotten as mere aberrations from his normal game, probably the result of some external distraction from his partners or from the world around them.

At six years old, Tommy was on his way to becoming a golfer.

His father was a powerful man and an optimist. This is rarely an effective combination when golf is the sport. George smote the ball vast distances, but only rarely on the line which was required. His sons were impressed by his drives, but intrigued by the places from which he had to play his second shots. Martindale was a big man, but definitely not at his golfing best when he was bent almost double beneath birch trees or standing on one leg against a fir.

'You'd be better taking a drop,' advised his elder boy gravely. Nicky was offering the accumulated golfing wisdom of an eight-year-old.

His father would undoubtedly have counselled a drop to any of his normal golfing companions, with the resultant penalty of one shot, and a free swing. He now waved away his son's advice and told him to stand clear of danger. This splendid figure of a man then crouched on one knee, swung back the club for the eighteen inches which was all the tree allowed him, and swatted at the ball with the arthritic twitch of an octogenarian. It moved a foot, into a totally unplayable lie against the base of the tree.

George Martindale uttered the word he had deplored in his younger son. The boys' laughter was unseemly as well as disrespectful.

But each of the trio hit three or four very good shots in the six holes they played. That was sufficient to make them think that this game was in essence really rather simple; only practice was needed to create consistency. They went happily back to their holiday home with three enormous appetites.

'Dad got into some horrible places,' Nicky told his mother happily. 'He's not really as good at this game as he lets you think he is.'

'He's never pretended to be very good,' said Mary Martindale loyally. 'You should be grateful that he's prepared to give you his time and teach you about the game.'

'The man on television said you should have a professional to teach you when you start,' said the precocious Nicky loftily. 'He said you get into bad habits if you don't.'

'You get started in the game and show some interest. Then I'll think about lessons for you,' said his father sternly. But he patted the boy's head with affection, and Nicky knew, as he had always known, that Dad was a soft touch.

'Dad used a rude word,' said Tommy delightedly. 'It was one he said I hadn't to use.' He shook his head censoriously, as he'd often seen his teacher, Miss Fletcher, do. 'And when he was crawling under the trees to get his ball, he did a big fart!'

Both boys collapsed in helpless laughter at this, as much because Tommy had produced this daring word in the home as for the event itself. Mary kept her face straight with some difficulty as she told them to wash their hands and come to the table.

The boys were in bed and it was quite dark when George Martindale came out for a breath of the clear, cool night air. He sauntered round the side of the lake, close to the two boathouses where the woods began, before he produced his mobile phone. He knew exactly what he wanted and it didn't take him long to make the call. He rapped out the quantities, waiting each time for the person at the other end of the line to make a note of his requirements.

George Martindale waited whilst his order was read back to him, then rang off after a terse confirmation. There was no social exchange, no polite leave-taking. This was strictly a business call. He was back with Mary and the sleeping boys in no more than fifteen minutes.

He would have been amazed to know that his call had been overheard.

The bar restaurant had closed and the lights were going off around the site by the time the last car to arrive on that Friday night drove quietly through the gates.

The three-litre Jaguar was a powerful car. It made very little noise, easing almost silently between the gates and around the site to the home beside the lake, which was now silvered by a crescent moon. The thickset man and the statuesque woman beside him sat for a moment and looked across the water, then climbed softly from the big vehicle and carried their bags without a word into their unit.

She said, 'I'll make us a hot drink, shall I?' but he took her into his arms and held her tight against him, running his hands softly down the length of her back and the soft curves at the base of it.

'Switching off for the weekend, are we?' she said into his ear. She held the back of his head carefully in both her hands and pressed his lips softly against hers.

He kissed her for a long moment, but tenderly, without the brutal fierceness he could display on other occasions. 'Rest Assured,' he quoted and they both chuckled a little, whilst he glanced at the closed door of their bedroom.

The man's name was Richard Seagrave and earlier in the evening he had been much less relaxed. At six o'clock, he was still in his office. His PA and almost everyone else in the building had gone home. The cleaners moved in, anxious to complete their work and leave the big modern building clean, shining and ready for the new week's work on Monday morning. Richard Seagrave told them they could not yet enter his office, nor indeed any of the rooms in the large section of the floor which he controlled.

He carried that sort of authority.

At ten minutes past six, two Asian men entered the lift, rose to the second floor which housed Seagrave Enterprises, and moved swiftly through the PA's anteroom and into the head man's office. 'The thing is going ahead,' said the one who was slightly the taller of the two. He had a beanie hat pulled down over his forehead, almost masking his eyes, as if he was deliberately playing a sinister stage villain.

'The thing?' said Seagrave, with a curl of the lip.

'Area Seven,' said his visitor hastily.

'That's better. It's important to me that you use the correct code. I have many concerns. I cannot afford to be vague.'

'I'm sorry, sir.' He glanced at the man waiting expectantly beside him. 'I understand that we must be precise, because you have many concerns. We ourselves have only the one concern. It occupies much of our lives and we are determined to get it right.'

'I also am determined that you will get it right. I hope you see that it is highly important that you get it right, for your own sakes. I hope you also see that if it blows up in your faces, I will not be around to defend you. There is no way in which I can afford to be connected with this, if it goes wrong.'

The second Asian man spoke for the first time. His Pakistani accent was more marked than that of his companion, whose English had been almost perfect, save for the flattened northern vowels which emerged strangely from his sallow features. 'That does not seem entirely fair, Mr Seagrave. We are taking all the risks. You should surely be prepared to do your best to protect us, if things go wrong.'

Richard Seagrave gave him his unpleasant smile again. His friends said that his face had a lived-in look, but he hadn't many friends. Ugly or malevolent were more usual descriptions. His attitude now matched his features. 'You're right. It is not "entirely fair". Life itself is not "entirely fair", Mr Anwar.' He mimicked the precise, careful pronunciation of the man who had dared to question his attitude. 'No doubt some of the girls you've recruited for us would also think that you in turn were not being "entirely fair". In case you hadn't noticed, I fund all this. And we have a saying in Britain that he who pays the piper calls the tune. You won't hear any piping, but I'm calling the tune, Mr Anwar. You would do well to remember that.'

The taller and more senior of the men who stood before his desk hastened to intervene. There was big money at stake here, and they'd run major risks to get it. The squat man behind the desk was going to take by far the biggest share for the smallest risk, but he'd financed the whole enterprise; they couldn't have done it without Seagrave. He didn't want to jeopardize his own share at this stage, after the trouble they'd gone to, the dangers they had run, and the months it had taken them to get here. 'We understand what you say, Mr Seagrave. It's only right that you should be kept clear of any risks.'

'If I'm not, I shall know who allowed my name to become involved; you two are the only ones who know anything about my financing of your little scheme. I have some rather nasty people who work for me: I don't even like them much myself, to tell you the truth. I shouldn't like them to feel they had to take any sort of action against you.'

'I'm sure that won't happen, Mr Seagrave. Nothing will go wrong, but even if it does, we shall make sure that you are in no way involved.'

Richard left a couple of seconds for the words to reverberate around his office, then stood up. 'I can't see why anything should go wrong. I look forward to years of profitable cooperation with you.'

They thought he was going to shake their hands, but he did not do that. He waited until they had gone, looking down from his office as they moved to their car in the almost deserted car park below him. Then he made two swift phone calls. Twenty minutes later he picked up Vanessa and drove out of the city. The roads were quiet as he drove towards Twin Lakes and the weekend.

He reached across a couple of times to grasp the slim forearm of the blonde woman in the front passenger seat of the Jaguar. He was working hard on himself, trying to contact that other and better Richard Seagrave, the pleasant, responsive man who had almost disappeared beneath his recent business ventures.

He could be that man at Twin Lakes. No one knew anything about Richard Seagrave there, did they?

SIX

Spring moved into summer, England played Australia for the Ashes, and Detective Sergeant Bert Hook almost forgot about the fears expressed to him by Lisa and Jason Ramsbottom.

The spring had been cold and late. It had needed tornados in Oklahoma and the loss of over thirty American lives to remind Britons perennially complaining about their weather that there was much to be said for a climate without extremes. At Twin Lakes the summer, when it eventually arrived, was warm and dry and the people who were to become the main protagonists in the dramatic events of July congratulated themselves on their choice of venue.

In some respects, the site was like a medieval city state. Its eighty acres of water, trees, rolling parkland and recreational facilities represented a haven from the harsher and busier worlds outside. The long pole of the barrier beside the office, firmly preventing the entry of others into that world, was a welcome protection for the fortunate few who had residences here and thus free access to its escapist world. The barrier symbolized for them this closed and privileged world of theirs.

The Ramsbottoms came to Twin Lakes with their daughter Amy. Jason introduced her to sailing, which she enjoyed, and golf, which she alternated between enjoying and furiously rejecting, a variation which almost exactly mirrored her performance on the agreeable little course, as her father gently pointed out. Amy rejected bowls entirely after a single experimental twenty minutes on the green and a brisk command from the passing owner to keep her back foot on the mat as she released her woods. Fourteen-year-old girls do not take kindly to correction, nor is the image of crown-green bowling one to set their hearts dancing.

Freda Potts had no children. She came here with her husband for a couple of weekends, when he was home from the oil rigs. Matthew liked the peace of the site and the mirror-like summer sheen of the lakes, which was such a welcome contrast to the turbulence of the North Sea around the rigs. He began to make himself into a golfer, and had his handicap cut accordingly by the diligent Walter Keane. He was amused that people here could take life on the site so seriously. For Matthew Potts, this place was a welcome and strictly temporary respite from the challenges of his work outside, which brought him rich pickings but also the sort of challenges which most of the people here could not even contemplate.

Freda Potts was glad that Matthew was something of a loner, so that he did not get heavily involved with the people on the site. She watched anxiously his limited but perfectly polite conversation with some of her neighbours on the site. Freda had now been here twice with her supposed nephew, Wayne Briggs, but to her mind Wayne had not been convincing in the role. He had regarded it as a rich joke rather than a vital precaution. She felt guilt when she was here with Matthew, but an overwhelming excitement and danger that set her pulse racing when she drove in here with Wayne Briggs beside her.

George Martindale, the Jamaican with the huge friendly smile and the ability to attract and amuse most people, came here with his family almost every weekend. People looked forward to seeing his two bright and lively children, who were so 'well brought up' and polite. George's wife, Mary, was even more popular than he was, because she would do anything to help people, assistance which was welcome in a community where most people were older than she was. In the conservative and largely middle-class world of Twin Lakes, where racism, conscious or unconscious, still lurked beneath many skins, the Martindales were excellent ambassadors for more modern attitudes.

At the edge of the site, Geoffrey Tiler and his partner Michael Norrington were more conscious than others of the opportunities of escapism offered by Twin Lakes. If there were still instances of casual and unthinking racism, which occasionally declared themselves in people's speech, there was also still suspicion of gay people in this sort of community. Geoffrey and Michael approached the closed world of Twin Lakes with caution, but found to their delight that they were generally accepted here for what they were.

Norrington had been open about his sexuality for years, but Geoffrey Tiler, although at Twin Lakes he made no secret of his feelings, had still not declared himself in his working environment. It was somehow more difficult when you were the managing director of a small company, he maintained, although even Geoffrey was not quite sure how far that was true and how far it was merely a convenient excuse for not boldly declaring his new lifestyle. He cherished the seclusion of this place – but that was merely an evasion. He liked Twin Lakes, because people respected your privacy here and weren't too anxious to ascertain how your persona on the site related to your life outside.

Geoffrey had never been much of a sportsman, but he took up bowls and enjoyed the quietness of the green on the long summer evenings. He often played alone, exploring the subtleties of the turf and the effects he could achieve with the bias on his woods. Michael Norrington was more outgoing and confident. He joined up with anyone to get a game on the golf course, and was delighted to win the mixed doubles championship with Debbie Keane, Wally having graciously invited him to partner his very short-hitting but very straight-hitting spouse. Debbie was highly pleased with their success. The indefatigable gossip contrived over several rounds of the competition to find out quite a bit about the backgrounds of Michael Norrington and Geoffrey Tiler.

Richard Seagrave and Vanessa did not mix much with the other residents at Twin Lakes. They were perfectly polite, but cautious, even standoffish, in some people's view. Yet as the summer advanced and the sun shone into most people's lives, even Richard and Vanessa unbent a little and joined in with the rest. It was surely harmless to do so, Vanessa told her man, because the people here were harmless and incurious. Well, not entirely incurious – she had to concede that when Richard cited Debbie Keane and her cheerful investigation of every-one's background – but surely harmless.

Richard increased his popularity by purchasing a dinghy from one of the older residents who was no longer able to use it and paying a generous price for it. He then spent many hours on the lakes, increasing his sailing expertise and waiting patiently for bites from some of the seven varieties of fish which swam in the waters beneath him. This was the sort of life he had envisaged for himself as a boy, he thought, during his quiet hours upon the lakes. This was the real Richard Seagrave, not the man who operated so ruthlessly during the week in Birmingham.

Debbie Keane was very anxious to know whether Vanessa was married to Richard, but the pair delighted in keeping her in suspense whilst they danced conversationally around the issue. Wally and Debbie Keane had to give a lot of attention to Vanessa's golf handicap, because the Junoesque blonde proved to have quite an ability for the game. She hit the ball much further than any woman on the site and out-drove many of the men. Her handicap tumbled as she won a series of events, so that the Keanes had difficulty in keeping up with the rate of her improvement. She was never short of male partners when she went out for a friendly round, but Richard Seagrave did not seem to mind that.

Seagrave put up a handsome silver cup for the young golfers to play for, and was on hand to present it graciously when Nicky Martindale became the first winner. The picture of the presentation, with the beaming black boy reaching up to shake the hand of the donor of the trophy, surrounded by other children and with proud parents applauding benevolently, delighted the site's owners. They had it enlarged for display in the office and used it in all the literature they devised to advertise Twin Lakes and its attractions.

On the morning of Saturday 20th July, Michael Norrington lay on his back in bed and listened to the dawn chorus. It was one of the splendours of the rural world of Twin Lakes, with birds large and small joining in to herald another day and stake their claims to their own patches and their own mates in the harsh world of tooth and claw.

Having to make your way in a hostile world gave you some understanding of the need to be joyous over the very act of survival, thought Michael. He was fifty-three now, but he had known about his sexuality since he was fourteen. The world in those days had been generally contemptuous of homosexuality. It had been legal for some time in 1975, but there was still much hostility, and even those who declared themselves liberals had tended to regard the boy's sexual preferences as suspicious. Well, unfortunate, anyway. Even Michael's mother, who had always been sympathetic to his leanings, had regarded them as unfortunate. He smiled fondly at the memory of her. She'd been dead for six years now, but he still missed her. Missed her foibles, he thought, just as much as her unstinting love for him.

The birds were finishing their concerted greeting of the new day now, but a single blackbird trilled on as a solo, flinging its soul from some tree towards the rising sun and the warmth which was taking over from the cool darkness of the short summer night. Michael lay and listened to it with the slight, unconscious smile which Geoffrey Tiler found so attractive. He knew that he was not going to get back to sleep again. Geoff was still dead to the world, snuffling occasionally into the half-snore which was the only thing that disturbed his quiet sleep. It would be better not to disturb him. From what Geoff had said last night, it seemed that he'd endured a testing week at his factory. He would need his rest to recover from it.

Michael rose and dressed quietly and slid softly out into the glory of the morning. He stood for a moment and watched the young moorhens at the edge of the lake, marvelling that they could have grown so much in a single week. The sun was still low and there was a thin white mist over the lakes, but there was scarcely a cloud to set against the vivid blue of the sky. He'd been planning a moan about being unable to sleep on into the day, but it was surely good to be out and savouring a morning like this. Good to be alive; that old phrase was fair enough, when you felt nature awakening all around you.

A quarter to six. He'd planned to walk around the lakes and watch the summer mist dissipate in the gathering warmth of the sun, but now he changed his plan. He'd stroll round the site and inspect the gardening labours of the residents. He was interested in their efforts, but too shy to inspect them when the owners were there to meet him and quiz him about his own tastes and his own movements. He looked first at the begonias and pelargoniums which Geoffrey had planted around their place a couple of months ago. They were doing well now; there had been helpful and quite copious rain in the weeks after he had planted them, and now they were burgeoning under the long days of sun. He bent and removed a single weed and a couple of spent flowers from the geraniums – he'd always called them that, despite Geoff's insistence upon the correct botanical name.

You could deduce which people came here most frequently by the plants around their homes, he thought. Some had plants in large pots which must need regular attention. Many had small beds like the one Geoff had made – strictly speaking, the terms of your occupancy didn't allow you to do that, but the site owners didn't seem to mind, so long as you didn't go overboard and so long as you kept your handiwork tidy and well weeded. The annuals people had planted in their small oval or rectangular beds were now coming to their best. There were splendid bursts of colour from antirrhinums, busy lizzies, lobelia and alyssum, as well as begonias and geraniums, some of which were almost as good as the ones Geoff had planted and cherished – Michael was studiously loyal to his still-sleeping partner.

This was definitely the best time to see them, when they were opening fresh petals to the bright light of the new July day and there was scarcely a breath of air to disturb their effects. Some people said many of these annuals were brash, with their sustained displays of vibrant colours, but Michael Norrington didn't subscribe to that view. To his mind, these sudden and brilliant displays amongst the green that dominated the site put man securely amidst nature. They were highly acceptable assertions of the presence of men and women amidst the water and trees which were the *raison d'etre* of Twin Lakes. And at this time of day, you could observe them at your leisure, without having to exchange polite and meaningless conversation with the people who had planted them here for their own and others' delight.

As if to counterpoint this thought, a woman appeared suddenly at the edge of his vision. A woman whose normally neat grey hair now flew uncombed and whose normally neat clothing was now dishevelled and unheeded. So much so that it took Michael a moment to realize that this was Debbie Keane, the woman whom he normally took pains to avoid as he moved around the site. There was no avoiding her now. She was seeking him out.

'Thank goodness there's someone!' shouted Debbie. There was no need to shout in this quiet place, and for a moment Michael wanted to counsel silence, so that she would not waken the residents who were still enjoying their rest on this perfect morning. But her speech, as well as her demeanour and dress, was so much the opposite of her usual mode that Michael felt an immediate surge of sympathy for this normally rather tiresome woman.

He smiled reassuringly at her. 'What can I do for you, Mrs Keane? Or Debbie, I should say, shouldn't I? We agreed on Debbie last week, didn't we?'

Normally she herself employed roundabout methods of address and cheerful questions like this. They were the methods she found most effective for her own inquisitive nature. This morning she brushed them aside. 'It's Wally. I can't find Wally.'

'I expect the sunlight woke him early. He's probably gone for a walk around the site on this glorious morning, like me. I'm really enjoying myself. I expect Wally is too. I haven't seen him, but I haven't moved very far yet. I was appreciating people's horticultural efforts. Yours included, Debbie. I think you've got a really good display going beside your unit.'

'I don't think his bed's been slept in.'

Michael Norrington didn't want to know about the bedroom arrangements of the Keanes and he wasn't going to enquire into them now. He said lamely, 'Are you sure of that?'

'I'm pretty sure, yes.' For a moment, his enquiry brought a slim hope to her. Then she said, 'No, I'm sure. I don't think he's been here since last night.'

For a moment, the bizarre prospect of the staid and elusive Wally Keane conducting an affair on the site and sleeping in someone else's bed reared itself in Norrington's undisciplined imagination. The notion was so evidently ridiculous that he switched immediately back to the banal. 'I'm sure we shall find that there's a simple explanation for this.'

'He doesn't do this. I'm worried about him.' It was direct, brusque and to the point; exactly the opposite of her round-about, insinuating style when she was searching for gossip.

Michael had his first moment of real fear. He'd been about to offer to accompany her on a stroll around the site to look for her husband, but suddenly he did not want her with him. Suddenly he was afraid of what they might find. He said as cheerfully as he could, 'I'm sure there'll be a simple explanation. I'm sure it will turn out that he couldn't sleep and went out for an early walk, like me.' He saw that she was about to point out again that his bed hadn't been slept in and went on hastily, 'I'll tell him he should have more consideration for you, when I find him.'

'Can I be of any help?' The deep voice startled both of them. They turned to find George Martindale standing behind them at the corner of the Keane home. His weight was a little on one leg and he had the awkward, diffident manner which descends upon big men when they are not quite sure whether they are intruding. Everyone on the site, including even those whose visits were least frequent, knew Debbie Keane, who made it her business to introduce herself to every newcomer. But Martindale paused, looked at the man beside her, and said, as if wishing to fill the awkward silence, 'It's Mr Norrington, isn't it?'

'Michael, please. And you're George, aren't you? I've seen those delightful boys often enough – they get everywhere at that age, don't they?'

Martindale smiled his pride in his children. 'It's those boys who've got me out here at this time of day. I've told them to keep quiet and let their mum sleep, but that won't last for long.'

'Mrs Keane – sorry, Debbie – has lost her husband.' Norrington watched the previously cheerful black face cloud with sudden concern. 'Temporarily, I mean. I was just volunteering to go and find him. I think Debbie should stay here, in case he returns whilst we're searching for him.'

'Yes. You should certainly do that, Debbie. Michael and I will find Wally for you. And tear a strip off him for worrying you, if you like.' George Martindale was back in smiling mode.

Debbie was grateful. She flicked her errant grey hair back

from her forehead, and managed a bleak smile. 'This isn't like him at all.'

The very thin white man and the burly Jamaican turned naturally towards the woods on the far side of the lake from the residences. Unless he was in one of the many homes and buildings, it was the obvious place for a man to conceal himself. Or simply to get away for a while from a garrulous wife, thought Michael hopefully. They walked in silence for a few minutes. They had never held a conversation or been alone with each other before, and you could hardly have had two more different men. Eventually, Martindale said, 'Do you know much about Wally Keane?'

'No. He seems to be a bit of a loner. But perhaps you get that impression because his wife's so talkative.'

'Nosey, you mean.'

Norrington grinned and felt the tension between them slackening. 'I suppose I do, yes. She's quite a busybody, Debbie, isn't she? But harmless, I think. Perhaps her life with Wally is a little sterile, without a bit of gossip to liven it up.'

George didn't comment on that. He didn't tolerate people who pried into his affairs, but you had to make an exception for a small, grey-haired woman of sixty-one who seemed to have no motive beyond curiosity. 'He's a bit of a loner, Wally. He knows everything that goes on here, but he doesn't broadcast it.' George glanced sideways at Norrington to see if he would comment, but there was no reaction.

They were in the woods now, on the far side of the lake from the residences. It was still only quarter past six; although the sun was rising rapidly, there was no visible sign of life in the homes. The boys would be dressed by now, George thought, creeping about the place and communicating in those stage whispers and giggles which would certainly waken Mary.

They were almost at the end of the woods when they saw it. The path wound in and out between the major forest trees here, so that the thing had its back to the light and presented itself initially only as a black silhouette against the low rays of the sun in the east.

The corpse was so still as it hung from the bough of the tree that it might have been something else entirely. Until you looked up and saw the features. The face was a livid crimson-grey, turning rapidly towards black around the tongue, which stuck out oddly on one side of the distorted lips. The eyes were so bulbous that they looked as if they might at any moment spring forth from the head.

There was but the slightest movement on the rope which suspended Walter Keane from the branch of the oak.

SEVEN

The owner of Twin Lakes was tight-lipped and strained. There had been reports of the death, first on local radio and then on the national bulletins. Foul play had not been ruled out, the official police release said. The familiar phrase was repeated with relish by the newsreader on Radio Gloucester. That got the journos interested. Jim Rawlinson's phone had scarcely stopped ringing during the last two hours. He had tried to ban reporters and journalists from the site, keeping the barrier beside his office firmly lowered.

But journalists are insensitive beasts, as he already knew. They were finding other ways on to the site, which was almost impossible to defend against unscrupulous human parasites in search of news and quotes. He had been relieved when the police had banished reporters and sealed off a wide area on the far side of the big lake with their plastic scene-of-crime tapes. But Jim Rawlinson had searched the site and found two reporters still snooping around, trying to get quotes from his residents about the site and the man who had been found hanged.

And now he had Detective Chief Superintendent John Lambert in his office. This was perhaps the most famous detective in the country and certainly the one whom almost everyone had heard of in this area. If the papers got hold of the fact that he was at Twin Lakes, they'd descend like locusts upon the site. And they'd be looking for the sensational and the bizarre, not the pleasant rural solitude and relaxation which Jim sold as the keynotes of this place.

Rawlinson said gruffly, 'I can't see why the top brass should be here at all. Not for a routine suicide.'

'If that is what this proves to be, we'll happily leave you in peace. DS Hook alerted me to the fact that threats have been issued to people on this site by a person or persons unknown. In view of that, any death needs to be thoroughly investigated.'

Rawlinson accepted that, reluctantly. The fact that he didn't query the threatening notes probably meant that he knew all about them: Bert had always known that Debbie Keane wasn't going to keep her mouth shut after he'd questioned her about the threats to the Ramsbottoms.

Jim Rawlinson said, 'This isn't the kind of publicity I need. I'm running a business here.'

The tall man nodded gravely, though he did not seem much impressed. 'We'll keep this as low-key as we can, but we can't control the media.' He smiled sourly. 'This might even be good publicity for you, Mr Rawlinson, if you take the long view. Murder – if this is murder – has a horrid attraction for many of the public. It would certainly put you on the map. Whether it would help you to sell your units might be another matter. But that's not my business. We need to determine whether there has been a serious crime here, and to find the culprit if there has been. We shall need your records of everyone on site. I'm sure you don't allow people to come here without recording a good deal about their backgrounds.'

'Our records are confidential.'

'And we shall treat them as such and return them to you. I assume your documentation of the home-owners is computer-ized. Detective Inspector Rushton at Oldford CID will require a full copy of them. Providing he has that, we needn't take anything away from here.'

Jim Rawlinson was reluctantly agreeing to this when DS Hook's mobile rang, sounding shrill and ominous in the high, quiet office. 'They're ready for us at the scene of crime, sir.'

Lambert glanced at Rawlinson. 'Don't worry, sir. We always describe the area as that, until we are sure that no crime is involved. Guilty until proved innocent, I suppose you could say, in this case. Do you think this was a suicide?'

The sudden baldness of the query took Rawlinson by surprise. 'I haven't even thought about it – I haven't had much chance to think, with these damn media people swarming around. I can't think anyone would want to kill Wally Keane. He was helpful and friendly. He even helped us out in the office here, when we were pushed for staff, with holidays and sickness. He was always ready to lend a hand, and he was almost a permanent resident at Twin Lakes. As far as that's allowed, of course.' He remembered hurriedly that he was speaking to what his father always called the long arm of the law.

'We'll let you know as soon as possible about the findings of our team. I'm afraid the woods are going to be inaccessible for your residents for at least the rest of today. And for considerably longer, if foul play has been involved.'

Lambert kept his face as blank as possible, implying that he would be pleased if this proved to be no more than the personal and individual tragedy of a suicide. But even as a veteran, he felt that quickening of the pulse which all CID men feel at the prospect of something more sinister.

The scene of crime area was not only taped off but protected by high screens. The sinister burden which hung from the tree had grown even darker as the sun had risen higher and the corpse had turned slowly backwards and forwards on its rope. It had now been photographed from every angle and carefully lifted down.

The two CID men, with plastic coverings over their feet to avoid contamination, moved slowly along the designated path, skirting the man and two women who were painstakingly gathering whatever they could glean from the area that might signify a recent human presence there. Lambert stared dispassionately at the small form upon the ground. Hook looked at it with more emotion, for he had known this thing as a living, speaking man, who had spoken to him and smiled at him on his last visit here three months earlier. Both men had seen hanging suicides before. Of the common means of suicide, this was the one which most affected you, because the evidence of the desperation which drove the decision to end life was somehow more apparent and stark with a hanging than with any other of the usual forms of suicide.

This was not a suicide.

The pathologist who had been examining the mortal remains of Walter Keane was quite definite about that. The body lay face downwards, looking pathetically small amidst the grass between the trees. 'This man was either dead or unconscious when he was strung up on that oak.' He glanced up at the tree which had been here already for a couple of centuries and looked good for a couple more; somehow that extended presence seemed to make human death and human activity beneath its branches less significant. 'I suspect the man was insensible rather than dead when he was strung up, but I'll tell you definitely when I've had him on the slab.'

Every profession has its own jargon. It is a long time since post-mortems were conducted upon slabs, but the men who conduct them still use the term, in a world of stainless steel. This one pointed at a wound at the back right of the dead man's head. It seemed at first insignificant, as there was little blood and the damage was concealed by Keane's lengthy grey hair. 'Someone hit this man very hard with the traditional blunt instrument. We haven't so far found anything round here which fits the wound.'

'And the rest of this was then arranged to suggest suicide.'

The pathologist nodded. 'Unless the victim was already wearing a rope around his neck, which seems highly unlikely, the person who hit him then fastened this rope around his neck and hauled him up into the tree.'

Lambert looked automatically from the body on the ground to the limb of the tree above them. 'So we can probably assume it was a man, because of the strength involved.'

'No.' The pathologist's prompt and definite rebuttal suggested he was enjoying increasing their problems. 'The victim is small and lightly built. We'll have an accurate weight by the end of the day, but I suspect it will be less than ten stones. Slinging the rope over that branch and using her own weight intelligently, any reasonably healthy woman could have got him up there.'

The scene of crime officer in charge of the team, a retired sergeant who knew a little of Lambert from his days in the service, said quietly, 'We don't know for certain that only one person was involved in this. We've found various bits and pieces within twenty yards of here, but it may be that none of them is significant. I understand that many of the residents walk through these woods. It will be difficult to pin anything down to last night.'

Lambert glanced automatically at the pathologist with the mention of a time. The man nodded. 'Almost certainly late last night, from rectal temperature and the progress of rigor. I might be able to give you something more accurate when I get to analyse the stomach contents.'

He sounded almost eager. Lambert, who had attended many a post-mortem in his younger days, could almost catch in his brain the sickening smells and sounds which would shortly proceed from what lay on the ground beneath them. He'd never developed the stomach needed for post-mortems.

He said without great enthusiasm to Bert Hook, 'We'd better speak to the wife of the deceased.'

For obvious reasons, the spouse of any murder victim and the last person known to have seen him alive always excite police interest. Debbie Keane was both of these. But neither man held any great hope that they were speaking to Walter Keane's murderer.

Lambert made his stock opening to bereaved wives. 'We're very sorry to have to intrude at a time like this. You're naturally very upset, but you might be able to offer us scraps of information which will help us to establish how your husband died.'

'It wasn't suicide?' Debbie Keane had been looking much older than her sixty-one years, with her face drawn and very pale, but obviously her brain was working well enough. She had picked up the implications in phrases he had hoped might pass her by.

He glanced at Hook, who said, 'It seems possible that he didn't die by his own hand, Mrs Keane.'

She was silent for such a long time that they thought she wasn't going to speak. But experienced CID men often let silences stretch; they realize that people who are accustomed to the normal social conventions will usually feel the need to fill a silence. And sometimes what they say under emotional pressure will be revealing. What Debbie Keane said was simple and quiet. 'I knew that. I knew that Wally wouldn't have gone up there and killed himself.'

She seemed relieved by the thought, even though it raised the possibility of the worst crime of all. It meant that Wally hadn't felt so desperate that he wanted to get away from her, that he hadn't felt that his life with her had nothing left save a suffering so crushing that even oblivion was preferable to it. There was another long moment during which she said nothing but allowed her mind to race. Then she said, 'You told me when you were here before that someone had been sending notes around, threatening people with death.'

'I did indeed. I asked for your help, Debbie, didn't I? But you had no more idea than anyone else who'd been sending those notes. Have you had any thoughts on it since?'

Again a pause, when this time they would have expected an immediate answer. She looked for a moment as if she might volunteer something. Then she brushed the strand of grey hair which strayed persistently over her forehead impatiently away and said, 'No, I haven't come up with anything. And neither has anyone else I've spoken to about it.'

Bert Hook gave her a quiet smile, which was designed to be encouraging but also had an element of resignation. He'd told her clearly all those weeks ago that what he'd said to her had been confidential, yet he'd known even as he'd given her the information that she would swiftly spread it around the site and through the very varied community which constituted Twin Lakes. And in a way that seemed to have served its purpose. There had been no reports of any further threatening notes like the ones which had so disturbed the Ramsbottoms. Perhaps the news from Debbie Keane that a detective sergeant was on the case had silenced the mischievous brain which had devised those melodramatic and distressing messages.

Hook said gently, 'Probably Walter's death had nothing to do with those notes. But it looks to us at present as though someone killed him. There'll have to be a post-mortem, I'm afraid. But we shall know more after that.'

'They'll cut him up, won't they?'

'Post-mortem examinations tell us all sorts of things, Debbie. We shall learn more about exactly how Wally died. Perhaps even things about whoever else was involved in his death.'

She nodded quietly, then repeated her previous reaction with some satisfaction. 'I knew he didn't kill himself. Wally wouldn't have done that. He enjoyed his life here far too much to do that.'

'When was he last with you, Debbie?'

'They always ask that, the police, don't they? They think the wife is a possibility for the killer, don't they?'

She seemed more excited than disturbed by the thought. Perhaps even a little local infamy was better than obscurity. Bert Hook said sturdily, 'I'm sure no one thinks that in this case, Debbie. But we need to establish whatever we can of Walter's movements last night.'

Her eyes filled suddenly with tears. She was in that febrile state which results from shock; she was experiencing swift changes of mood and emotion that were as much a surprise to her as to the onlookers. 'We ate at about seven. We don't like to eat too late in the evening nowadays; we need the time to digest the food during the evening. We had quiche and new potatoes and broccoli. Wally always likes new potatoes – he says they're a meal in themselves, when you get salt and butter with them.' She stopped, and for a moment they thought she was going to weep and lose control of her speech. But then she swallowed twice and continued. 'We had apple crumble for afters; he always liked that. It was much later that he went out for a walk; he often did that in the evenings in the summer. He liked to see what was going on around the site. See who was on the golf course and the bowling green. Find if there was anyone sailing or fishing on the lakes. But I think he would have been too late for that last night, by the time we'd finished watching the telly.'

They waited again to see whether grief would take over and destroy her coherence, but she merely shook her head sadly, as if she were speaking of a distant acquaintance rather than the man who had shared her life for over thirty years. Lambert said gently, 'Can you recall exactly what the time was when he went out, Mrs Keane?'

She looked at the older man sharply, as if she had forgotten for a moment that he was there. She had been concentrating upon the homely features of Bert Hook, the man she had met months ago in happier times. 'It must have been quite late, I think. We watched Gardeners' World until nine. We like Monty

Don, because he's a real gardener. Then we saw a couple of comedy programmes on BBC One. It must have been somewhere around ten when Wally went out.'

'Thank you. That is precise and helpful. And as far as you know, he didn't return here after that?'

'No.' She was suddenly brimming with tears, after the control she had shown in giving her account.

Lambert left it to Hook to ask the most difficult question. Bert gave her an encouraging smile as he said, 'But you didn't raise the alarm last night. Weren't you anxious then, when Wally didn't come back?'

She was suddenly anxious to speak, her tragedy forgotten for a moment in the necessity to explain herself and her conduct. 'I didn't know he hadn't come in. He moves quietly, does Wally. And he has his own room. He spends hours in there with his computer. Sometimes he's studying things on it long after I've gone to bed. He has his own bed in there, you see. But he comes in and we have a cup of tea together in the mornings. That's in my bed.' It was plainly important to Debbie Keane to explain that even if they slept apart they were not estranged from each other. It did not seem to have struck her yet that there would be no more companionable cups of morning tea.

Hook nodded. 'So it wasn't until this morning that you realized he hadn't come back from his evening walk.'

'That's just it, yes. I woke early with the sunlight. The place felt very empty. There was no noise from Wally's room. No flushing of the toilet or running of taps. And he didn't bring in the tea.'

Now she did weep, but softly and steadily, not in the great sobs they would have expected. Hook, who had never grown hardened to death, was suddenly full of pity for this woman who had been translated overnight from annoying tittle-tattler to tragic widow. She looked small and very helpless, as if she would never cope without the man to whom she had deferred so readily. She would survive, of course, when she had taken the time to grieve and to establish the rails upon which her new life must run. But she looked at this moment as if she needed someone to put arms around her and hold her for a long time, whilst she wept away the first and most wracking bout of her misery. He said softly, 'Do you have relatives who can help you? Children, perhaps?'

'We have one daughter. She's in Aberdeen. It's a long way away, and we're not close.' It was almost Chekhovian in its stark negativity.

'Perhaps you could go to her for a few days.'

'I wouldn't want to go there. My friends are here. This is where I belong, now.'

'I see. Debbie, I'm sorry, but I have to ask you this. Do you know of anyone who would have wished to harm Wally?'

'You mustn't be sorry, DS Hook. We all want to find out who did this, don't we? And I can think of a few people around here who weren't keen on Wally. He could be irritating sometimes, you know. He thought he knew everything and people didn't always like that.' She was suddenly shaken by a sigh which seemed almost too much for her thin frame to contain. 'But no one would have wanted to kill him, just because he was irritating, would they? You don't go killing people because you're annoyed about an adjustment to your golfing handicap, do you?'

Lambert, who was a member of the Handicap Committee at Ross-on-Wye Golf Club, said hastily, 'No, you don't do that, Mrs Keane. Perhaps when you've time and you're less upset you could give a little more thought to this. If you come up with any names you think we ought to consider and investigate, would you ring this number immediately, please?'

She took his card and studied it intently for a moment, as if the simple print was confirming to her that this awful thing had really happened and must be attended to. 'I'll do that. Someone must have done this, mustn't he?'

'Yes, I'm afraid that's so. And it might be a he or a she. We must keep an open mind on that, until we know more.'

She was suddenly animated by that thought. The gossip in her responded through all her suffering to the thought that this might be man or woman, might be someone to whom she had spoken, someone with whom she might have shared a joke in the days before Wally's death. 'I'll think about it. Other people on the site might have ideas about it too, mightn't they?' For a moment, she was beguiled by thoughts of the exchanges she would enjoy; she would be the centre of attention for those from whom she normally merely gathered material.

Lambert said, 'We'll need to take away Wally's computer, I'm afraid. We may be able to get clues about his enemies from what's in there, you see. We'll let you have it back, in due course.'

'Don't you worry about that, Mr Lambert. I never liked the thing – never understood why he spent all those hours playing with it. I don't know anything about computers.'

'You won't be able to give us his password, then?'

'Oh no. I never wanted anything to do with the damned thing. Will that stop you getting what you want from it?'

'No. We have people who are experts in these things in the police service, Mrs Keane. It will take a little longer, but I'm sure they'll get in there quite quickly. Unless it had anything to do with his death, whatever we find will be kept strictly confidential. And unless it's needed for a court case, everything will be returned to you in due course.'

It was perhaps this glimpse of the nuts and bolts of a murder investigation which brought home to her finally the thought that Walter Keane was gone forever. They left her standing alone in the doorway of her unit, a tiny, weeping figure for whom the world was suddenly far too large.

EIGHT

There should have been a golf tournament on that Saturday. It was postponed. The Twin Lakes residents had no stomach for competition, after the sensational death of the man who had watched their golfing efforts and controlled their handicaps. It would not have been fitting; everyone was agreed on that.

But the police spread the notion that people should carry on as normally as possible, apart from avoiding the scene of crime area – that cordoned-off section amongst the trees on the other side of the lakes which had been transformed overnight from picturesque to sinister. So people came out to play golf on the little course, even though the serious competition had been postponed. Surprisingly quickly, the fairways became quite crowded on this perfect July day. Conversation was muted at first, with everyone conscious of what had happened three hundred yards from the first tee, but gradually golf's own petty triumphs and tribulations took over, so that the laughter and anguish rang more loudly from the green acres between the trees.

Vanessa Seagrave was one of the participants. She billed herself under that name now, though Debbie Keane still doubted its authenticity and conveyed her thoughts to anyone who cared to share her speculations. Vanessa, the woman who was now the best female golfer at Twin Lakes, was playing with Freda Potts and two men whose wives did not demean themselves with golf.

Freda was talented but erratic, whilst Vanessa was talented and consistent. Their handicaps reflected this and offered them a close contest against each other. The two men who were partnering them did not care too much about the contest. Their form and their conversation were muted by Wally Keane's death when they began, but they were soon radically cheered by the contours and the movements of their female partners.

It suited Richard Seagrave that Vanessa should be playing golf and helping to ensure that the course was a centre of attention. He had watched the activities of the police from his residential unit, whilst remaining carefully concealed within it. He made a phone call which lasted no more than thirty seconds, agreeing a time and a place. He didn't like phone calls, even from mobiles. You never knew what was being recorded. And from what he read of police activity, it seemed to be possible to track down all kinds of phone conversations which you would once have thought untraceable.

He recognized Chief Superintendent John Lambert and noted grimly that the case was already high profile. The news of a suicide had flown round the site, but this was clearly no suicide. Not if bloody Lambert had been assigned to it. Wally Keane had had this coming to him, from the moment when he'd moved out of his comfort zone. He was a meddling old fool who'd strayed beyond the harmless area where he should have operated. Like Polonius in Hamlet, thought Richard, with a small, satisfied smile. He was an educated man: people sometimes forgot that.

It was when Lambert and Hook were within the screens at the scene of crime site that Seagrave slipped quietly into the driving seat of his dark blue Jaguar. The office staff and the police were stopping anyone coming on to the site, but they couldn't prevent residents from leaving. He watched the long barrier pole rising slowly towards the perpendicular, then eased the big car out into the anonymity of the world outside Twin Lakes.

Britain wasn't yet a police state, whatever the left-wing press said, and you could take advantage of that.

The Ramsbottoms hadn't left their home by the lake during the morning. They had watched what was happening on the site and remained tight-lipped. They hadn't even spoken much to each other, beyond terse statements of fact about what was happening around them.

Jason hadn't felt like playing golf, even after he'd seen others trundling trolleys past them on their way to the course. Three hours crept by as if they were waiting for something.

Neither of them was surprised when they saw Bert Hook marching towards their door with a tall man alongside him.

Hook gave them no more than a token smile. Lisa thought Bert looked almost as nervous as she felt. He said, 'It would be good to see you both again, if it wasn't for the circumstances. You've heard what's happened?'

They nodded in unison, not quite trusting themselves to speak.

'This is Detective Chief Superintendent Lambert. We need you to answer a few questions for us. We've come to you first, but there's nothing significant in that. We shall be speaking to other people who knew the deceased. Everyone on the site will be interviewed by a member of our team in due course.'

Lisa glanced at her husband, then back at Hook's weather-beaten, reliable features. 'It wasn't a suicide, was it?'

'That has yet to be confirmed officially. But no, it wasn't: we're pretty certain about that.'

Jason addressed himself directly to John Lambert. 'You're now investigating a murder, then. You wouldn't be here unless that was so.'

The tall man with the long, lined face gave him a brisk nod. 'And we hope you may be able to help us with the first stages of that investigation. Murder and manslaughter are almost unique among crimes, in that the victim cannot speak for himself. Yet almost always we need to gain a knowledge of the type of man he was, the way he lived, his likes and dislikes, the people he liked and the people he hated. These are crucial to solving the problem of who ended his existence. We have to find out all of these things from other people. We've spoken to Walter Keane's widow. You are the next people we decided to contact.'

It sounded quite threatening, in Lambert's calm, measured tones. Lisa Ramsbottom wondered if it was meant to do so. She was already disconcerted by the steady scrutiny she felt from those clear grey eyes, which seemed to study her as no other eyes had ever done during normal social exchanges. She said nervously, 'We know Sergeant Hook. He's a neighbour of ours. He came here and played golf with Jason, back in May.'

'But that wasn't the primary reason for his visit, was it, Mrs Ramsbottom?'

He made her feel as if she'd been concealing something. 'No. We'd received some rather disturbing notes. I spoke to Bert and he agreed to come to see the set-up here and conduct an informal investigation.'

'Yes, Bert would do that. He's good at the informal. Especially if a game of golf was part of the deal.' It was the first hint of humour, but accompanied only by the most minimal of smiles.

'The golf was deliberate. We wanted the people here to think that Bert was just an ordinary visitor.' Jason sprang to the defence of the inscrutable Hook. 'You have to bear in mind that it was almost certainly someone here who shoved those notes under our door.'

'Agreed. And DS Hook told me about those threats and named to me the people he had questioned about them. He didn't mention his score on your golf course. We agreed to do nothing about the notes unless there were more of them. I understand that the agreement was that Lisa would let Bert know if there were any further developments on that front.'

'Yes. I'm away for most of the week.' Jason gave a small, encouraging smile to his wife.

'And I'm the one who was most upset by the messages. Jason was more ready to shrug them off.' Lisa wondered why she felt it necessary to explain that it was she who had made and continued the contact with Hook.

'And have there been any more of them?'

'No. I'd have been straight round to tell Bert at home if there had been.'

The mention of home was a reminder to the CID men that these were second homes to the invisible people around them, that this was a kind of permanent holiday village where the occupants knew each other but worked all over the country and had other and perhaps very different lives away from Twin Lakes. Lambert said, 'Has anyone else received similar notes to the ones sent to you?'

'No. Well, not as far as we know.' She glanced at Jason, who gave her a taut nod, which seemed to signify approval as well as agreement.

Lambert nodded. 'Of course, other people might have received them and said nothing about them. You yourselves chose to ask Bert Hook to look into the matter, rather than comparing notes with people here. Which was, incidentally, the right thing to do. Such things rarely lead to any serious injury, but it's much better that the police are informed about them. Apart from anything else, it often brings about an abrupt end to the trouble. People who send messages like the ones you received are usually no more than unpleasant mischief-makers. They cease activity at the prospect of police investigation and possible legal action.'

Jason said firmly, 'It's my belief that this is what happened here. We've had no more notes, and I don't believe that anyone else has.'

'But if everyone acts as discreetly as you did, how can you be sure of that?'

Jason glanced at Hook and received a grin which encouraged him to proceed. 'It's public knowledge around here now that we were threatened. Bert questioned Debbie Keane about it when he was here. That was because we told him that Debbie was the one most likely to know the source of anything untoward like this. She lives here permanently, apart from the month when she has by law to be somewhere else. And she makes it her business to know everything that goes on around here.'

Bert Hook spoke for the first time in many minutes. 'It was a deliberate decision on my part to speak to her. She was the person most likely to know of anyone making a nuisance of himself or herself in this way, because she's a great gossip. But discretion isn't in her nature. I was aware when I spoke to her that she simply wouldn't be capable of keeping such a juicy titbit of news to herself. But that wasn't necessarily a bad thing. The knowledge that the police were aware of the threats which had been offered to Lisa and Jason might at least frighten off the twisted mind which was behind this, in the manner you just mentioned.'

'Which is what seems to have happened,' said Jason Ramsbottom. 'We haven't had any more notes.'

'And has Debbie Keane unearthed any other similar threats to other people who have units here?'

'No. The whole thing seems to have gone very quiet. Hopefully it's died the death.'

'As has Debbie Keane's husband, Walter,' Lambert said grimly. 'That is our greater concern now, as you will understand. Do you think there is any connection between the threats you received and what happened to Walter Keane last night?'

'No,' said Jason promptly. 'I think those notes we received were from someone who was no more than a mischief-maker, as Bert suggested at the time. There's been no sign of any activity from him – or her, as you pointed out it might be – in the last three months. I can't see that person suddenly acting against Wally Keane. And who'd want to kill Wally?'

'Someone certainly did,' said Lambert dourly. 'Our business over the next few days will be to find an answer to the question you've just asked. Have you any ideas yourself?'

Jason felt almost as if he'd been slapped in the face, because the question he should have expected had been flung at him so abruptly. 'No, I haven't. This will be a shock to everyone on the site.'

'Not to one person, it won't. Or possibly two.' Lambert glanced from one to the other of the shocked faces opposite him. 'We can't rule out a joint effort. In fact, we are in no position to rule out anything at the moment, so your views as regular weekend visitors will be welcome.'

There was a moment of silence before Jason said brusquely, 'Wally was a loner.'

'Was he a likeable man?'

'Likeable wouldn't be the right word. He wanted to be in charge of things, and that doesn't always make people popular. Some people resented the way he adjusted their golf handicaps without reference to anyone else. He could be a law unto himself and he liked to assert his opinions about everything that goes on here. But he was prepared to put in a lot of unpaid work and he was here for most of the time, as others aren't. So you could say that he had a right to do the things he did.'

Jason hadn't looked at his wife through this, but she now supported him. 'And he didn't offend people, as his wife sometimes does. He didn't seem to want to know everyone's business, as she did. Jason is right when he says people sometimes resented

Wally, but that was all very petty. I can't think of anyone who would have wanted to kill him and I'm sure Jason would agree with me on that.'

Her husband immediately nodded his confirmation. Lambert looked at both of them for a moment, as if weighing the likelihood of accuracy in what they said, then gave a nod of acceptance. 'Give some thought to the matter over the next day or two, will you? However unlikely it may seem, the overwhelming probability is that it's someone to whom you have spoken many times, perhaps even someone whom you would call a friend, who has done this thing. It will be better to ring this number at Oldford CID than to wait to contact Bert at home. He's likely to be working long hours until we have an arrest.' He gave them the card with the number and appeared to have finished with them.

It was left to DS Hook to complete the exchanges. 'You'd better tell us where you both were last night, please. For elimination purposes. It's just routine.'

Jason glanced at Lisa, giving her a small, encouraging smile. 'I expect you use that phrase about routine a lot, Bert. You hear it in police series on the telly, don't you? Well, I think we were together for the whole of the evening, weren't we, darling?'

It was the first time he had used the endearment and it dropped a little oddly into the tension in the room. Lisa didn't look at him but at Hook's substantial feet: perhaps she was concentrating on her memory, or on what she had to say now. 'We arrived here at about half past five, I think. We unpacked what we'd brought with us, which only took a few minutes. Then we went across to the bar-restaurant and got ourselves something to eat there. We saw quite a few of our friends in there. They'd remember us, I'm sure, if it's necessary.'

'What time did you leave there?'

She glanced at Jason, who said immediately, 'Around eight o'clock, I'd say. It's difficult to be completely accurate, when you don't think you're going to be questioned about it by CID the next day.'

He gave a nervous laugh, which brought no response from Lambert or Hook, who said merely, 'And during the later part of the evening?'

'We were together all evening and all night.' He made another attempt to lighten the tension. 'That's the kind of alibi the police don't like, isn't it, the husband and wife one?'

This time Hook did allow himself a rueful smile. 'We often suspect it, when we're dealing with known crooks. But it's difficult to break down, and the known crooks know that as well as we do.'

Lambert stood up, then paused to deliver a final sobering thought to them. 'It's early days, of course, but as I said, we haven't ruled out the thought that more than one person might have been involved in this crime. Two people would have made it easier in several respects.'

The two detectives walked a hundred yards away from the little bungalow by the lake, watching the swans cruise majestically away from them over the water. Hook voiced the thought they had both had a hundred times before in similar circumstances. 'I'd like to hear what those two are saying to each other now.'

Lambert's eye followed a skein of wild geese flying purposefully over their heads. 'I expect they're wondering what we are saying to each other about them, Bert. And I'd put money on the fact that your first thought about what we've just heard is the same as mine.'

It was a challenge, of sorts. But they had worked together for so long now that Hook found it stimulating rather than stressful. He reviewed the conversation in his mind for a moment before he said, 'They didn't seem at all surprised when we told them at the outset that this was murder, not suicide.'

'That's it. Might be significant. Might mean nothing.'

Richard Seagrave felt himself relax as he drove the big Jaguar unhurriedly along the lanes around Leominster. He'd been quite tense that morning at Twin Lakes, he realized. He smiled at the thought. He wasn't used to stress nowadays.

He opened up the engine for a few miles as he moved northwards on the A49. He was pleased that he still felt the aura of superiority, of having arrived in life, which three litres of engine and the big, sleek car still gave him. Schoolboy-ish really, but that was all right. Richard still cherished the notion that all men were boys at heart and did not mature as women did. It was fond and foolish, in view of the many things he had done to banish the innocence of childhood.

He met the men in the village of Tenbury Wells. That too was an indulgence: he had chosen it purely because the name of the place appealed to him. But the village had a good hotel and restaurant; he had eaten there with Vanessa only six weeks earlier. The men he was meeting wouldn't like it. Snooker halls and lap-dancing clubs were more their scene, and they would be thoroughly uncomfortable in this place, but he liked that. People were less likely to speak up for themselves and demand things when they felt ill at ease.

They were there when he arrived, sitting in the car park in their silver Ford Focus. They hadn't gone inside to wait for him, because this wasn't their sort of place. He parked only three places away from them, reversing in with a wide sweep to make sure that they could not miss him. He gave not a glance in their direction, but flicked the button on his key to lock the Jaguar and walked unhurriedly into the inn.

It was too late for coffee; people were already beginning to move into the dining room for lunch. He strolled into the luxurious bar and ordered two pints of lager and a whisky and water for himself. The two men had joined him at his table by the time the barman brought over the tray. They looked around them and sat down carefully, plainly not at home in these surroundings, as Seagrave had intended. He was still absurdly pleased by small things.

He leaned back in his chair, deliberately unhurried, motioned towards the lager, and watched them take a gulp each. Only then did he say, 'Is it done?'

'It is, sor.' The bigger of the two men had a Northern Irish accent, which became more pronounced when he was nervous.

'As planned? No hitches?'

'No hitches, sor. Like a military operation.'

'A smooth and successful one, I hope. No prisoners taken in this one, eh?'

The big man recognized a joke and gave a dutiful smile. 'No prisoners, sor. But you won't be hearing any more from those two who were giving yees the trouble.'

Richard Seagrave glanced unhurriedly round the almost empty bar, noting that the other occupants were busy with their own conversations. He produced the envelope and put it on the table. The men had their eyes upon it, but neither of them made any move towards it. Seagrave said, 'You'll tell me of anything that went wrong. I wish to know if you had any problems.'

These were orders, not suggestions. The big man said as firmly as he could, 'It went like clockwork, sor. Just as it was planned. We're professionals.'

'Very well. You'll be paid as professionals. The better you execute these things, the better it is for you as well as for me.' Seagrave gestured towards the envelope. 'Take it. There's two thousand in there in used notes. There's no need to count it.'

'Indeed there isn't, sor. Not with a man like you. Glad to be of service. Hope you'll use us again.' They downed the remainder of their pints whilst he watched them, plainly anxious to be on their way.

'I expect I shall use you again, when I have need of you. You came highly recommended. Keep it that way.'

But now that it was over, he was glad to be rid of them. They were vile and he despised them. As Macbeth did the murderers he had to employ, he mused. Shakespeare again: just as well to remember that he was an educated man. He said sourly, 'Be on your way, then.'

'Indeed we will, sor. And 'tis grateful for this that we are.' The man from Ulster shuffled to his feet and moved awkwardly out of the bar with his companion. The second man gave Seagrave a quick nod before he turned away. He had uttered not a word throughout their ten-minute interchange.

Seagrave gave them five minutes, affecting to read the newspaper he had bought on his way here. He checked the car park before he drove away. No sign of anyone observing his movements. That was the way it should be, in an efficient organization.

NINE

'Elfrida Potts?'

'Freda, please. That's bad enough: I've never liked the name. But we don't get to choose, do we? But it was my choice to put Potts on the end of it, which doesn't help. It shows how much I must have fancied this man, I suppose!' She gave a high-pitched laugh and took hold of the sturdy arm of Matthew as he came and stood beside her in the entrance to their unit.

Her husband glanced down at her, then at the tall man with the lined face and the powerful, burly man who stood beside him. 'How can we help you?'

Matthew Potts was a man who was not at ease with words. He distrusted them and tended to use as few as possible until he was fully relaxed, which always took some time in new company. On the oil rigs, where he worked exclusively with men, actions spoke louder than words, and Matthew preferred it that way. He did not give much attention to his appearance and still less to fashion. But his black hair was neatly parted, his dark eyes were clear and observant, his flesh was scrupulously clean, and the short-sleeved red leisure shirt he wore was freshly laundered and of good quality.

The two CID men took in all of this immediately, just as they noticed that his wife was twitchy and nervous. They noted these things, but made no deductions: there could be all sorts of reasons why Freda was nervous. It might be no more than a natural reaction to being drawn into a murder enquiry.

'I'm Detective Chief Superintendent Lambert and this is Detective Sergeant Hook. We're conducting an investigation into the death which took place here last night and was discovered this morning.'

Freda said almost before he had finished, 'Wally Keane. It wasn't suicide, was it? I saw poor Debbie this morning and she told me foul play is suspected.' It was a jittery reaction to their presence here. Like many people, Freda Potts had a compulsive need to talk when she was agitated.

Matthew Potts looked as if he would like to clap his large hand over her mouth and compel her silence. Instead, he slid his arm behind her and set a hand on each of her shoulders to move her gently aside. 'You'd better come inside, if you wish to speak to us. But we shan't be able to tell you anything useful.'

Freda glanced quickly up at him. 'Perhaps the officers would like to question us separately.' She turned quickly back to Lambert with a determined smile. 'That's what you like to do, isn't it? In case our stories don't tally?' It sounded almost like an appeal as she looked hopefully into the experienced face of John Lambert.

'That won't be necessary at this stage. These are just preliminary enquiries. We might need to speak to you separately later, when we have learned more about Walter Keane and the people who were closest to him.'

He made it sound almost like a threat. He intended to do that; certainly it was a warning that they should hold nothing back from him. Matthew Potts said, 'Sit down and ask us whatever you need to ask. We shan't be able to help you. I hardly knew the man.'

Freda said quickly, as if apologizing for his churlishness, 'Matthew's right. He's speaking for himself, you see. He's only been here three times since he examined the site and decided to buy a property for us at Twin Lakes. He works on oil rigs in the North Sea. The money's good, but the work is hard and he's away a lot.' She did not look at Matthew, but he put his hand on top of hers. It was more an attempt to still her tongue than a gesture of affection.

'But I understand that you have been able to make more frequent use of this unit yourself, Mrs Potts.'

She wondered how much he knew, how much Debbie Keane had told him about her. It must surely be Debbie who was the source of his information. 'Yes, I've been here quite a few times. This is a pleasant place, and I find that my weekends are less lonely here than in our home in Bristol. People here are very friendly.'

'Do you work yourself, Mrs Potts?'

'Yes. I'm Head of History in a comprehensive school. So I'm far too busy to be lonely during the week!' Her short, high-pitched laugh echoed beneath the low ceiling, whilst she watched Hook make a careful note of her occupation.

'So you've come here alone on some occasions?'

A tiny pause. Freda willed herself not to look at Matthew. She was wondering what Debbie had told them about her visits here with her 'nephew'. But there was only one reply she could make, with her husband at her side. 'That is correct, yes.' It sounded curiously formal. 'There's plenty to do here. I'm developing my golf. I played a little when I was a teenager, but it was almost twenty years since I'd touched a club when we came here, I suppose. I've even had a go on the bowling green, though I'm not very good at that yet. But people here are very friendly, as I said. You feel part of a little community, which I don't do at home. Big cities can be very impersonal.' She knew she was talking too much, but she found it difficult to stop. She feared what others would say, when her own compulsive lips were eventually still.

She had not looked at Lambert throughout this, but she was nevertheless conscious of his unrelenting scrutiny of her face and her movements. He waited for a moment to see if she would resume her account of herself before he said quietly, 'And now this happy, supportive community at Twin Lakes has been disturbed by a sudden death. A sudden death which was not a suicide, as someone tried to pretend it was. Who would want to kill Wally Keane, Mrs Potts?'

The sudden, brutal statement and the immediate question felt to Freda almost like an accusation. 'I don't know. Why is it that you think I should know?' Her voice rose towards hysteria. Matthew reached towards her and put his hand on top of both of hers, which were clasped on her lap, as if he wished to prevent them from fluttering in front of her.

'There is no reason why you should be able to give us anything significant, Mrs Potts. But you knew the deceased, and there you have the advantage of us. We shall be asking similar questions of everyone who was on the site last night.

Some people will be able to help us; that doesn't mean that they will have any responsibility for this very serious crime.'

'I knew Wally, yes. He was always polite and kind to me, but we didn't speak much. I've spoken much more with Debbie Keane, when I've been here. It's difficult not to speak with Debbie.' Freda's brief grin and flash of irony showed for a fleeting moment how she might be a lively staff-room colleague in a busy comprehensive school. It was a glimpse of that alter ego which almost all the people at Twin Lakes must have, in their normal working lives. 'Wally controlled a lot of things and did a lot of voluntary work around this place. Apart from that, he was a bit of a recluse, I suppose.'

'You say he did a lot of voluntary work. What kind of work was that?'

'Well, he helped Mr Rawlinson in the office sometimes, when he was short-staffed. And Wally and Debbie did all the golfing handicaps. That was him, really. He fed all the information into his computer, or so he said, and came up with scientific answers.'

'You sound as if you have your doubts about the accuracy of his findings.'

She grinned again. 'I'm no computer expert. But I know a little about their workings and what they can do, from their use in schools. Wally never bothered to demonstrate how he'd arrived at his findings, and that irritated some people.'

'Including you?'

She was increasingly at her ease now. 'No. It didn't concern me. I haven't even got a golf handicap and I don't play in the competitions. Wally was talking about allotting me a handicap this year, so that I could join in, but I told him to leave it for the moment because I'm still just a beginner, feeling my way into the game. Tennis was more my sport, really, but we don't have that here.'

'You mentioned that Walter Keane irritated some people. Could you enlarge on that for us?'

Freda paused, striving to relax even further. 'I couldn't really. I meant just what I said. It was irritation people felt, no more than that. Most of us treated Wally and his idiosyncrasies with a sort of amused tolerance.'

'Can you give us the name of anyone who would have wanted to kill Walter Keane? Any suggestions will be treated as strictly confidential, but it is your duty to give whatever assistance you can to the police in a situation like this one.'

'Of course it is, and of course I want to help. He was a decent man, Wally, from what I saw of him. I hope you arrest whoever was responsible for his death very quickly. But I can't think of anyone who might have done this. It seems inconceivable, in this place, where people come to enjoy themselves.'

'It has happened, nevertheless. What about you, Mr Potts? Have you any thoughts on the matter?'

Matthew took his time. He had remained apparently very calm even through the earlier minutes, when his wife had been disturbed. 'No. I've seen passions rise and I've watched small disputes get out of proportion on oil rigs, where people are cooped up together for weeks on end. This place is the opposite of that, in most respects – people come here to relax and enjoy themselves, and there's plenty of space around them. But the homes themselves are close together, and in that sense people live on top of each other in a closed environment. Perhaps things grow out of proportion here at times.' He paused, mentally comparing the wild waters and the challenges of the North Sea with this altogether softer environment. Then he concluded quietly, 'I'm not able to help you with any suggestions. I've scarcely been here, as yet. I hope to use this place more in the future, but I know hardly any of the people here. I think I spoke to Wally twice, just to pass the time of the day, really. He did tell me a little about the fishing on the lakes, because I expressed an interest in that.'

Bert Hook made a note of that on his pad. He thought this man would be capable of killing, if he felt the necessity for it. But he could see no possible motive at the moment. He said, 'No doubt you spoke a little more with Walter's wife.'

'With Debbie? Yes, I did. As Freda said, you don't get much choice about that. I think that when I'd been on the site for about three hours on my first visit, Debbie knew exactly what I did for a living and what I'd done previously. She isn't at all afraid to ask questions, Debbie.' Like his wife, Matthew seemed more amused than annoyed by the thought.

'What did you do before you worked on the rigs, Mr Potts?'

He looked for a moment as if he would refuse to answer. He didn't like this invasion of his private life. But these were policemen, one of them very senior, and both his training and his temperament determined that his instinct now was to answer them. 'I was in the army. Royal Engineers, initially, which was where I learned some of the things which I now use on the rigs.' He pursed his lips and was silent for a moment, then said with what seemed reluctance, 'I was then in the SAS for four years. Then I met Freda and we got married and I decided that the army was no life for a married man.' He smiled grimly, squeezed his wife's two small hands beneath his large one again, and then withdrew it. 'You might say that the rigs are also not ideal for married life, but the work pays well and you get generous periods ashore to compensate for working away from home.'

'You've worked in much harsher environments than Twin Lakes, Mr Potts. Your views on who might have committed what I fear we must treat as murder would be much appreciated.'

'Possibly. But I have to disappoint you. I know virtually nothing of the people here. I couldn't even hazard a guess at who might have seen off Wally Keane.'

The CID pair noted his casual, almost heartless phrase for the murder of a seemingly harmless man. It was probably no more than the honesty of a man who had seen much violent action. Hook said, 'Could you both give us an account of your movements last night, please?'

Matthew ignored the gasp he heard from his wife beside him. 'That's easily done. It will be a joint account, because we were together throughout the evening.' He didn't even look at Freda. 'We arrived here at just after five o'clock: I picked Freda up from school and we came straight here. I made us a curry and we had rhubarb and cream as a dessert. I'd bought the ingredients for the meal during the afternoon, before I collected Freda. I like to cook occasionally.'

'And I much appreciated his efforts, after a hard week in school.' Freda came in loyally to support him. 'Matt's a much better cook than he pretends to be, and it's a real luxury for me to sit back and let him wait upon me.' ·

'We finished eating at around eight, I'd say.' Matthew came in again quickly, as if he didn't want his wife to say too much. 'We watched television for a while. Then we both read our books for an hour or so.'

'But we went out for a stroll around the site. You mustn't forget that!' said his wife, and her brittle, high-pitched giggle rang round the room again.

'No, I hadn't forgotten it,' said Matthew with a touch of impatience. 'It was a warm, quiet evening, and we had a stroll along the edge of the lakes and down the deserted fairways of the golf course.'

'Did you use the path through the woods?'

'No. We kept to the more open ground. With no street lighting and no major town in the area, you get a very good view of the stars here, on a clear night. I was pointing out some of the better-known constellations to Freda. We were probably out for about twenty minutes. Certainly no more than twenty-five.'

'I'm very ignorant about the sky at night, and Matt knows a lot about it,' said Freda quickly, as if she felt it necessary to give substance to his statement.

Lambert had watched the pair very closely whilst Matthew Potts gave his account of their evening. He'd delivered it almost as if it had been a prepared statement. Perhaps it had been just that; men who distrusted words often liked to prepare exactly what they intended to say. The CID instinct was to disturb this measured control. 'What time was this?'

Matthew nodded, as if he had expected the question and welcomed its arrival. 'It must have been well after ten, I think. We could see the stars quite clearly, but there were still the last vestiges of light over the hills to the west.'

'We do not yet know when Walter Keane died. We shall have more accurate information on that after the post-mortem examination. He may well have died at around the time when you were strolling around the site. Did you see anyone else whilst you were out?'

Potts paused, giving the matter thought, as the question required him to do. 'No, I don't think we did. Can you recall seeing anyone, Freda?'

She gave a little shudder at the thought of there being a

murderer abroad as they had innocently studied the sky and strolled arm in arm through the warm and friendly night. 'No. We heard voices and laughter from some of the homes, as you'd expect. And I think I remember seeing a few shadowy figures away to our right when we were on the golf course. I thought at the time that they were going down to the bar for a drink, or perhaps moving away from there. But they were much too far away for us to identify anyone, and we were more interested in what we were doing ourselves.' She glanced up into Matthew's face and received a small, confirmatory smile.

'How long are you here for?'

'For the next few days certainly. Probably for the week, we thought. We're both on holiday. Getting to know each other again, you might say!' Freda managed this time to suppress her giggle, whilst Matthew looked as if he wished she had not volunteered her last thought.

'Carry on thinking about this and keep your ears open, please. If you hear anything which might help us, or indeed have any further thoughts of your own on the matter, please ring this number immediately.'

The couple watched through the long window in their sitting room as the CID officers walked away from them. Then Freda said, 'I probably sounded very nervous when I was speaking to them.'

He didn't look at her but watched their late questioners until they disappeared. 'They won't make anything of that. You've ample reason to be nervous, after all.'

The Martindale boys were excited by the news of death and the numbers of policemen and police cars that poured on to the site during the day. Their mother told them repeatedly during the morning to moderate their shouting and their laughter and to refrain from racing around their unit.

It was futile, of course. Boys of eight and six are incapable of retaining instructions in their heads for more than three minutes when they are together and excited. And they were not alone. On this July weekend, there were many children on the site. Most of them were at least as excited as Nicky and Tommy and many were less responsive to parental control.

Mary Martindale was relieved when someone took the boys away to the golf course and organized an informal children's competition. In this the prizes were small, the competition fierce, and the carelessness accorded to the rules of golf would have scandalized the late Wally Keane. Mary heard the distant cries of happy children and marvelled at how swiftly tragedy could be shrugged away by those too young to recognize it for what it was.

George Martindale was normally ebullient and happy at Twin Lakes, but today he was in a sober mood. He had given a formal statement to the police about his discovery of Walter Keane's body with Michael Norrington. Perhaps that had depressed him, Mary thought, for he did not speak much during the rest of the morning, even to her. You only realized how cheerful George was most of the time when that bright face and flashing smile disappeared for a while.

George was in fact preoccupied with something else entirely. Mary knew nothing of this and he was determined that she never would. He had received a text on his mobile which had disturbed him. He knew that he couldn't afford to ignore it, but it took him some time to respond. Eventually he told Mary that he would slip down to the golf course and check that the boys were behaving well and not getting too raucous on this sombre day for Twin Lakes.

Mary approved of that. She was proud of her boys and proud of the reputation they had established here as being 'well brought up'. People thought of Nicky and Tommy as the key members of a happy and popular family. She had not the slightest doubt that George intended to do just what he had said he would: they did not have secrets from each other.

The big man set off towards the golf course, then turned sharply away from it as soon as he was out of his wife's view. He found a quiet place by the smaller of the two lakes, well away from the spot where Wally Keane had died and from the police activity which surrounded it. He moved beneath the canopy of a sycamore and reluctantly dialled the number on his mobile. 'You took your time!' said the aggressive voice which responded.

'It's a bad reception area here for mobiles,' said George.

That was in fact perfectly true, but he didn't for a moment think that he would be believed.

'Change of plan. You're doing an extra drop.'

'But I don't operate from here. My weekends and holidays here are my time away with the family.'

'You don't have a choice, Marty boy!'

This man always called him that and he hated it. 'There was a clear understanding that I wouldn't be contacted here.'

'Fuck your clear understanding, Marty boy! You're a well-paid operative, not a virgin being violated. You do as you're fucking told.'

'But I have an image here as a family man. We don't want to jeopardize that, do we? It's safer for me if I'm left alone here, which means that it's safer for you as well.'

'Since when did you become a planner, Marty? Moved up the ranks, have you?'

'I was just pointing out what seemed—'

'Well don't! Leave the planning to the big boys. You're a very small cog in a very big wheel. You could be replaced at any time. Not just replaced, but cast aside and never seen again! You would do well to remember that, Marty boy.'

For the hundredth time, George Martindale wished that he had never got himself involved in this. But he was enjoying the results, wasn't he? He would never be at Twin Lakes and Mary and the boys he loved wouldn't have all this without that odious man at the end of the line and the anonymous tycoons who controlled both of them. He was a hypocrite to enjoy the pickings and yet ignore the way in which he obtained them.

And there was no way out, even though he wanted one. He had no choice in the matter. He had known in his heart since the moment he received the text that he would do whatever he was directed to do. He said hopelessly, 'I want you to know that I am doing this under protest. I do not wish to be disturbed whilst I am here and I tell you again that there was a clear understanding that I wouldn't be.'

'Shut the fuck up and move your arse, Marty boy! You don't want me to lose patience with you, do you? I'm telling you that you don't!'

'Where?'

'Lay-by on the A49. One mile south of a village called Hope Under Dinmore. What could be more innocent than that, Marty boy?' The voice hardened even further. 'Be there in one hour from now. Stay in your car until you are approached. As usual, we do all the work for you whilst you sit on your arse and wait.'

The phone went dead before he could confirm that he would be there, leaving him staring at the instrument in frustrated resentment.

'I have to go out,' he said to Mary when he returned to the unit.

'Must you? I thought we might take the boys to the river this afternoon. Have a family picnic. It's the right day for it.'

He couldn't deny that. So he didn't respond to the suggestion in any way. He said sullenly, 'I have to go. I don't have a choice. I shouldn't be away for very long.'

Mary wondered where he was going and what was so urgent that he had to desert her and the boys for it. But in her Nigerian culture you didn't question your man, didn't even try to find out what he was about. She wasn't stupid. She had wondered several times as she looked out over the sunlit acres of Twin Lakes where the money for all this came from. Not from what the council paid George, that was for sure, even though he was now a foreman on the road works team.

But you didn't ask about these things. You trusted your man absolutely to provide for you and your children, and George did that handsomely and lovingly. Lovingly was a big bonus. George had given her love, and given her Nicky and Tommy. She wasn't going to start questioning him now. She said only, 'Get back as quickly as you can. I'll make up a picnic. It won't be wasted: we can eat it here, if we have to.'

He nodded, but didn't speak to her again before he left. She wondered if he had even heard what she said.

TEN

They seemed an oddly matched couple, Geoffrey Tiler and Michael Norrington. That was Lambert's first impression and it had nothing to do with their sexual orientation.

Nor did he think his view significant. He had met many oddly matched couples over the years, and their oddness usually proved to have no bearing on the crimes he'd been investigating. And people who did not match each other physically, like the old seaside-postcard pair of huge-busted wife and diminutive and downtrodden husband, often complemented each other and handled life's problems well. It was sometimes the couples who seemed most at ease with each other, like the gruesome Fred West and his equally appalling wife in Gloucester, who perpetrated the most unbearable of crimes.

Moreover, John Lambert's impression of oddness in this pair was completely subjective and based merely on appearances. These men very probably got on perfectly when they were alone and away from the world. Whatever got you through the night, in the old phrase: the long hours of darkness during a winter night were surely the best test of any relationship.

Geoffrey Tiler was short and thickset. He had plentiful grey hair and watchful brown eyes, which registered every movement of these visitors to his chalet but betrayed no obvious hostility. Michael Norrington was five or six inches taller than his partner, blue-eyed and very thin. His dark hair was so free of any greyness that Lambert fancied he resorted to a bottle to keep it that way. He was more obviously nervous than Tiler at this intrusion; his quick physical shifts betrayed that. It seemed that the movements of his hands were sometimes a surprise to him as well as to the men who had come here to question him.

Lambert said to him, 'It was you who discovered the body, wasn't it, Mr Norrington?'

'Yes. I've made a full statement of how I did that. I wasn't alone. I was with George Martindale.' He asserted that firmly, as if it established his innocence in the matter of Walter Keane.

'Yes. I've read your statement. You were abroad very early this morning. Can you tell us why that was?'

'There were perfectly innocent reasons for it.'

'Then give them to us, please.'

Norrington looked as if he was being upset by this directness. Geoffrey Tiler said calmly, 'No one is accusing you of anything, Michael, and you've nothing to hide. Just tell them what happened.'

Norrington looked at him for a long moment, then turned back to the CID men. 'I awoke to find the sun filling the bedroom with light and the birds trilling their hearts out in celebration. The curtains are much thinner here than in my room in Stourbridge. I lay and listened for a while and enjoyed the birdsong. Then I tried to go to sleep again. I dozed a little, but I couldn't get off. Geoffrey was fast asleep, of course: he's a good sleeper. He was snoring a little – well, more of a snuffle really.' He turned his head abruptly back towards Tiler and smiled at him, as if it was important to him that he had asserted their intimacy.

Lambert said with a trace of impatience, 'But you didn't stay in bed for long, did you?'

'I wasn't able to get back to sleep. I think I probably dozed a little, but further sleep proved impossible for me.' He smiled, as if the formality of this phrasing gave him satisfaction. 'I eventually decided to get up. It seemed a shame not to be in the fresh air and enjoying Twin Lakes by myself, on such a glorious morning. You may find this strange, but I thought that this would be a good time to examine people's horticultural efforts. There are lots of flowers which people have planted in little plots near their units, but you aren't able to appreciate them properly when there are people around and you have to make conversation. Well, I feel that I do, anyway.' He glanced suddenly at Hook, with one of those swift and unpredictable movements of his head. Perhaps he thought the man with the countryman's exterior might be the one most likely to confirm his sentiments.

It was Tiler who tried to explain what he meant. 'Michael

is an excellent conversationalist, but he doesn't like making small talk, especially with people he hardly knows. He's a shy man.' He spoke as if he was providing some sort of verbal testimonial for his companion.

Norrington nodded. 'I did indeed inspect many of the annuals which are now providing such colour around the site. I'm happy to say that Geoffrey's begonias and geraniums are more than a match for anyone else's efforts.' He knew he sounded pompous, but he was prepared to accept that, to create the nerdish impression he wanted them to take away.

'They don't want to hear that, Michael. They're busy men.' Tiler was apologetic to the police officers, affectionate towards his partner.

'Yes. Yes, I'm sorry. Well, I remember seeing the new moorhen chicks at the edge of the lake and feeling glad to be alive. And then I met Debbie Keane.' He giggled at the unwitting joke he had made with this juxtaposition, revealing again how nervous he was. 'She was very upset, as you'd expect, because she couldn't find Wally. Apparently he'd been missing since late last night.'

'Yes. Did she tell you why she hadn't looked for him earlier?'

'She said she'd gone to bed without knowing that Wally hadn't come back to their home. Apparently he spends a lot of time using the computer in his own room. She said they sleep apart and she didn't realize he wasn't around until he didn't appear with their morning cups of tea.' Norrington clasped his hands and wrung them together, as if he needed some gesture of apology to mitigate this betrayal of the Keanes' domestic arrangements. 'I said I'd have a look round to see if I could locate Wally. Fortunately, George Martindale turned up at that moment and more or less took over. He's a much more practical man than I am, is George.'

Hook, who had his notebook open but who had so far made scarcely an entry, said briskly, 'And the two of you discovered the body hanging from the oak tree, in the wood beyond the larger lake. We have your statement about that.'

'Yes. I'm glad I wasn't on my own for that.'

'Mr Norrington, this is very important. Did you see anyone

else around the site? Was there anyone near the place where you found the body?'

'No.' He spoke very promptly, then apparently felt the need to explain himself. 'It was still very early, you know. The sun was climbing, but it was still only around six o'clock.'

Lambert said curtly, 'Who do you think killed Walter Keane, Mr Norrington?'

'Not me, for a start.' His hands flicked in the air in front of him as if they were not within his control. 'Sorry. Bad taste, that. Frivolous, as well; this is a serious matter. I've been thinking about who might have killed him, ever since your officer indicated to me that it wasn't suicide. But I haven't come up with anything. I didn't know Wally as well as some people around here, but I can't think why anyone would want to kill him. He could be irritating, I think, but no more than that.'

He looked to Tiler for confirmation, and his companion said calmly, 'We've been discussing the matter for most of the day, as you can imagine. We haven't come up with anyone who might have done this. We thought it might be an outsider, but that's probably wishful thinking. You don't want it to be anyone you know, still less someone you consider to be a friend.'

Hook said firmly, 'We need to know where both of you were last night, so that we can eliminate you from any suspicion. This is routine. It's part of the process we are applying to everyone on the site.'

He had expected an overwrought reaction from Norrington, but the two had obviously anticipated the question and discussed their reactions to it. Norrington did not look at Tiler as he said, 'We were together for the whole of the evening and the whole of the night.'

Geoffrey Tiler said quietly, 'I can confirm that. It may not be what you wanted to hear, but it is the truth.'

'The truth is all we want, sir, from everyone on the site. One person, possibly two people, will probably be lying. It will be our job over the next day or two to find out who they are.'

'Possibly two?' said Tiler.

'It is very possible that more than one person was involved

in this death. A partnership would have made murder easier in several respects.'

Tiler saw them through the door, then moved to the flower bed beside their home and removed a couple of weeds from it as his visitors departed. He went back into the unit and said to Michael evenly, 'Possibly a partnership, they think.'

There was a steady stream of traffic on the A49 between Leominster and Hereford. You would have expected that on a sunny Saturday afternoon in midsummer. Not many lorries or trailers, of course. George Martindale would have welcomed some heavy commercial vehicles around him. Somehow, the great wall of a high van in front of him would have offered him greater cover than a string of cars on pleasure outings.

His new red Ford Focus seemed shiny and far too noticeable on this mission. The boys had wanted that colour when they saw it in the showroom. He would have chosen some more muted colour himself, but he'd been happy enough to defer to them at the time. The sign that told him he was entering the village of Hope Under Dinmore came up all too quickly. Such an innocent-sounding name, to be selected for a sinister transaction.

That was stupid thinking, George told himself firmly. The transfer which would take place here was but a tiny segment of the evil abroad in the world; the merest fraction of the vice that must be occurring even in a rural and thinly peopled county such as Herefordshire. He was helping to supply a demand, that was all. A demand which would be met, whether he was part of the supply chain or not.

Thus the old arguments and the old evasions swam through his mind. They remained as unconvincing as they always were.

The lay-by came into view precisely when he expected it, exactly one mile south of the village of Hope Under Dinmore. They were nothing if not accurate, these people. He indicated in good time, then swung carefully into the parking provided. His was the only car here; he felt very conspicuous in the bright red Focus. He should have brought a newspaper. The map-book was all he had to pore over as he waited. There was no reason why a man in a bright red Focus should not be consulting maps to find his way, but he felt very noticeable and very spurious.

He didn't actually wait in the lay-by for very long, but the minutes felt to the naturally active George Martindale to stretch towards hours. Seven minutes after he had cruised into the lay-by, a Mondeo Graphite drew up not more than four feet behind him. The same make of vehicle, and a single black man of about his own age at the wheel. That might have made Martindale feel easier, but it didn't.

The man behind him was very visible, even magnified, in George's rear-view mirror. He was broad-shouldered. He had short, grizzled hair and he wore sunglasses with wide black lenses. They were appropriate wear for a sunny July day, but they made the man look even more threatening. That impression was not mitigated by the man's movements, or lack of them. He sat there motionless for a full two minutes, gazing at the car in front of him and the driver at its wheel.

When he eventually detached himself unhurriedly from his vehicle, it was almost a relief to the man awaiting his attention. George had fully opened all the windows in his vehicle whilst he waited, but the Focus still felt altogether too warm. The man was bigger and wider when he stood upright than he had appeared to be when sitting in the Mondeo.

He had to bend quite low to put his elbows on the sill of the driver's door of the Focus. Although he was now very close, George could still not see his eyes behind the black spheres of his sunglasses. It made people more sinister when you could not see their eyes, because it made it much more difficult to follow what they were thinking. The eyes were windows to the soul. Mary had told George that. He didn't wish to investigate this man's soul.

'Payment up front.' The Mondeo driver was a man of few words.

'This isn't a normal drop. This is an extra I've been forced to accept.'

The merest quiver of those huge shoulders. Nothing as violent as a shrug. 'I've got my orders, same as you've got yours. Payment up front.'

Barbadian, George reckoned, by his accent. No help there.

Those from the small island of Barbados had little sympathy for men from their bullying bigger West Indian neighbour, Jamaica. He glanced behind him, saw that the lay-by still held only their two cars, and slid a polythene package containing a bundle of notes swiftly from beside his seat into the big receiving hands. 'There's a grand there in tens and twenties.'

The sunglasses dipped briefly towards it. 'I won't count it. You wouldn't be stupid enough to try to cheat these people. Neither of us would.'

For a moment, they were two men united by a mutual resentment of the anonymous and powerful forces which controlled them. Then the man outside the car stooped and produced the box which had hitherto been out of Martindale's vision. 'It's good stuff. Mostly coke and horse. Make sure you make the most of it.'

George took the box, nodded sourly and pressed the switches to raise his windows. He needed to isolate himself, to get away from here as quickly as he could. The transaction was over and the Barbadian was as anxious to be away from here as he was. He was back in the Mondeo with the engine running by the time George had stowed the box in the rear footwell of the Focus. Seconds later, he was away, swinging across the road into the stream of the northbound traffic, not troubling to wave to the man whose thousand pounds he had just collected.

Martindale shut his eyes for a moment and took a long breath. Then he eased back into the traffic and took the first opportunity to turn round and head back towards Twin Lakes. He passed the Mondeo, now moving south, a hundred yards after he had turned. The drivers made no acknowledgement of each other.

After he had run through Leominster and turned on to the lane which led to Twin Lakes, he stopped the car and transferred the box from the back of the car to the boot, where he hid it as well as he could under his golf waterproofs. You couldn't be too careful, with the place alive with policemen, both uniformed and plain-clothed. He'd much rather not be taking drugs on to the site at all, but he'd been given no choice in the matter.

Mary Martindale wondered why her normally cheerful spouse

looked so worried as he parked the car outside their unit. He mustered his usual smile for her as he climbed the three steps to the elevated entrance, but she wasn't deceived by that.

George summoned his resources of cheerfulness. 'We can have that picnic now, if you want it.'

'It's too late to go out. We'll eat it here. But we've got visitors first. The police want to speak to us about last night.' She glanced at the clock beside her cooker. 'They'll be here in ten minutes.'

George had just enough time to wash his face and change his shirt. These were the first steps towards presenting an innocent front to the forces of the law. Its representatives arrived as they had promised at four thirty, punctual to the minute.

He sized them up as well as he was able. There was the tall man he'd seen questioning others earlier in the day. Chief Detective Superintendent John Lambert, he said his name was. George knew a little about him already, but he didn't acknowledge that. The solid man beside him looked less threatening. But you couldn't trust the police, any of them. Especially if you were black: everyone knew that.

It was the sergeant who gave him all the usual stuff about this just being part of the police routine. Maybe it was, but that wouldn't make him any less careful with these bastards. Then Lambert said to him, 'It was you who discovered Mr Keane's body. We've read your statement about that.'

'Then you'll know that I wasn't alone.'

'We do indeed. We've already spoken to Mr Norrington.'

'We were the only people around at six o'clock this morning. We were trying to help Debbie Keane. She couldn't find her husband and she was in a state.'

'Which proved to be well justified by subsequent events. Did you believe her when she said she hadn't missed him earlier?'

'Earlier?'

'He hadn't been in her home since last night, but she says that she only realized he was missing this morning. You accepted that?'

'I'm not sure I even heard it. I arrived to find her talking to Michael Norrington and gathered that Wally had gone missing. I registered that and we said we'd look for him. I'm not sure I was aware at the time of anything except the fact that he was missing and needed to be found.'

'That is understandable. It is to your credit that your first impulse was to find out where he was and what had happened to him.'

'If Debbie says that she hadn't found he was missing until the morning, that will be correct. She enjoys a bit of gossip – well, she thrives on it, to be honest. But there's nothing vicious about Debbie. I'm sure you can trust whatever she's told you.'

'Thank you. You'll appreciate that I know no one here, although DS Hook has met a few of the residents before and knows a little about what goes on here.' He contrived to make that fact sound quite sinister, as if Hook knew all sorts of facts and George and Mary had better be very careful to give him the truth. 'So you and Mr Norrington, being the only people around at six o'clock this morning, set out to look for Walter Keane.'

'Yes. Debbie wanted us to do that.'

'Whose idea was it to take the route you did, Mr Martindale?'

George hadn't expected that question. He thought feverishly about the implications of it. 'Does it matter?'

'Probably not. But the information isn't in your statement.'

'I think it was probably my idea. Michael isn't a very prac-tical man. I think he was glad I turned up when I did. I'm sure he was anxious to help Mrs Keane, but he didn't seem to know what to do next. I suppose I suggested that we should look in the woods, simply because that was the most obvious hiding place for someone who was missing. We were still presuming at that stage that Wally might have chosen to hide himself away for some reason. Or of course that he might have met with some sort of accident.'

He was choosing his words carefully; this wasn't the time to make any kind of mistake. Lambert nodded slowly. 'How did Mr Norrington react when you discovered the body hanging in the woods?'

'How do you think he reacted? He was horrified, just as I was.'

'You didn't detect any sign that he had in some way expected this?'

'No. How the hell could he have done?'

'Someone on the site, and maybe more than one person, knew what you would find in those woods. It's our job to find out who they might be. It's a legitimate question.' John Lambert allowed himself a mirthless smile, as though an idea had just occurred to him. 'We might ask him the same thing about you. We have a large field of suspects and very few clues at the moment.'

'Well, Mike Norrington and I were both horrified by what we found up there. That's unless he's a damned good actor. We assumed at the time that it was suicide. That was quite bad enough. Murder makes it worse. It probably means that someone we know has killed Wally.'

'Quite. Who do you think that might be?'

George ignored the gasp from his wife beside him, willing himself not to look at her. 'I've no idea who it might be.'

'And what about you, Mrs Martindale? I expect you've both been thinking about it all day. It's only human to do so, don't you think?'

Mary glanced at George, who was staring hard at his shoes. 'You can't discuss anything like that when the boys are here. And the word didn't get round that it wasn't suicide until about lunchtime. We've had rather a hectic day, so George and I haven't had much time to talk about it, really.' She didn't want to draw their attention to the fact that George had been off the site for over two hours this afternoon. She said almost brightly, as if the thought had just occurred to her, 'I think you were upset and shocked by finding the body this morning, weren't you, George?'

She should have said that at the outset, thought Lambert, not as an afterthought. Mary Martindale might be one of life's innocents, as her broad and innocent black face suggested. Or she might be something much more malign; you had to keep all possibilities in mind, until you could establish more facts about a death. He said calmly to her husband, 'Why did you go out this afternoon, Mr Martindale?'

'It had nothing to do with Wally's death. Are my movements subject to police surveillance now?'

'We have a record of everyone who has left the site today and how long they were away for. You are helping the police with their enquiries. You can refuse to answer, if you wish to do that.'

He wished to do exactly that. But it would attract their attention, and that was the last thing he wanted to do. He said carefully, 'I have a cousin in Hereford. I was delivering some paint to him. He's going to paint the outside of his house, so he needed gallons of the stuff. Because I buy quite a lot for the council, the supplier gives me a big discount. It's all quite above board.'

'Thank you. Have you any thoughts on who might have killed Walter Keane?'

'No. We know a few people here quite well, but others hardly at all. It wouldn't be fair to speculate, even if I had any thoughts on this – which I haven't.'

'But you'll go on thinking about Mr Keane's death. That's the normal human reaction. And however little you know about the people here, it's more than we know at the moment. So if you have any thoughts, please ring the number on this card immediately. Your thoughts will be treated confidentially.'

'I'll think about who killed Wally. I'm sorry if I was touchy just now. When you're black and you've grown up in a city, you get used to being stopped and searched whenever there's trouble. It makes you anti-police. But black men have good reason to be so.'

'I'm sure they do. You'll be treated exactly the same here as everyone else who had contact with Walter Keane.'

'Which is everyone around here. Everyone knew Wally; everyone knows Debbie. You can't have a property here without doing that.'

'So I gather. Solving this one isn't going to be easy. Where were you last night, Mr Martindale?'

'With my wife and children, as you'd expect. All evening. And all through the night. Until Tommy and Nicky woke me, early this morning, and I went out and discovered a body.'

'And you can confirm this, Mrs Martindale?'

'Yes. You may not believe me, but it's true. The boys will confirm it, for the time they were awake.'

'That won't be necessary.' Lambert stood up. 'Thank you for your co-operation. We may need to see you again, when we know more about this killing.'

Mary stood at the window of her kitchen and watched the CID men departing. She continued to look up the line between the chalets, even after they had disappeared. She was looking there and not at George as she said dully, 'You don't have a cousin in Hereford, George, and you don't have a concession on paint.'

ELEVEN

John Lambert was up early on Sunday. He had almost finished his bowl of cereal when Christine came into the kitchen in her dressing gown.

She looked at him and felt a sharp, protective pain at the signs of ageing in his bent shoulders. But they weren't really old, were they? Late fifties was nothing nowadays, everyone told her. Well, everyone who was older than sixty told her. She said, 'You need to take it easy, John. You had a long day yesterday.'

He was on the verge of turning tetchy and impatient, as he would have done thirty years ago. It was a good thing that he had to chew and swallow before he spoke; that instant was enough to modify his reaction. He said quietly, 'I had a good night's sleep.'

'You need to delegate. It's time you let younger men do more of the work.' She felt she was repeating a script she now knew by heart.

'You can't delegate in a murder enquiry. You either take charge and accept responsibility or you don't. I've already delegated all I can. Chris Rushton does all the computer work. He logs everything we find and cross-references it with other crimes. He's welcome to that and he's good at it. I'm fortunate to have him.'

She knew that she wasn't going to win the argument, but it was nonetheless an exchange she needed to conduct. She came and stood behind him, kneading his shoulders, feeling the hard muscles of his neck relax as he dutifully slackened his body to take account of her efforts. 'It's Sunday. You should be out in your garden, enjoying the results you've worked hard to achieve there.'

'I will be. This is the exception, not the rule. I'm usually here at weekends, nowadays.'

'You should be here all the time. You've earned the right.'

She hadn't mentioned the taboo word 'retirement', but he did that, or came near enough to it. 'You're a long time on a pension, Christine, with any luck. You're enjoying your part-time teaching. Let me go out with a bang rather than a whimper.'

If they let me, he thought. But hadn't the new Chief Constable told him only a couple of months ago that he wanted him to stay on for the foreseeable future? For as long as he got results, that meant. He needed results, almost as urgently as he'd needed them a quarter of a century ago, when he was making his way in CID. But he couldn't tell Christine that.

She threw in the last trump card from this hand which could not win. 'Caroline may be round with the kids this afternoon.'

'I'll try to get home. I can't promise anything, so don't wait for me if you're eating. It will depend on how the day develops.'

So even the grandchildren couldn't get him home. Christine said dully, 'Don't worry about the time. I'll have something for you, whenever you get in.'

She watched him go out and lever his long frame into the old Vauxhall he stubbornly refused to change. She felt more anxious for him and more tender about him than she had ever felt when he was younger. It must be another of the unwelcome effects of age.

Sunday was not a day of rest for Mark Patmore. He had always felt more at risk on Sundays. All of his days dragged, not just Sundays. Yet all of his days were highly dangerous. When you were working undercover, you had to be alert the whole time, even when to others you seemed out of your mind on coke.

And the police who paid your wages every few months were no use to you. To be fair, they couldn't offer you direct help or support, without risking blowing your cover. But when they wanted something, they soon muscled in to tell you just what. A daft inspector who was desperate to up his conviction rate had almost got him killed three months ago. Too many chiefs, not enough Indians: the old complaint. Some of the sods who held your life in their hands didn't have a bloody clue what was going on.

Patmore had had his head shaved close, two days ago. The idea had been to make him fit in, to make him unnoticeable among the fighters and drinkers and muggers who inhabited the world around him. Now he wondered if the shaving had been done too well, whether his bare skull was too neat and perfect among the scruffier and filthier ones around him. Perhaps he should have damaged the skin a little, or made the cutting less even, more amateur. He was unusual among the people in the squat in having no major scar to parade as a badge of his belonging to this harsh and dangerous underworld.

He wondered how balanced his mind was now. It was difficult to tell, when there was no one to warn you that you were running off the rails. He hadn't been the same since he'd broken up with Amy. He knew that, but he couldn't be certain how much the rift had affected him. You couldn't expect to keep a partner, when you were undercover. She'd told him that, two months before they split up. You couldn't keep up a relationship when you saw each other once every five or six weeks, without prior notice. You shagged each other silly in the first hours after the long deprivation and hoped that sex would bring you together. It did, for a while, but you needed the small, stupid, insignificant things as well.

You weren't good at the small things, when you worked undercover. And you became less good at them with each passing week. After two years of it, you found you were no good at all. You didn't even know after two years quite what small things were, still less why they mattered. Amy had been right to go. He felt now that she was a stranger whom he'd hardly known at all. Perhaps he was unbalanced, as she'd said he was. Well, of course he was: you had to be unbalanced, even to consider working undercover.

Patmore was enjoying the bright Sunday-afternoon sunlight. Correction: he was enduring it, while other people were enjoying it. He heard them telling each other all around him that they were. Stupid sods. Hadn't they anything better to think about than the damned weather? And in any case, it wasn't a beautiful day, as they all kept saying it was. Sunlight wasn't good, when you worked undercover. You wanted thick clouds when you were outside and shut curtains when you were inside. Instinct told you to seek whatever shield you could. That's what working undercover was all about, though the daft sods who'd sent him here had no idea about that.

Mark opened up the Sunday paper he had picked out of the litter bin. He sat very still on the park bench as he pretended to read it. England were doing well in the Ashes, apparently. He looked at pictures of bright young men in white clothes and stupid postures. He told himself that they were older than him, even though he felt that they surely couldn't be. There was a lot of stuff about who was going to win the Open Championship, with pictures of Tiger Woods looking very strong and very aggressive. The Tiger looked much like some of the men you worked with in this real and more deadly game. Stupid game, golf. Quite popular in the police, nowadays. Why the hell couldn't they get real?

It was late in the afternoon and the park was less peopled now. Most of the Gloucester citizens had taken their small children home for tea, Mark supposed. He could remember tea with his Gran when he was a small boy; he could picture the table full of good things, when his wide eyes had been almost on a level with them. But the figures in that picture seemed to be from some old and outdated book, not from this world.

He listened to distant teenager shouts from somewhere behind him, but did not move his head. They were playing some sort of game, but he wasn't going to turn and see what it was. That would be a sign of weakness; Mark wasn't sure why, but it would. He rose, flung the newspaper violently back into the bin whence it had come, thrust his hands into the pockets of his jeans, and walked towards the exit from the park.

He found that he was happier when he was back on streets which were a century old. The wide-open spaces of the park seemed to expose him, like a fly crawling across a window pane, and he was happier with bricks rising high on each side of him. This assignment would be over soon now, he decided. He didn't know why he thought that, but as soon as the idea had entered his head it became as concrete as any fact. Either he would deliver what was required of him to his police paymasters, or he would be sucked into the dark recesses of the world where he was operating and disappear for ever.

He didn't know why he was so certain that the climax was

at hand. Nor was he frightened by the idea. He had lived with
fear for so many months that his thought processes and his
very mind were blunted by it, as if he were operating under
some strange sort of anaesthetic. The bold steps he had used
to leave the park did not last for long. His trainers were very
worn and the wear was not even. The heels were gone almost
completely on one side, so that he dropped quite naturally into
the swift shuffle which was now his normal gait.

He could have afforded good trainers; the best, he supposed,
if he'd wanted them. But they would have been a dead give-
away, an announcement to anyone who cared to notice him
that he was not what he pretended to be. You did not have
new clothes or new shoes in the squat. Unless you stole them,
of course. Some of them did that, but it wasn't an option for
Mark Patmore. You weren't allowed to break the law when
you were undercover. Those daft buggers who made the rules
had no bloody idea.

He should have felt easier when he was back in the squat
and lying in the darkness, but he felt only depressed. It would
be over soon, whatever happened, he told himself. That wasn't
much of a consolation. He looked at his watch. It was one of
the things he had kept as he gradually discarded all the rest.
You needed to know the time, when you worked for these
people. You had to be there exactly when they said you should
be, if you wanted to go on working for them and go on finding
out more and more about them.

Two hours yet. He lay on his back and blanked his mind.
He could do that now; he could let the time swim past him
whilst he lay in limbo. He wouldn't sleep, but he would lie
here for ninety minutes in some sort of self-induced trance.

He wasn't even sure who the woman was, at first. Someone
from the squat, obviously, but that could be any one of five.
He had his mattress tight under the gable to guard against any
attack, so that the light here was very dim. She lay for a while
against him, her slim body cool despite the summer heat. Sam,
she called herself, he thought, if it was the one he thought it
was. She must have come up from the floor beneath this one;
he hadn't heard her on the stairs. If it was Sam, she used horse
to get her kicks. She was perhaps not yet an addict, but on

the way there. She hadn't shown any interest in him before. He shifted on to his side and tried to assess whether she was drugged or not.

Presently, he felt her stretch her body against his, then slide an arm tentatively around him. Two minutes later, she moved her hand to the back of his neck and stroked the short, shaved hair there for a moment. He reached his hands experimentally to the small of her back, caressed it softly, ran his hand down to the cleft of her bottom and the softness beneath it, pressed her against him. Both of them could feel his arousal, despite the fact that he had moved only minimally since she had joined him. Seconds later, she had her legs round his thigh and his erection in her other hand.

She was reaching for the fastening of his jeans when he put a hand like steel on her thin wrist and whispered an urgent 'No!'

'It's all right! I'm clean. And I won't get pregnant.'

'It's no good! I have to go.'

It was brutal. Unnecessarily so. He couldn't even be certain enough of her name to use it as he pulled her away from him. He hadn't thought of Amy for days now: a couple of weeks probably. But an image of her face had reared itself before him when he had least required or expected it, vivid and accusing.

He needed all his strength to detach the woman as she clung to his body like a snake. 'You bastard!' she said as he clawed her away. 'You rotten bloody bastard!'

He was all of that and he knew it. But his sensitivity had been blunted long ago. He knew only that he couldn't do this, that he must detach himself now before it got worse. He grabbed a thin shoulder in each of his large hands and threw her off him. 'Piss off, you stupid bitch! I didn't ask for you and I don't bloody need you!'

She was gone then, slinking away as silently as she had arrived. He lay for a long time with his eyes shut, feeling lower than ever. But not guilty. You couldn't afford guilt or any other emotion when you were working undercover.

'We'd prefer that you talked to us together. We've nothing to hide. We want this cleared up as quickly as possible.'

Richard Seagrave looked at Detective Chief Superintendent Lambert steadily, refusing to let his eyes drop in the face of the older man's scrutiny. His words sounded like a challenge.

Lambert said quietly, 'You are helping us voluntarily with our enquiries into a serious crime, as we expect all normal citizens to do. We are quite willing to speak to you together at this stage. If at some future stage of the investigation we feel it advisable to speak to you individually, we shall arrange to do that when it is necessary.'

Vanessa Norton smiled, trying to relax the tension she felt. She was good with men and well aware of it. These were experienced policemen, but that didn't mean she couldn't use her influence on them. She smiled unhurriedly, swept her very blue eyes swiftly across all three of the faces, and said, 'You would learn nothing additional by speaking to us separately. We both know exactly the same amount about this, which is very little. You will save your own time as well as ours by speaking to us together.'

Lambert was used to resisting the charms of women. This one seemed to have some of the most impressive of those charms. Early thirties, he reckoned; possibly mid-thirties. Very well preserved – but then he had reached an age where it seemed ridiculous to think of anyone in their thirties being well preserved. He wondered how important looks were to this woman. Her hair was probably genuinely blonde; there seemed to be no darkening at the roots and she had that clear light skin which appeared Nordic. There were no wrinkles apparent around her eyes or on the elegant exposed neck, two areas where he looked instinctively for the first signs of ageing.

He said abruptly, 'We shall need your full name.'

'Of course you will. For the records.' She gave a calm smile with this reference to police bureaucracy. 'My name is Vanessa Norton. I am not married to Richard, though I let some of the nosier people around here think that we are. I am not engaged.' She watched Hook making a note. 'You'll have to put me down as his bit of stuff, if you need a technical designation. Or is that too old-fashioned, even for the police?'

Hook glanced up at her with the merest suggestion of a smile. 'Spinster of this parish would probably suffice. But we'd better have a home address as well.' He took down addresses for both of them, studiously unreactive when they were different. Vanessa felt now that she was going to enjoy this little contest, but she warned herself not to be so self-indulgent.

Lambert asked her crisply, 'What did you think of Walter Keane?'

'I didn't like him. He was an interfering busybody. So was his wife, but I felt that Wally was more malicious than Debbie. I suppose convention requires me to say now that I shouldn't be speaking ill of the dead, but I prefer to be frank.'

'We much prefer honesty.' He put just enough stress on the word to imply that it might be something different from what she was offering them. 'You are the first person to confess to an active dislike of the deceased.'

'Then I hope you will applaud my candour rather than deplore my bad taste. I'm not sure you should call it an "active" dislike. I didn't take any action against Wally. I like to think I treated his behaviour with an amused tolerance.'

'Vanessa was very patient with the man.' Richard Seagrave clearly felt it was time to offer a little support to his lady. It was almost a snippet of Jane Austen, save that with his squat and scowling exterior this was no Mr Knightley.

Lambert ignored the interruption to the verbal joust he had commenced with Ms Norton. 'In what context did Mr and Mrs Keane irritate you?'

'Irritate is the right word, Detective Chief Superintendent.' She articulated his title deliberately, as if emphasizing to him how few of the members of the public he spoke with got it exactly right. 'Debbie was an amusing nuisance, if that's not a contradiction in terms. She wanted to know all of your business, and you knew from what she said about other people on the site that whatever you said to her would be told to others, probably with further imaginative speculation from her. She pried as fully as she could into my relationship with Richard. I took some pleasure from stonewalling resolutely.'

'And Wally?'

'I disliked Wally much more. He wanted to control every-thing on the site. Jim Rawlinson, who owns this place, allowed him to help out in the office whenever they were short of staff there. I wouldn't have done that, if I'd been Jim. Wally was cheap labour – well, free labour, I think – but I wouldn't have wanted him anywhere near anything confidential. Wally was a control freak: he wanted to take charge of anything and everything that goes on at Twin Lakes. He and Debbie were here more than anyone else – for every day of the year that it's possible to be here, in fact. They sometimes made the rest of us feel like intruders.'

'You say you disliked Walter Keane much more than his wife. In what context was this?'

'I think I'm making this sound more serious than it was. Your notion of irritation is nearer the mark, I'm sure. I've taken up golf since I came here, and I think I've made some progress.' She smiled appreciatively at the affirmative murmurs from her partner on her left. 'It's only a short course here, but ideal for someone who's hardly played the game before, like me. But Wally controlled the golf here and took it very seriously. He liked to strut about as if he was the Secretary of the Royal and Ancient at St Andrews. He gave everyone their handicaps and adjusted them regularly as he saw fit. Most of us just grinned about it behind his back and let him get on with it, because we didn't want to be bothered with all the boring administrative stuff ourselves. But it's only a little nine-hole course here and we play for fun: we don't want a Gauleiter looking over our shoulders and constantly tinkering with our handicaps. You'd play one good hole on your own on the edge of dark and find Wally creeping out of the trees and telling you he'd decided what he'd seen warranted knocking another shot off your handicap. It was daft. But irritating, as you say, rather than anything more serious.'

'Where were you on Friday night between seven and midnight?' Lambert addressed his question to her, but his glance took in both of them.

'That's when he was killed, isn't it? That's pretty obvious, from what we've heard from others on the site. Things fly around, once you've questioned people, in a place like this. But perhaps you like to encourage speculation, at this stage, when you still don't know much.'

There was an unspoken question in her last phrase, but

Lambert did not react to it. 'We need to know where you were on Friday night. Each of you.'

Vanessa smiled, conveying how much she was at her ease. 'Shouldn't you say that it's just routine, so that we can be eliminated from your enquiries? We know that everyone on the site has been asked these questions, so we're not going to be upset about it. But not everyone has been visited by the top brass, have they?' She glanced at Seagrave. 'Perhaps we are rather special, after all, Richard, though I can't think why. Well, I'm afraid we have to disappoint you, Mr Lambert. We were both here, in this very room for much of the time. We cooked a Marks and Spencer's meal for two. I say "we", but Richard confined himself to opening and pouring the wine – that's the male way, isn't it? Not that the salmon and vegetables took a lot of cooking: it was beautifully prepared for me by the M&S chefs.'

'Did you go out at all during the evening?'

'No. I'm sure we didn't. Can you confirm that for them, Richard?'

He spoke carefully, sounding curiously stilted. 'I can indeed. I stood on the balcony outside for a couple of minutes at around half past seven, enjoying the evening sunshine whilst I opened the wine. But I didn't leave our home. Neither of us did, throughout the evening.'

Vanessa smiled her assent to that. 'We had a leisurely meal and a quiet evening, accompanied by an excellent bottle of New Zealand chardonnay. And then we turned in for an early night. I shall not give you a detailed account of what happened after that.' Vanessa taunted them a little with her smile of remembrance.

Seagrave enjoyed the moment and then added, 'So we're each other's alibis, you see. I know the police don't like such things, but there's nothing you or we can do about that, as it's the truth.'

'The truth is what we always welcome, from everyone,' said Lambert evenly. 'There will be at least one person, and probably at least one couple, who were at Twin Lakes on Friday night who are not delivering the truth to us.'

'And of course we wish you the best of luck in uncovering those people as quickly as possible,' said Vanessa sanctimoniously.

'Who do you think killed Wally Keane?' This was Bert Hook, looking up from his notes and abruptly terminating this display of insouciance.

'You're very direct, Sergeant! But I expect I'd be the same in your position. Anxious for a quick result. After all, murder is murder. Whether I liked Wally or not, I certainly didn't want to see the poor bugger murdered, irritating as he was. But I'm afraid neither of us can help you. We've discussed it for most of the weekend, as you might expect. But that's just the problem, you see. He was an annoying bloke, Wally. He really got on Richard's tits, didn't he, darling? I wouldn't use such a crude expression about myself, of course, but I've already been quite frank about how he infuriated me at times. But that's what he was: irritating. I can't see anyone caring enough about what he did to murder him. And I'm not the murdering type, and neither is Richard.'

She giggled and took her partner's hand to reinforce that sentiment. Hook studied the two of them without emotion for a moment and then said, 'What about you, Mr Seagrave? Can you think of anyone with a motive for murder?'

Richard pursed his lips, emphasizing that he was according the question due weight and deliberation. He hadn't been allowed to say much, but his vanity determined that he should now convey to these senior CID men that he was an educated man, not a rich fool. 'No. Wally Keane struck me as rather like Polonius in Hamlet. A meddling old fool who was determined to have a finger in every pie.'

He wondered if this stolid-looking sergeant would be out of his depth here. But Hook made some sort of note and then said, 'But Polonius meddled his way to his death, didn't he? Perhaps Wally Keane did the same thing. Perhaps we shall have to find who was most seriously affected by his meddling. You left Twin Lakes at eleven thirty-four yesterday morning and returned at thirteen twelve. Would you tell us where you went when you were off the site?'

Richard was shaken for a moment by the precision of the figures. But he realized that he should not have been. It was easy for them to check times for anyone leaving the site, and natural that they should do so once a murder investigation was under way. He said curtly, 'It has no relevance to your investigation. I had a business meeting in Tenbury Wells. I had arranged to speak with one of my head salesmen and he had travelled some distance to be there.'

Hook made a note but offered no further comment. He looked into their faces for a moment and said, 'If either of you have any further thoughts on who might have committed this crime, you should get in touch with us immediately.'

Vanessa put the card he left them beside the clock in the kitchen. Richard grinned at her. 'You promised me you were going to do most of the talking. You certainly did that.'

She answered his smile, then held his broad hand for a moment in her much more delicate one. 'It's what we agreed before they came, wasn't it? You have a lot more to hide than I have.'

TWELVE

Lambert was back in time to see his daughter and his grandchildren, to exchange views with his son-in-law over the successes of the England cricket team against Australia and to indulge in the various joys of the extended family.

Yet through all of this there was a portion of John Lambert which was not present in this happy gathering, however much he wanted it to be there. Murder investigations and the people you met in the course of them had that effect on domestic life, however much you willed that it should not be so. He could not thrust from his mind the disquieting image of the menacing, almost silent Richard Seagrave and his bright and intelligent blonde partner, Vanessa Norton. His grandsons were only seven and five, but even amidst their innocent cacophony, the cadences of the earlier interview at Twin Lakes refused to leave him.

It had been routine stuff, on the surface. They had given their account of Friday night and it had been officially noted. It might be that everything they had said about those hours was entirely true. Yet he had a feeling about the exchanges that he could not dismiss. Bert Hook and he had been bested by the cool, intelligent Vanessa Norton and the watchful man who had sat beside her. The interview had been conducted on their terms, not on his. La Norton had told them exactly what she had planned in advance to tell them, whilst Richard Seagrave had contentedly overseen the process.

John Lambert would have instructed Hook and the rest of his team to assemble facts before they formed opinions. Yet, with precious few facts as yet, he was already sure in his own mind that Seagrave and Norton were a dangerous couple who had won the first round of the contest.

He arrived at Twin Lakes early on Monday morning. Jim Rawlinson had allotted them one of the unused units near the entrance as a murder room. The place was rapidly filling with materials gathered and bagged around the scene of the crime, together with pictures of the deceased and of various other objects and scenes which might have significance. DI Rushton was completing his filing of interviews conducted with everyone who had been on the site at the time of the crime. Many of them had been with not one but several people on Friday night, so that their alibis were much more convincing than those supported by just a spouse or partner. It was too early to be certain, but it seemed likely that Lambert and Hook had already conducted preliminary interviews with the people closest to this crime.

By ten thirty, they had the post-mortem report. Lambert called Chris Rushton and Bert Hook into his office to review the findings. As they had feared, these added little to what they already knew. Walter Keane had been hit fiercely on the back of his head with an object which had so far not been located. There were no traces of wood in the wound. The likeliest implements were a bottle or a section of metal piping. It seemed unlikely that even if the murder weapon was discovered it would reveal much about the assailant – it was unlikely to carry fingerprints, since the killer would almost certainly have worn gloves or wiped it clean.

This assailant might have been male or female. Walter Keane had weighed just under ten stones, or sixty-three kilograms, in the pathologist's preferred term. As he'd pointed out before, any woman in reasonable health could have hauled his inert corpse aloft once she had secured the rope around his thin neck.

The rope on which the corpse had swung from the tree until discovered was substantial but not individual enough to offer any clues as to its user. It was the sort of strong rope often used for a variety of purposes in boatyards, and indeed three lengths of very similar rope had been found in two of the three boathouses which sheltered craft at the edge of the lake and were within eighty yards of the scene of death. The coarse surface rarely yielded decent fingerprints, and on this occasion there was no residual sweat or grit from whoever had used it to string up the corpse. All indications were that the killer had worn stout gloves for the task.

'On a warm summer evening, that strongly suggests pre-meditation,' said Rushton. 'You'd hardly take gloves with you on a night-time stroll unless you intended some sort of assault on Keane.'

Lambert was studying the paragraph which carried the details of the analysis of the stomach contents. 'Some sort of quiche, with broccoli and potatoes. Followed by apple crumble, probably consumed two to three hours before death. Recall for me what time the Keanes ate on that evening, Chris.'

Rushton did not need to consult his notes. 'They ate at seven and finished by eight, Debbie Keane says. That puts the probable time of death at between ten and eleven. If, that is, we accept the times she's given us. We've unearthed nothing so far which implies that she had any connection with her husband's death.'

Lambert frowned. 'The time suggests a prearranged meeting with his murderer. Debbie said he liked to walk round and check what was happening on the lakes and the golf course, but this time in the evening was much too late for that. It's possible that his killer was waiting in the woods and surprised him, but we know that it wasn't his habit to wander through there in the dark. I think he'd arranged a meeting with someone who either was already planning to end his life or panicked during their meeting and resorted to violence.'

It was Bert Hook who voiced the question which comes first to any experienced policeman. 'How many people who were here at the time of this death have previous form?'

Chris Rushton frowned. Some people expected you to perform miracles; he'd spent most of his weekend organizing the collection of statements from everyone on site and filing the results. 'I'd begun the trawl when you called me in here. I'm expecting a smaller percentage than normal with criminal histories; the people who have homes here tend to be middle-class and respectable. But there'll be some, for sure. There always are.' He delivered the sentiment with satisfaction. Policemen are rarely bright-eyed about the integrity of the public; they have seen too much vice to be other than cynical.

Hook smiled, thinking of his earlier visit to the site at the invitation of Lisa Ramsbottom, as well as the current high summer situation, when Twin Lakes was much busier. 'This doesn't strike you as a place for desperados, when you wander around it.'

Lambert said acerbically, 'That will make it much easier for us, then. The violent man or the violent pair who strung up Wally Keane will leap out at you from the innocents all around them.'

Bert was suitably chastened. 'I'm not saying it will be easy. I was talking about the people who find places like this attractive. But when you look beneath the surface, there are always people who strike you as different from the norm. Maybe we've found a few already. Richard Seagrave and Vanessa Norton didn't seem typical, for a start.' Hook had clearly found the exchanges of the previous evening as unsatisfactory as had John Lambert.

'No one is normal, once you scratch away the surface.' Chris Rushton was surprised to find himself voicing a thought he had heard from a forensic psychologist, a beast viewed with perennial suspicion by the police service.

'What about Keane's PC? Do we have anything from that yet?' asked Lambert.

'Nothing yet. I'm hoping for something by the end of the day. Tom Jameson, the DS who's the expert at getting into the computer stuff that people don't want anyone else to see, is back from holiday this morning. He's already been assigned to this as a priority. I've never known him beaten by a computer. Sometimes it takes him an hour to get in, sometimes two or three days, but he gets there.'

'From what everyone tells us, Keane seems to have been an irritating busybody, but scarcely an interesting man. I expect we'll find nothing of great interest on his computer.'

Lambert spoke with the weary pessimism of the senior detective who has in his time investigated many blind alleys. On this occasion, his views would prove quite spectacularly mistaken.

There was a tension between Jason and Lisa Ramsbottom which neither of them cared to acknowledge.

Perhaps it was only to be expected, thought Lisa, with a murder committed scarcely two hundred yards from where they now sat in the sunshine outside their unit. Especially so when the most serious of all crimes might have been committed by someone with whom you spoke daily as you moved around the site; someone with whom you had perhaps exchanged a laugh and a bit of harmless gossip. Jason had voiced that thought over breakfast.

It didn't bear thinking about. And yet it was difficult to think of anything else. She said, 'Freda Potts has been here two or three times with that boy, Debbie Keane says. She doesn't think he's Freda's nephew at all. She said the lad doesn't behave like a nephew.'

They should have laughed over that, but each of them gave no more than a sickly grin. Lisa wondered if Jason was seeing in his mind's eye the same images she had, of a randy boy tumbling staid Freda Potts the schoolteacher as she begged him for more. Most unworthy and reprehensible.

Jason obviously felt the same as she did about the murder on Friday night, for he too could settle to nothing. He kept shifting his position on his chair and turning the pages of the sports section of his newspaper, but he plainly wasn't reading much or developing any positive train of thought. Both of them were startled when his mobile phone rang. Its note sounded unnaturally loud in the rural silence.

Jason snatched it up and checked the caller. 'It's Ellie.'

It was a relief to both of them to hear their daughter. The fourteen-year-old was full of her own life and her own news. She translated them for the duration of her call from this doom-laden world to her more innocent one. She was thoroughly enjoying her school trip. She had tales for them of the mischief perpetrated by her daring contemporaries and of the comical discomfort of the long-suffering staff who were accompanying them. Her animation and her obvious happiness cheered her parents, despite their closing injunctions to her that she should be careful not to go over the top and seriously offend the staff in charge.

Jason seemed to settle a little more to the reports of Ashes cricket and the Tour de France, though Lisa noticed that he kept glancing at his watch. He seemed relieved when she said she must drive the mile or so to the nearest village and its store to buy provisions for the next couple of days. Probably he just wanted a little time on his own to digest what had happened and what was coming next for them in the police investigation, she thought. She was glad now that she had brought kindly, normal Bert Hook here a couple of months ago, even though Jason had said at the time that she was over-reacting and shouldn't have bothered their neighbour. She couldn't explain how, but that move seemed to her to have put them a little ahead of their neighbours amidst all the speculation around the site.

Jason waited until she had been gone five minutes before using his mobile. The conversation didn't take long. It was too urgent an exchange to allow any pleasantries. He kept a wary eye on the quiet ground around him in case of unwelcome eavesdroppers. He uttered the briefest greeting, listened to the reply, then glanced once again at his watch. 'Lisa's gone to the shops. She won't be long. I should be with you not later than one.' He terminated the call immediately, then sat for a moment smiling down at the silent mobile.

Mark Patmore was trying to relax. That was a contradiction in terms, when you were a police officer working undercover: the first and greatest rule was that you should never relax. You had to live the part, to force yourself into it so completely that your previous existence was forgotten and the man you had been was just a memory.

Except that it was all crap. You weren't allowed to observe this most vital rule of all and become the person you were pretending to be. Because every so often you were reminded vividly who you had once been, who you still were when it suited them. An officer in the police service. A sergeant in the Drug Squad, to be precise. The police liked precision. Someone today would take away the disjointed information he had to offer and turn it into a neat report. Someone with rank, some fucking Inspector. Someone who had never and would never undertake the risks Mark had run to provide him with this information.

He'd tried to apologize this morning to the woman he'd rejected so brutally last night. She'd told him bitterly to fuck off, before he had even begun an explanation. Her reaction had brought a small measure of relief to both of them. All reliefs were small, in the squat. And yet it was a refuge, the only one available for every one of the assorted misfits who occupied it.

There weren't many windows left intact now. The wind would howl through the cracked and broken glass, when autumn and then winter came. The house might not be habitable, even when you wrapped yourself in the filthy blankets which most of them had acquired. But you didn't think long-term, when you were in the squat. Unless you were an undercover man. Then you were supposed to crawl patiently towards long-term intelligence about the men you never saw, the ones who controlled the dangerous and highly lucrative world of illicit drugs.

Mark was going through his ritual of silent complaint against the drug barons who controlled him here and the police barons who had sent him here. He realized what he was doing. He realized also that it was a prelude to action. It was a motivator to drive him to do what his instincts told him he no longer wished to do. He must leave the dark anonymity of the squat and move out into daylight and the world which he had left behind to come here.

Five minutes later, Patmore stood blinking resentfully in the sunlight. He moved automatically to the shady side of the street and kept as close as he could to the fronts of the derelict terraced houses, moving reluctantly away from the squat and the security that it afforded him. He dropped into his swiftly shuffling gait, with his battered trainers scarcely leaving the ground as he walked. It was the movement of a much older man. Strangely, that was a kind of defence. Many of the aggressors in this underworld were strong young men, who found it necessary to confront strength when they saw it in others.

It was quite a long way. It seemed to get a little further each time. Something over a mile, he thought. He didn't mind that, though he hated the sense of exposure. He felt more and more defenceless now when he moved out into the open. He'd had a car, once, before he'd undertaken this assignment. That seemed a long time ago, and the man who had driven the car and been interested in other cars was a man he scarcely knew or remembered. He'd thought once that he'd get back to that Mark, but it now seemed an unrealistic goal, one in which he had little interest.

He didn't like it when the narrow streets finished and he had to move along wider and more modern roads. The houses here were set back from the pavements and there were lots of cars parked in front of them. But there were spaces too. It was Monday morning and most people would be back at work after the weekend. Mark remembered that world.

There weren't many people about and he liked that. A woman with a toddler's hand in hers crossed the road to avoid him. He must look pretty sinister, with his shaven head and his unshaven face. He grinned his secret grin and did not look at her again. He was nearly there now. He couldn't see the football posts; they should have been visible now, over the low wall to his left. They must have taken them down for the summer, to stop the kids using them. The pitch had been mown recently; the straight lines of the cutting made the grass look quite neat. He stopped near the entrance and looked around, but there was no sign of a groundsman. Probably he was employed by the council and directed to somewhere else today; that was good.

Mark Patmore knew exactly where he had to go. He shuffled across towards the long wooden building which was a cricket pavilion in summer and changing rooms for the football teams during the winter. There was no sign of life within it today. He moved to the rear of the ramshackle edifice, where the shed which housed the maintenance equipment for the playing fields was attached.

There was no padlock on the door today. That was as it should be. He opened it and slipped quietly inside. The only light was from the single small window in the side of the wooden hut. He felt at home in the dimness.

The man sitting in the chair beside the tractor did not move. He wore neatly creased fawn chino trousers and a bright yellow shirt with the Pringle logo prominent. Casual wear, but as clean and smart as Patmore was grubby and dishevelled. The man's hair was precisely parted and as neat as if he had come here straight from a barber's shop. Patmore sat on the wooden chair opposite him and ran both of his hands briefly over the stubble of the scalp he had shaved three days earlier. He had never seen this man before and he resented him already.

Yellow-shirt flashed a warrant card that signified he was a Detective Inspector. Mark didn't bother to register the name. The DI studied him wordlessly for a few seconds; you needed to assess men like Mark Patmore before you decided how much to rely upon what they told you. If they moved beyond a certain point, they could sell out and disappear into the murky underworld they were supposed to be illuminating for you. When he said, 'What news, Sergeant?' the rank was meant as a reminder that they were on the same side: he had caught a whiff of the under-cover man's disillusion.

'I saw them last night. Well, saw Mercer. They're promoting me. Me and one of the others.' Patmore curled his lip on the thought, as if promotion merely emphasized what a dangerous farce these bastards had devised for him. 'They want to move us up – they're putting each of us in control of a group of dealers.'

'Congratulations.' Yellow-shirt kept any hint of irony out of his tone, but it was a strange thing to be acknowledging the promotion of your own man amongst the enemy. 'Have you any names for us beyond those of the dealers around you? It's the men further up we need to nail, if we're ever going to break this.'

Mark was suddenly enraged that the smug bastard should remind him of something so obvious. He wanted to crash his fist into the small straight nose and the prim, successful mouth beneath it. 'That's why I'm here! That's why I've been risking my life for the last eight months. And no, I haven't any names for you. Not yet. Perhaps by the time I have them, I'll be doing so well out of drugs that I won't want to reveal them. Sir!' He delivered the last word like an expletive, after a lengthy pause.

'Take it easy, Sergeant Patmore.' But the DI knew that the reminder of rank meant nothing here, that he was dealing with a man near to the end of his tether. He was on ground where he had not ventured before, and he felt it crumbling beneath his feet. 'When you have names, we'll take them and get you out. Meanwhile, you're doing a good job.'

The phrase fell limply amidst the wisps of dead grass on the wooden floor of the room. Who the hell knew what a good job was, in this extraordinary context? Even Mark Patmore, who was at the centre of it, had no idea whether he was doing a good job or drowning in vice. He had no comparisons, no measures by which he could judge himself and his performance. He knew now that he wanted it to end, but how it would end and what he would do if he survived he could not even contemplate. He stood up, wanting to be out of the presence of this smooth bastard, back in the squat with the losers he suddenly loved. 'I'm seeing them on Wednesday.'

'Good. And you'll let us know if you get any names of the men issuing orders to you at this new level.' He didn't wait for assent, since it might not be voiced. 'What about the other dealer who's being moved up with you? Do you have a name for him?'

'It's the black man.' But there were a lot of them among the dealers as well as the users. Mark liked this one, what little he'd seen of him, and the other half of him didn't want to deliver the name. But he sighed and said, 'He's not a user. That's why they think he'll be reliable, I suppose. His name's Martindale.'

DI Rushton had completed his initial trawl of criminal records by early afternoon. He was not optimistic when he reported to his chief superintendent.

'We've turned up two previous instances of violence which have led to court proceedings and convictions. One was fourteen years ago and was a domestic. The man assaulted his former wife. He broke a cheekbone and two ribs but claimed she was threatening him with a knife at the time. The court must have believed him, because he got away with a suspended sentence. He is now forty-nine, apparently happily settled with his second wife, with whom he has two children. The family were here on Friday night and are still on site. He was with other people throughout the evening and has no connection with this crime, unless we think he brought a killer in from

outside, which seems highly unlikely because of his background and present income. I doubt if he'd have the contacts
or the money to bring in a contract killer.'

'And your other man with form?'

'He was involved in a pub brawl eight years ago. Put a man
in hospital. Seems to be a man handy with his fists and with
his boots who lives on the edge of the law. But he's small-
time. He doesn't like us and the two officers who took his
statement didn't like him. I had a look at him myself and
agreed with them, but I don't think he had any involvement
in this crime. He has an impeccable alibi for Friday night and
no apparent motive: he's only just bought one of the homes
here and scarcely knew Keane. Other people have confirmed
that. Again, I think a contract killer would be beyond both his
experience and his resources.'

'So how does this crime look to you, Chris, now that you've
assessed all the statements and the previous form?'

DI Rushton was now used to being treated as an equal and
being asked his opinion as such by the great man. Lambert
had overawed him, when he had first been assigned to him as
a young and newly promoted detective inspector. 'I suppose
it's still possible that someone totally unconnected with what
goes on here came in from outside to commit murder, but that
seems highly unlikely, especially if we posit a prearranged
meeting at a specific place in those woods. More important
to me is that Walter Keane's life revolved totally around Twin
Lakes and what happens here. The Keanes have been virtually
full-time residents here for the last eight years. Walter's death
must surely be directly connected with previous events here.'

'Agreed. So what next?'

'I'd be pretty confident that the killer is among the five
couples whom you and Bert have already spoken to. Everyone
else with even the flimsiest of motives seems to have several
people to attest his or her alibi.'

'And you've come up with nothing in the way of form on
any of these ten people?'

Rushton smiled grimly. 'Enquiries are ongoing, as we
tell the public when we've nothing to report. In this case,
they really are. There's nothing useful on record, but I'm

still exploring the police grapevine in the case of two of the ten.'

Lambert's answering smile was rueful, but even more grim than Rushton's. 'We can't afford to wait for you to gather information, Chris. Tell me what you have, and where you have nothing, give me your thoughts.'

'Let's take the easy ones first. Lisa and Jason Ramsbottom. He got in with a bad set when he was younger. He was a member of a gang with whom he had a series of Saturday-night rumbles up in Lancashire, where he grew up. I suspect that there were a couple of occasions when his youth protected him from charges, because we all know it's hardly worth the bother of charging kids under eighteen. But all that's a long time ago. Marriage and a daughter, who's now fourteen, seem to have settled him down. Most important of all, it was the Ramsbottoms who brought Bert Hook on to the site more than two months ago to investigate threatening notes. They'd hardly have done that, if they'd been contemplating murder.'

'Only one person needs to be involved in murder, but I take your point. Go on.'

'George and Mary Martindale. George was a jobbing builder for several years, taking work wherever he could get it, but almost never unemployed. He seems to have been involved in a few fights and scuffles, but nothing serious; I expect as a black man in that environment, he had to learn to use his fists. He's been working for the council in the road works department at Kidderminster and I've spoken to his bosses there. They're very well satisfied with him and have recently promoted him, making him foreman of a road works gang. They say George is popular with the other men, looks after youngsters well, and is generally a good example. He and his family – he has two boys aged eight and six – seem to be well liked on the site. Several of the other people we've interviewed have told us that, without any prompting.'

'All round good egg, then. If a Jamaican can be such a Bertie Wooster thing as a good egg. Life being what it is, we'll probably find he strung up our victim on Friday night.'

Chris Rushton grinned. 'I doubt it. He has the physique to do it, but hardly the motivation. He seems to treat Debbie

Keane's nosiness with an affectionate tolerance. From what they've said to us so far, we could probably say the same of Matthew and Freda Potts – well, of her, anyway. Matthew hasn't been here often enough to have many dealings with the Keanes. He works on oil rigs in the North Sea and is away for lengthy periods. But Freda has been here two or three times with her nephew. Neither of the Potts seems to have any criminal record. Matthew Potts was in the SAS for several years and I'm still trying to check his army record: the military authorities are notoriously stingy with information, as you know. I suppose with his background he'd be able to kill someone like Wally Keane with great competence, but I can't see why he would want to do that, and no one else has suggested a reason. He seems to have hardly known the victim. His wife, on the other hand, was quizzed and irritated by the Keanes when she was here without Matthew.'

Lambert came back to the people who had been in his mind for almost twenty-four hours now. He said hopefully, 'Have you turned up anything useful on Richard Seagrave or Vanessa Norton?'

'No criminal record for either of them. Seagrave went to Rugby public school as a day boy and Norton was at Roedean for a time. Her father was an army major and her parents were abroad for most of the years of her schooling. Seagrave and Norton aren't married and we've no evidence about how long they've been together or how serious the relationship is.'

'Pretty serious, I'd say, from what we saw. Bert and I interviewed them yesterday afternoon. She did most of the talking and I felt that was something they'd agreed on before we saw them. We got very little out of them.'

'Neither of them has any criminal record, as I said. They seem pretty high-powered people to take a place here, but perhaps it's a bolt-hole from taxing lives elsewhere. She writes a fashion column for the Mail on Sunday and he has his own successful business, Seagrave Enterprises. Office supplies. Highly successful, apparently, for a small business which is run almost entirely by the owner.'

'Could it be a front for something larger and darker?'

'It's possible, I suppose. I'll make unofficial enquiries. There's a DI in Birmingham who trained with me and owes me a few favours.'

Lambert grinned. 'I'm the one who always tells my team members they mustn't assess people's characters without assembling the proper factual basis, so I don't want this to go any further at present. But I didn't like Mr Seagrave and I didn't trust his partner, if that's what the blonde goddess is. How have they been received here at Twin Lakes?'

'They're more popular here than they are with you, by the sound of it. No one seems to know much about him; he doesn't mix a lot, though people find him pleasant enough to speak with. He provided a fine silver cup for a junior golf competition, and presented it to the first winner himself, as well as providing other generous prizes. That hasn't done him any harm in this holiday environment, where families are so important. Vanessa has taken up golf herself and made rapid progress, apparently. There was some amusement because Wally Keane kept having to adjust her handicap and was reputed to resent her progress.'

'I must send Bert Hook out for a round with Vanessa. I'm sure they'd both enjoy that.' Chris Rushton and John Lambert grinned for a moment at the thought of the Junoesque and fashion-conscious Vanessa Norton with the staid and persevering Bert Hook, whose golf gear was usually just too worn to wear socially and just too good for gardening. Chris was delighted to enjoy even the smallest of jokes with Lambert, whom he had held in awe for far too long.

Rushton now said, 'There's one little mystery which has emerged. Probably perfectly innocent, but intriguing nonetheless.' Chris liked to save what he considered his best or most meritorious discoveries until last, so as to leave the chief with the best impression of his industry and efficiency. 'It concerns Geoffrey Tiler and Michael Norrington.'

'Our gay couple. I hope you're not going to exhibit any evidence of prejudice.' Lambert kept his face studiously straight. Chris was a modern man and well aware of the dangers of sexual bias, despite the police service's well-earned reputation for homophobia.

'Nothing to do with their sexual orientation,' said Rushton stiffly. He still found it difficult to know when Lambert was giving his leg a gentle tug. 'No criminal record for either of them. Tiler runs a successful plastics business in Wolverhampton. Small but highly successful, it seems. The attitude towards them here could best be described as reserved. Amongst the conservative community of Twin Lakes, gay couples are not treated as unthinkingly as they might be in London or Brighton. People may not be biased against them, but they treat them cautiously. Having said which, I get the feeling that people are warming to this couple after a cool start. Norrington in particular is popular, because he's always ready to help people out.'

'As when he offered to look for Debbie Keane's husband and discovered a corpse.'

'Along with George Martindale, yes. Nothing has come up so far to connect either of them with the killing. But it's Michael Norrington who has provided me with my little mystery. I was checking him out on the electoral register to make sure of his address. He appears to have changed his name – a few years ago, probably, but I can't be sure exactly when as yet. That's not illegal, of course, but I thought it might be of interest.'

He looked up to find John Lambert staring at him intently, with his head a little on one side and his grey eyes wide and inquisitive. 'Now why would a man want to do that, Chris?'

THIRTEEN

Jason Ramsbottom tried to disguise his impatience. Lisa had been longer at the village store than he had anticipated – shopping always took more time when you held conversations with the owner, as you were expected to do in country areas when the shop was quiet. He helped his wife to unload her purchases and to carry them up the steps and into their kitchen. She sank thankfully into her armchair in the sitting room. 'No cup of tea for a weary shopper?'

'I have to go out. They've phoned from work. Sorry.' He resisted the temptation to look at his watch. Instead, he looked at his wife's pretty face and buxom figure and thought how strange human nature was. And how stupid men were, not to be content with women like this.

'You didn't say anything about that. I was hoping we—'

'I didn't know this was going to happen. I had a phone call whilst you were out.'

'But you're on holiday. They surely can't—'

'They shouldn't, but they do. We're in a recession, Lisa. They're taking advantage of that. Everyone is scared of losing his job. It isn't pleasant, but we have to live with it.'

He was on his way five minutes later, glancing at the murder room on his right as he approached the exit of the site, wondering exactly what was going on in there and exactly how much those shrewd and experienced CID men now knew about him. Then he was out on the open road, driving away from Twin Lakes and what he thought of as his public life. He slid his window down a little and felt the exhilaration of air around his head as he accelerated. His spirits should have lifted now, but he felt only the heaviness of guilt and what he was doing to Lisa.

He drove thirty miles before his pulses quickened and elation took over from guilt. He put his foot down when he reached the dual carriageway, wanting suddenly to waste as little time on travel as he could. Then he glanced at his speed, saw the needle creeping towards ninety, and slowed immediately. It would be stupid to get pinched for something silly like speeding, when there were much greater issues at stake.

He wondered again what those policemen were doing back at Twin Lakes. 'Rest Assured' the notice said beneath the name of the place. There hadn't been much rest there since the discovery of the body on Saturday morning. How much had the CID discovered about him and Lisa? He'd been appalled when she'd brought that stolid and friendly Bert Hook on to the site all those weeks ago to investigate the notes they'd received. But perhaps it had been a good thing, as things had turned out. The CID surely couldn't suspect him now, when he and Lisa had invited one of their men in of their own free will a couple of months earlier.

The last four miles were through lanes. Here he had to twist and turn the Audi expertly round bends and over crossings. He had to crawl along behind a tractor for over a mile, whilst his impatience grew at the same rate as his excitement. And then suddenly he was there, cruising into the village which was scarcely more than a hamlet, turning into the tight drive of the chocolate-box cottage with the pink roses climbing beside and over the door. He wondered if those staid Victorians who had cherished and painted places like this had behaved as passionately within the dwellings as he did.

Anna Riley was waiting for him, in black jeans and a vivid green top. They looked at each other for a second, then said not a word as she flung herself urgently against him. He ran his hands over her small breasts, then up and over her shoulder blades, down the small of her back and on to the exquisite curves beneath. Then the green top and the jeans were off and they were naked together on top of the bed. The love-making which had begun with the first touch climaxed with penetration and the urgent and repeated thrusts of ecstasy which followed.

They held each other for minutes after they had finished, enjoying their gradual relaxation both as an expression of trust and as a conclusion of the intimacy between them. She had shouted exhortations to him during their coupling, but when he finally held her away from him and gazed fondly into her face, his single appreciative breathing of 'Anna!' was the first word he had uttered since he had entered her home.

Freda Potts was at her most understanding and considerate. 'You needn't come if you don't want to, Matt. You won't enjoy it. Dinners aren't your sort of thing and you wouldn't know many of the people there.'

Matthew was tempted but dutiful. He said after a pause to consider the matter, 'But it's meant to be couples, isn't it?'

'Yes. It's the staff dinner we always have just after the end of term, at the beginning of the summer holiday. But I've been on my own before. You were away when they had it last year. I don't mind, really I don't. I'm used to going to things on my own; it's not your fault that you have to be away a lot.'

'No, it's not. But that's all the more reason why I should support you, when I am here. I'm coming with you tomorrow night.'

She forced a grin. 'Very noble, I'm sure. But unnecessary. I don't mind going on my own. It's only an hour's drive from here and the roads will be very quiet when I'm on the return journey. I expect it will be after midnight by the time I get back here.'

'And you won't be able to drink unless I come.' He said it firmly, because he worried sometimes about her weakness of will over drink-driving. She was prone to push it a little, take the odd risk, and in a convivial gathering of staff he feared she might do just that. 'But you will be able to drink tomorrow, because I shall be driving. You can get paralytic if you like, so long as you don't start snogging everyone in sight.'

'I shan't get paralytic. That would be educationally indiscreet and make me a cause célèbre in the gossip stakes. And you obviously don't know my colleagues. You'd have to be tight to consider a kiss on the cheek from most of them!'

'You make them sound quite irresistible! It's obviously high time I got to know this fascinating cross-section of the intelligentsia. And I assure you, after the company I keep most of the time on the oil rigs, the teaching staff of a comprehensive school will seem richly diverse.'

And so it was settled. Freda felt strangely queasy at the prospect.

In the murder room, DI Rushton conducted a long, intense phone call with a former colleague, then sought out Detective Chief Superintendent Lambert.

'It looks as though you could be right about Richard Seagrave. Seagrave Enterprises might well be a front for something much more sinister. The local CID are working on it, but they're hampered because they've been told not to alert anyone at the firm to their enquiries.'

Lambert sighed. Complications like this were much more common than most members of the public appreciated. That was understandable, since most members of the public never heard about them. But where extensive criminal networks were involved, as for instance in the illegal drugs trade, local forces were often warned to hold off, in case a minor arrest alerted much bigger villains to the fact that their activities were under investigation.

This was logical and inevitable, since everyone wanted to pin down the faceless moguls who controlled the worst and most lucrative criminal enterprises in Britain. But it led to much frustration. Sometimes local CID sections had conducted an investigation which had occupied many months and much manpower, only to be told when they were near to an arrest that they should hold off and pass on their information to units with a national overview. When clear-up rates were often the measure by which their efficiency was judged, this could be highly frustrating.

'Seagrave is under investigation.' Lambert nodded thoughtfully. It was the blanket phrase which covered a multitude of different possibilities. 'Is Vanessa Norton involved?'

'There is no evidence that she is. My contact wasn't even aware of her. He made a note of the name.'

Lambert was vaguely pleased that Norton probably wasn't involved. He wondered if he would have felt the same measure of relief if an unattractive middle-aged man rather than a striking, curvaceous and highly articulate blonde had been involved. He said to Rushton, 'Any ideas about where we go

from here with the delightful Mr Seagrave? The people investigating him should be aware that he is now a murder suspect
here, whatever else he is also involved in.'

'I think we just have to proceed as normal, assessing whatever we find here whilst being aware that there is accumulating
evidence that this particular suspect may well be a major
criminal player elsewhere.'

'Agreed. Have we any idea where "elsewhere" might be?'

Rushton pursed his lips. 'My contact mentioned Oxford.'

'I've a couple of old friends in the Oxford CID. I'll see
what they're able to tell me. Off the record, of course.'

'Off the record, inevitably.' Both of them savoured the use
of the phrase which journalists offered so often when quizzing
them.

Then Lambert voiced a much more important thought. 'I
wonder whether anyone here was aware of Seagrave's activities
elsewhere? Whether Walter Keane, for instance, knew anything
about them?'

That idea seemed preposterous, but within twenty-four hours
it would seem much less so.

As Monday 21st July moved into a tranquil evening, Geoffrey
Tiler and Michael Norrington were quite unaware that the
identity of one of them was the subject of police investigation.
Murder brings heightened attention to any irregularity, but
neither of them had yet grown accustomed to thinking of
himself as a suspect in a murder investigation.

The site was busy. Children released for the long summer
holiday were making the most of each other's company in
boisterous games; no less than five dinghies sailed on the two
lakes which gave the place its name; the golf course was filled
with players displaying a wide range of abilities and epithets,
as well as the endless optimism which is a necessity for all
participants in the ancient game.

Geoffrey and Michael were walking in the quietest section,
on the edge of the woods which fringed the lakes. They skirted
the area which was still ribboned off as a scene of crime, studiously avoiding any glances towards the tree where Wally Keane
had been left hanging three days ago. Without any words of

agreement, each of them knew that they would not speak of Wally, nor of the progress of the police investigation, nor even of the questions the police had asked and the responses they had given when they had been interviewed about that death on Saturday. It seemed a long time since they'd spoken to the CID, but neither of them voiced even that innocent thought.

Norrington was looking across the lake, towards where three boys were trying to launch a rowing boat on the opposite side of it, when he said quietly, 'Are you absolutely sure you want to do this, Geoff?'

'I'm very sure. Are you?'

'I've been sure for months now. I think you know that. But I want you to be sure. I don't want you to be railroaded into this by things quite outside our control.'

Tiler smiled ruefully. 'Maybe I needed a little railroading. I'm happy with things as they are here, where no one has known us except as a couple. It's more difficult for me elsewhere.'

'In your normal life, you mean. In that life you live during the working week, when you have to leave behind our escapist world.'

Michael hadn't meant it to be an accusation, but it emerged as just that. He could hear the underlying bitterness which he thought he had banished for ever. Geoffrey Tiler wasn't offended. He nodded his head slowly and put his hand softly upon the forearm of his companion. 'I used to be like that. I wouldn't admit it, even to myself, but that's how it was at the beginning of our time together. But it's changed completely now: you must believe that.'

'I believe it. I can feel it.' Norrington looked down at the hand upon his arm for a moment as if he meant that literally. 'It takes time for things to develop and to deepen. Especially in your situation, when you've been straight and married. I've known I was attracted only to men since I was an adolescent, but you've had to discover that much later.'

Tiler nodded, eager to accept that analysis. 'I should have asked myself all sorts of questions years ago. But it wasn't until I met you and our friendship ripened that I became sure – it was only then that I was prepared and willing to ask those questions of myself.'

'Friendship.' Michael smiled wryly, then detached the hand from his arm and picked up a small flat stone. He crouched and skimmed it vigorously across the deserted section of the lake which was nearest to them. They watched its six swift splashes, then the widening ripples which spread from them across the calm water. A moorhen which they had not seen took off, flew no more than forty yards, and then settled on the surface again, immobile after a vigorous shaking of its tail.

'Don't decry friendship, Michael. It's a splendid thing. Ours was the beginning of my salvation, before it grew into something more.'

'And now you're ready to acknowledge us in the wider world outside Twin Lakes. The world where you live your working life and make your living. Are you sure you want to do that?'

'I'm sure. I should have done it long ago.' Geoff turned and looked at Michael and felt awkward and apologetic, as he always felt when they came to this issue. He was intensely aware of his tardiness when it came to going public over this most important thing in his life. 'You've been very understanding, Mike.'

'I know that it's different for you. You have a well-established public persona which is going to be completely changed by this. You run a business, employ almost a hundred people. It will affect the way people look at you.'

'I'm not interested in the people who will look at me differently when I announce that I'm gay. Fools like that are out of the Ark. If they want to go on living in the past, so much the worse for them.' But Geoff wondered even as he asserted it whether it was wholly true, whether he was strong enough to simply shrug off any opposition, as well as the welter of excited gossip which would follow the announcement of his revised sexual preferences.

'Will it affect the business? Will you lose orders?'

'No. The public won't even be aware of it. It's the quality of the goods we produce which will affect the orders, not the chairman's preference in partners.' He spoke very firmly and he spoke good sense, he was sure. But a small part of him wondered whether some of his older clients might be staid enough and conservative enough to hesitate over continuing to do business with him. Wolverhampton was not London, with its chattering classes and influential media, where it seemed almost more fashionable to be homosexual than heterosexual.

'Will you want me to come to your works social affairs? I wouldn't really enjoy that. I've always been a shy man. But if you want me there, I'll be there. It's the least I can do.'

'No. That won't be necessary.' Geoff wondered if his assurance was too prompt, whether it sounded relieved rather than reassuring. What a complicated business gay love was in public, when in private it seemed to him so natural and straightforward. 'I know you don't enjoy socializing unless you know the people involved quite well. I think I'm the same myself, actually, though of course I've known most of the people I work with and deal with for many years.'

'There's still a lot of you I don't know, Geoff, isn't there? Almost all of your working life, which means about three quarters of your life in all, I suppose.'

Geoffrey Tiler put his hand back on his partner's arm, this time very firmly. 'You know me, Mike. You know the private me and the real me. Everything else is irrelevant – well, not irrelevant, because my work is important to me and to the people who are dependent on me for their livings. But the real me, the one who matters, comes alive when I am alone with you.'

Norrington looked across the lake at the distant dinghies, at the boys noisily preoccupied with their rowing boat. He didn't like physical displays of affection in public, so that even Geoff's hand on his arm made him check to see if they were observed. 'We should be getting back. We arranged to eat with other people in the restaurant, if you remember.'

It was almost an accusation, as if he was stating his resentment at being paraded as part of a couple in front of others. Yet he knew that it was Geoff who was making the effort, that it was Geoff who was forcing himself to get used to appearing in public as half of a gay couple. He himself had been used for many years to such things. He tried to sound relaxed. 'I'm quite looking forward to a bit of company.'

Geoff had arranged earlier in the day for them to meet up

with the Potts and the Martindales in the unpretentious little restaurant on site. They had been comparing notes on what the police had asked them about Wally Keane. As they had stood beside the bowling green and swapped experiences, dinner had seemed an agreeable notion. Now, he wasn't sure it had been such a good idea. He could sense that Mike was a little uneasy about it. But then Mike knew nothing about the announcement he was planning to make, if things went according to plan.

They went back to their site home and put on their clothes for the evening, as the time dictated that they should. They didn't exchange many more words. Geoff sensed a nervousness in both of them as the appointed time approached. What had earlier seemed a chance to declare his love now seemed to have all sorts of dangers. But he was resolved, and his determination carried him through all of his doubts.

The Potts were already in the bar when they got to the long, single-storey building which housed the small dance floor and the restaurant. It was a relief to chat to Matthew Potts, whom they hardly knew. He was a quiet, reserved man, who observed what went on around him, missed nothing, and generally offered opinions only when asked for them. That probably stemmed from his army background and his present work on the oil rigs, Geoff decided. But Matthew was friendly enough; he seemed to appreciate being asked to join their small party tonight. Freda was more outgoing and seemingly more nervous. 'I'm really being spoiled this week,' she giggled. 'Treated to a meal here tonight and then out tomorrow to my school's staff dinner with my husband. It helps to make up for all those lonely microwave meals on my own in front of the telly when he's away!'

They chatted a little about her work as Head of History in the comprehensive and she emerged as altogether more grounded and less shallow than she had appeared earlier. She showed an eagerness for her subject which she normally concealed because she was afraid of boring people she scarcely knew. Geoffrey Tiler was glad to see how well Freda was getting on with Michael Norrington, who was both knowledgeable and enthusiastic about British history.

It was seeing Mike at ease that emboldened him to ask Jason and Lisa Ramsbottom to share their table when they came in for a meal. The pair hesitated for a moment before Lisa said, 'Thank you, that would be lovely. It might save us from grumbling at each other over our food; Jason's been out for most of the day, when I wanted him here!'

'Pressure of work!' said Jason, with a forced smile and a shrug of his shoulders. He didn't enlarge upon the thought.

The Martindales were last to arrive. Geoffrey, who now found himself acting as unofficial host, said with studious neutrality, 'You didn't bring the children?'

Mary said immediately, 'They're used to eating quite early. And young Alison, who lives next door, offered to babysit for us. She likes the boys and they like her. She's very responsible, for a seventeen-year-old.' She was anxious to get the girl's age in, to show that this was all quite proper and that her children were not being neglected. She glanced at Freda Potts. 'I think Alison wants to become a teacher eventually, and she says it's all good experience for her.'

George Martindale said more quietly, 'We love the little demons dearly, but it's good for us to be able to get out for a civilized meal without them for a change.' His dark-brown voice was as smooth as velvet, easing all of them towards relaxation with each other. Geoffrey Tiler took it as the cue to order two bottles of wine as they sat down to their meal. He had taken over, he realized, but that was appropriate enough, in view of what he planned as the climax of this modest gathering.

The eight of them got on remarkably well, as people of very different backgrounds sometimes do over food and drink, and the decibel level of the conversation rose steadily, punctuated as it was by outbursts of genuine laughter as the meal proceeded. The wine went down well, and when a third bottle was eventually ordered, the company seemed to accept that it would be Geoffrey Tiler who bought it, since there was a general recognition now that this had evolved into his evening, however informally it had been planned earlier in the day.

Geoffrey himself became very quiet as they finished dessert and waited for coffee, seemingly content to observe the pleasure his companions were taking in each other's company.

Because things had gone so well, they had now been here longer than any of them had expected, and the few other customers in the restaurant on a quiet Monday evening had mostly filtered away, with envious looks at the convivial eight and the clinking glasses at the end of the room.

It was a surprise, but not a major one, when Geoffrey Tiler rose to his feet with a nervous smile. As the owner of a prosperous small business, he had grown used to making short, generally humorous speeches on a variety of occasions, most of them concerned with retirements. He was more nervous before this speech than before any other he had made, but quietly determined, as he had been throughout the day.

'This won't take long, but it's very important. Thank you for joining Mike and me tonight.' He looked round at the suddenly expectant, wondering faces and took encouragement from them. 'All of you know that Michael Norrington and I are a partnership. We are grateful for the way you have received and befriended us here at Twin Lakes.' There were mutters of approval, then an assurance in Martindale's mellow base tones that the feeling was mutual.

Geoffrey Tiler smiled at his small audience. 'I want you to be the first people to hear the formal announcement that we have decided to cement our relationship for the rest of our lives. Michael and I will be taking advantage of the recent recognition of partnerships like ours in the laws of the land. We shall be getting married on the twenty-eighth of September and we'd like all of you to be there.'

FOURTEEN

Detective Sergeant Bert Hook was the one who was sent to question the grieving widow.

'You already know her,' Chris Rushton pointed out. 'And you are by far the most tactful senior officer we have in the team.'

'Not much competition for that title, is there?' Bert pointed out dryly. It was true that tact was not a highly estimated virtue within the CID ranks. But he had talked to Debbie Keane two months before tragedy had struck, and he had actually quite liked the sixty-one-year-old whom most people found an irritating busybody. Hook had known loneliness in his own life, and he recognized that an interest in the lives of others and garrulous gossiping could be an outlet for some people who were beset by it.

Debbie looked even older and greyer than she had done when he'd seen her three days earlier after the news of Walter's death. Her face was more noticeably lined and the puffiness round her eyes showed that it was not long since she had been weeping. Hook said he was sorry to intrude and she said, 'Do come in. I'm tired already of being treated like cut glass by the people around here.' She sounded surprisingly weary of the daily interchanges which had been the pulse of her life. 'Have you come here to tell me who killed Wally?'

'No, we can't do that yet, Mrs Keane. Perhaps we might have some news by the end of the week.' He didn't know why he'd said that: there was no basis for it, and it wasn't the kind of reassurance he should be offering.

'Call me Debbie, please. I feel that we've known each other for quite a long time – I suppose something like this brings you closer. But I shall continue to call you DS Hook.' She gave a little smile, more of relief than amusement. They were the first words she had uttered with even a suggestion of humour since she'd heard about Wally. She realized now how weary she was of hearing sympathy.

Bert smiled back at her, then said awkwardly, 'We're working hard and making progress, I think. One of the things we do in cases like this is to investigate the finances of the murder victim. It's all part of what we told you on Saturday: we have to take all possible steps to get to know as much as we can about someone who can no longer speak for himself.'

She nodded several times, staring past him and out of the window towards the busy, carefree happiness of others. 'He was quite a private man, Wally. We got on well together, and people thought we were very close. I suppose we were, in most ways, but he kept some thoughts to himself. There were a lot of things he shut away from me.'

Hook nodded, wondering if she had ever confessed this to anyone before. He recognized that this was his moment to speak and yet he felt that he was taking advantage of the defencelessness of grief. 'Did Wally tell you that you will have no need to worry about money, Debbie?'

She came back to reality with a sudden start. 'He said we were comfortable enough. This is where we live, you know. We don't have another home, like most of the people here.'

'Well, you won't have any financial worries. You could probably buy somewhere quite grand, if you wanted to do that. There's a lot of money in Wally's bank account.' She looked at him sharply, and he felt compelled to add, 'Bank accounts are normally kept confidential, but even the banks have to give us details, in the case of a murder victim. You'd be surprised how often it helps us with our investigations.'

'I suppose I'll have to start worrying about financial matters now. Wally used to do all that, and I was happy to let him get on with it.'

'The bank will give you all the advice you need, if you ask them about it. People think banks are very impersonal nowadays, but you can still make an appointment to speak with someone who'll answer all your questions.'

Debbie Keane sighed wearily. 'Thank you. I'll do that, when I feel up to it.'

Hook smiled nervously. He didn't want to press her now,

but he knew he had to do just that. 'You won't have any worries, as I said. There's a lot of money in Wally's account, and the bank holds some quite valuable stock market shares. The bank has the certificates and will give you the details. Debbie, there's an awful lot of money gone into the account in the last year. Do you know where it came from?'

She looked quite shocked and Bert was pretty sure that she wasn't simulating her surprise. 'No. Wally had a pension from British Telecom. He'd taken early retirement. He told me he'd made some investments with the lump sum he'd been given and that they were doing well. Would that account for this?'

Her eyes were wide with wonder. She was stunned, as Bert Hook had seen many widows shocked before, by the discovery that this man who had shared her life and her thoughts and her bed had kept part of his life completely denied to her. He said gently, 'No, his investments wouldn't account for this, Debbie. Almost a hundred thousand pounds has been paid into the account over the last year. We need to know where that money came from, because it might have a connection with his death. But you aren't able to tell us that?'

'No. I've no idea. We lived quietly here. Our whole life was at Twin Lakes. We know all sorts of things about people here.'

Bert glimpsed for a moment the lover of tittle tattle who had amused him when he had first spoken to her months ago. 'So you've no idea where these large sums of money might have come from?'

He had a shrewd idea himself, but he wasn't going to upset this bewildered and rather pathetic lady with that thought.

Vanessa Norton was enjoying herself. She was modelling clothes for a fashion photographer. She mostly wrote about fashion now, but it was good for her morale to know that her willowy figure and strong Nordic features were still in demand when it came to showing expensive clothes to their best advantage.

She had given up the catwalk years ago. She didn't need to have sweaty journalists staring up at her from all angles and assessing the flesh within whilst they made notes about the clothes in yet another spring or autumn collection. These days she sat among the hacks herself, compiling an informed commentary for her occasional columns in Vogue and her regular ones in the Mail on Sunday. But this assignment was different. She was treated as the most important person in the room. The gay man who was photographing her was both deferential and humorous, coming forward occasionally to adjust the fall of a skirt or the tautness of a blouse around her bust with no consideration except for his camera.

He provided her as he worked with a string of bitchy but humorous gossip about models of her own age and their decline, as well as news of the latest foibles of the big-name fashion designers. They controlled the industry, but were also at the mercy of it as soon as they followed a wrong trend. She knew that Nigel would speak to others in the same waspish vein about her, but she reflected that there was no real malice in his chatter. It was a tool in his professional equipment, the means he used to relax his models, so as to enable them to strut their stuff and make the very best of these ridiculously expensive creations.

It was a luxury for Vanessa to be working in Birmingham. Usually she had to race down to London on the train to view the latest creations in the salons of the capital city. Nigel was highly efficient beneath all his prattle. He was pleased to be working with an experienced model who understood what was needed and was able to react promptly to his every suggestion about the positioning of her excellent body and the rake of the clothes he had set upon it. He was finished and highly satisfied with his results within ninety minutes, when he had privately allotted three hours to this session. He would charge for three hours of his expensive time, of course. That was the agreement and if the clothes sold for anything like the price tags which were being allotted to them the designer could well afford it.

He offered to lunch with his model, but to his secret relief Vanessa Norton declined. Nigel wasn't anything like as good at conversation once he moved away from his work. His steady stream of chat and banter derived entirely from the fashion industry and those who worked within it.

Having finished early and being highly satisfied with the

session, Vanessa thought this a good opportunity to join Richard at his place of work. With any luck, they might be able to have lunch together. Her taxi dropped her off within fifteen minutes at the entrance to the high building which housed Seagrave Enterprises. She was so full of energy that she ignored the lift and raced up the four flights of stairs which took her to the second floor and the offices of Richard's firm.

Richard's PA told her that he had someone with him at the moment but she would let him know that Ms Norton was here. That was fine: she had expected him to be fully engaged and he wasn't expecting her. The PA made sure that the boss's lady had a tray with china teacups and teapot delivered to her in the spacious waiting area. Vanessa was happy to see that the PA was a no doubt highly efficient woman in her mid-fifties. She sipped her tea contentedly and virtuously ignored the home-made cookies which had come with it.

The two men who came in and sat five yards away from her on the other side of the room were Asian and looked very sinister. Vanessa wondered if that thought was racist, but then assured herself that it wasn't. These two would have been sinister whatever their colour, creed, or country of origin.

The older man had heavy jowls and was frowning fero-ciously. That seemed a habitual expression; his heavy-lidded eyes scarcely lifted during the ten minutes when they studied her. He was heavily built and powerful, running a little to fat, though she wouldn't have cared to be the one who told him that. His companion was thinner of face and body and even more contemptuous in his visage. He looked like the sort of man who would dart at you with a knife if he suspected any sort of insult.

They sat and looked at her with a scorn which they did not trouble to disguise. Indeed, their disdain seemed to be an active and aggressive weapon against her, rather than a mere reaction. She had become used over the years to men mentally undressing her. The less subtle ones did not even realize how transparent they were. Usually she contented herself with imagining these pathetic creatures in shabby boxer shorts, with pot bellies drooping over the waist elastic. She even managed to feel sorry for some of them, pity being the ultimate sexual insult.

These two were different. They gazed at her not surreptitiously but quite openly, mentally stripping the clothes away from her elegant body and treating it as a plaything for their perverted pleasure. She tried not to contemplate what they might wish to do to her, but she had no doubt that it would be abnormal, violent and humiliating. Their dark eyes surveyed her minutely and very slowly from top to toe and then moved upwards again equally slowly. Not a word was spoken, but she was left in no doubt of both their contempt for her and their inclinations.

Vanessa was very relieved when the PA appeared and said briskly, 'Mr Seagrave will see you now, gentlemen.' She wondered what sort of business Richard could be conducting with men like this. They did not look like men who would be placing large orders for office supplies.

They were in the head man's office for exactly seventeen minutes: Vanessa had no idea why she timed their meeting, but she did. The men left quickly, making for the lift, staring straight ahead of them, affording her not even a final lecherous glance as they passed. Vanessa was surprised, but felt in no way deprived.

And then Richard was with her, beaming his pleasure, planting a kiss on her forehead as she stood up, saying, 'This is a bonus and an unexpected pleasure. And I have a full hour for lunch with my favourite woman!'

It was a small pub round the corner, a place you would scarcely have noticed if you were a stranger. But they knew Richard and saw to his every need and the food was unexpectedly splendid. Her sea bass and his duck were both cooked to perfection and the vegetables were succulent and not too al dente. Half an hour had passed before she ventured, 'I didn't like the look of those two men you saw at the end of your morning. They looked like rogues to me.'

Richard frowned and stared studiously at his plate rather than his companion. 'Not very prepossessing, I suppose. But one can't pick and choose one's clients, when one's in business.'

People always switch to the indefinite pronoun when they're uncomfortable. An internal, unwelcome voice reminded Vanessa of that. She knew she should leave this now, but she picked at it as she had picked at scabs on her knee when she'd been a child. 'I found them quite unpleasant.'

'They didn't speak to you, did they?' He was looking her full in the face now; she suddenly had all of his attention.

'No. They looked at me and stripped me bare. Their eyes told me what they wanted to do to me.'

He relaxed a little, forced a smile. 'Penalty of being an attractive woman, I suppose. Someone with your attributes must be used to that sort of attention.' He touched her foot softly with his beneath the table.

Normally she liked him being slightly risqué, even found it stimulating when he made sexual references to what they might do later in private. Today she said simply, 'They were repulsive. I should screw them for everything you can get from them, and then get rid of them, if you'll pardon the expression.' She pasted a smile on to her words, feeling that she was over-reacting. 'I don't know much about your business affairs and the people you have to deal with, do I?'

'And you don't want to, my darling! I thought we were agreed that that is how it should be.'

'You're right. I've no intention of prying into your affairs and you've quite rightly got no interest in the highly superficial world of fashion. It's just that I didn't like the look of those two at all.'

'Don't you worry your pretty little head about it, my dear!' It was a joke between the two of them. He'd used the cliché before to send up other men who treated women as idiots, and now he was using it partly to send up himself. But he was fobbing her off without an explanation, and Vanessa Norton knew it. She felt that a small, invisible barrier had been raised between them.

Detective Inspector Rushton sought out John Lambert quickly. He was glad the chief was on site, because he had urgent news for him and he wanted to bear it himself.

'I told you DS Jameson was a wizard with computers. I've never known him to fail. It took him a while, because Walter Keane was evidently a more subtle operator than we thought he was. He'd built in all sorts of defences and it was difficult to crack his passwords, Tom says. But he's done it. And the results are going to surprise you.'

'Not for long, they're not. Because you're going to tell me everything the wizard DS Jameson has discovered. Right now and very simply.'

Chris Rushton grinned. 'I've had to listen to a detailed account of how intricate the codes were and how clever Tom was to work them out. I'm not sure I understood it all and I'm certain I couldn't relay it to you accurately. The gist of it is that Keane investigated certain people at Twin Lakes in much more detail than we had previously realized. He not only recorded their weaknesses but he kept full chapter and verse on them. There's an amazing amount of information there on all of our main suspects. Keane had begun files on four other people on the site whom he thought possibilities, but there's scarcely anything about them.'

'Possibilities?'

'We all know that the Keanes pried into the lives of people on this site. We've been given the impression that they were great gossips, who found out whatever they could about people's lives, then retailed it to others in exchange for more scandal.'

'Bert Hook thinks that Debbie Keane did just that, and from what I've seen of her I would agree with him.'

Rushton nodded grimly. 'When you see what Walter Keane gathered and recorded for his own purposes, you'll agree that he was a lot more than a mere gossip. It seems to me that he used whatever Debbie picked up as a mere starting point. He's contacted all sorts of other people who've never set foot here to follow up anything he saw as incriminating.'

Lambert struggled to recall the words of the grief-stricken widow from three days earlier. 'His wife said that he spent many hours alone with his computer. That he often worked on into the night. This must have been what he was about.'

'And he had more information than Debbie Keane could ever have imagined. Carefully filed on his computer, to be used if he ever needed chapter and verse.'

'Dangerous stuff. Stuff which now gives us motive, where there was no motive before. It's pretty obvious where these large sums of money Keane banked during the last twelve months were coming from.'

Bert Hook appeared beside them, almost as if responding to a cue. 'I've talked to Debbie Keane. Wally was up to things she knew nothing about.'

Lambert smiled grimly. 'And we finally have the details of what was on Walter Keane's computer. Information about our leading suspects.'

Hook nodded. 'We have a blackmailer as our murder victim.'

FIFTEEN

Freda Potts was right about the staff dinner: Matthew wasn't comfortable with the other people there.

She wore the low-cut green evening dress which had seen far too few special occasions. The pendant which she sported at her neck held mostly semi-precious stones, but the delicate framework was of pure gold and the workmanship was good; she was complimented on it throughout the evening. She would have liked to say that Matt had bought it for her, but he was there and he would have denied it, so she had to tell everyone that it had belonged to her grandmother and was probably Edwardian.

Some of the other spouses at the staff dinner felt as awkward as Matthew Potts at the beginning of the evening, as the teachers who had worked with each other exchanged in-jokes and reminiscences about problem pupils. But most of the other partners had been to these or similar functions before, so that they could renew acquaintances and talk with each other on how careers and families were developing.

Matthew was quite new to all of this. He decided after ten minutes of it that he was much more at ease in the company of men than in mixed gatherings like this. He had spent years in the army and was now building up years on the oil rigs. In both of these environments he had been respected for his own expertise. That was a basis on which he had been able to build the type of persona he wanted for himself. Men were easy: they talked about sport and sex for many hours, even when they were hundreds of miles from either of them.

After you'd been with men for weeks on end, you had to be careful what you said and what opinions you allowed yourself in mixed company. It wasn't just language you had to watch, but attitudes also; remarks which might have been run-of-the-mill stuff even ten years ago and were still current on the oil rigs could have you accused of sexism in the sensitive climate of modern-day Britain.

And particularly, it seemed, in education. Matt expressed what he thought was a conventional view when he said that girls performed badly in Maths because they thought they were less intelligent in that area than they really were. He was immediately informed that he was way out of date and an example of the attitudes which held back female development in education. Two men who were attending the evening like him as spouses hastened to leap on to the bandwagon and condemn him as a bigot.

One, a bespectacled accountant, added the thought that they should make allowances for Matt's army background and present work. 'Matt's a man of action,' he told his wife and anyone else who cared to listen. 'You can't expect men of action to be deep thinkers. I'm sure he doesn't mean any harm.' He laughed lightly and moved on to the government and the economy.

'Patronizing sod!' thought Matthew Potts. He smiled weakly and moved resolutely away to avoid confrontation and decided that he had never liked accountants.

Freda, appearing suddenly at his side to support him, did not help. 'Matt's the strong, silent type,' she said with a nervous smile. 'Not like me at all!'

She dwelt a little on his past career and his present work, which was exactly what he had been trying to avoid. 'We shall make allowances for him,' said his tormentor. 'I suppose you can't expect strong, silent men to join the twenty-first century for quite a while yet!'

The joke seemed to be happily received by all who heard it, though Matt told himself that he was by now scarcely an unbiased witness. Things improved a little when they went in to dinner. The food was good and the noise level rose as the conversation and the wine flowed. Matt was inhibited here, since he had assured Freda that he was driving home and so had to be very abstemious. He made his two glasses of red wine last what seemed a very long time as others, including his wife, grew more boisterous. He sat back and watched Freda and her colleagues and their spouses becoming happier and more inebriated.

It is a disturbing experience to remain sober whilst those

around you reach various stages of drunkenness. What seems to them irresistibly hilarious seems to you banal. Matthew was aware that he was becoming increasingly grumpy. He looked for but did not find a kindred spirit in this gathering of aliens. He respected good schoolteachers and there were no doubt several of those present tonight. Their wives and husbands seemed to him ever more tedious as the evening proceeded. He should not have come here; he should have heeded Freda's advice. He realized that now, when it was much too late. He must see the evening out and make the best of it.

He almost did that. Well, almost negotiated it without any serious incident. It was when everything was over and people were collecting their coats that things really went wrong. An ugly incident, Freda called it later. It was certainly that.

Many of the couples had taxis ordered and some were sharing. Coming seventy miles from Twin Lakes, that hadn't been an option for the Potts. It was outside the hotel, in the car park, that things went seriously wrong. The coolness of the night air hit the revellers and made the effects of alcohol more evident. Freda reeled a little and clutched at Matt's arm to steady herself. 'Watch your step, Head of History! Keep one hand on your man and the other on your ha'penny!' said a drunken voice behind them. A chemistry teacher, who had clutched Freda's bottom as they rose from the table five minutes earlier and been summarily rejected.

Matt whirled to confront him whilst Freda said urgently in his ear, 'Ignore him! He's drunk but harmless. Let's go!'

Matt glared menacingly at the unsteady figure in the gloom and would probably have done just that. But the man then yelled at him. 'Take the bloody prick-teaser away! Take her where she can't cradle-snatch while the cat's away!'

Matt had him by the throat and against the wall in a second. Freda tugged at his arm and shouted, 'Leave him, Matt! He's not worth it!'

It was her cliché which drove him on: he couldn't explain it afterwards, but it was the vapidity of her words which made his blood pound, where previously there had been only a cold depression. He lifted the man off his feet, heard the thump of the back of his head against the bricks of the wall as he held

him there. 'Explain yourself, you fucking prat!' he yelled into
the terrified face. All the frustrations of the evening surged
through his body. He wanted the man to argue, to raise his
hands. He wanted to let go with his right hand and pound the
terrified face, which was suddenly sober in the face of this
assault. He'd beat the stupid sod insensible and leave him here,
given half an excuse.

But hands were on his shoulders and on those of his victim
and Freda was screaming in his ear. He was dragged away
from his quarry and the man was taken half running from his
presence. A calm voice said through the darkness, 'I think
we've all had rather too much to drink. Best forget about these
things and get away home now.'

Matt wanted to tell the emollient voice that he wasn't drunk
at all, that this young twat had groped his wife and then
insulted her and that he wanted to see him off. But there was
a general murmur of assent and the company melted away
into the night as taxis pulled up at the kerb. Freda clung
desperately to his arm and eventually succeeded in dragging
him towards their car. They sat panting heavily in their seats
whilst other vehicles pulled away around them.

'You've shown yourself up and embarrassed me in front of
my colleagues,' she said eventually. 'Charlie was a bit drunk,
that was all! I could have handled it.'

'What did he mean about cradle snatching?'

'What? Oh, nothing. He was very drunk. It was just talk.'

Matt started the engine, gunned it as though to wake the
neighbourhood. 'You've got some talking to do yourself, I'd
say.'

'We'd like to speak to Mr Ramsbottom. On his own would
be best, I think.' Lambert glanced around the living room and
the kitchen beyond it, which were very tidy, even at ten past
nine in the morning.

'Jason isn't here. He's gone out to get a morning paper and
some shopping. He may be quite a while.'

'Do you know exactly where he is?'

'No. And he won't have his mobile switched on.' Lisa forced
a smile. She knew Bert Hook, but she was suddenly apprehensive

at his return to her home with the man in charge of a murder case. 'I suspect he might be popping into a betting shop in Leominster to have a fiver each way on some nag. That's not a crime, is it?'

Hook smiled. 'It certainly isn't. Do you know when he'll be back?'

'I don't, I'm afraid. I'm going round for coffee with a friend later, so he has the whole of the morning at his disposal. But probably I can help you. I'm sure I can tell you anything that Jason could.'

There seemed to be a touching naivety about this trim, alert woman. Lambert frowned briefly, then said, 'Those threatening notes you received months ago. Has there been any recurrence?'

'No. I'm happy to say that we haven't had any more of them since DS Hook came to the site and asked around about them. It seems that whoever was sending them got the message and was scared off.'

'And have you had any further thoughts yourself on who might have been responsible for them?'

'No. We've discussed it several times, but it remains as much of a mystery as ever. We haven't even talked about it during the last two or three weeks. I'm just glad that the notes have stopped.' She glanced at Hook. 'I think what you said at the time was right. It was probably someone being mischievous, or even someone with a mistaken sense of fun.'

Bert smiled and explained to Lambert. 'I only spoke to Debbie Keane. We thought that would be quite sufficient to get the word all round the site that the threatening notes were being investigated. It seems that we were right.'

Lisa hesitated. 'I'm reluctant to say this. I don't like the idea of accusing a dead man. But do you think it might have been Wally Keane who sent us those notes?'

Lambert looked at her keenly. 'What makes you say that?'

'He must have known as much about us as anyone at Twin Lakes. Debbie pokes her nose into everyone's business and I'm sure Wally would have picked up everything she learned. They were a pretty close couple, even though he didn't seem to be as inquisitive as her.'

That was certainly true, Lambert thought. He'd recorded all the stuff that Debbie had gathered for him on his computer, plus much more damaging information which he'd gone on to gather for himself. But he wasn't going to tell Lisa Ramsbottom that, at this stage. 'But why would Wally want to damage you? You hadn't made an enemy of him, had you?'

'No. He'd no reason to hurt us. It's just that he and Debbie were here all the time and I know how he liked to control things. He seemed to me like one of the few people on the site who might have done this to us, but I can't think why. If it was pure mischief on someone's part, as DS Hook suggested it might be, I just thought that Wally might be the likeliest candidate. Especially as the notes ceased after Bert had spoken to Debbie about them.'

'It's entirely possible. I just can't see what Walter Keane had to gain from sending you such poisonous stuff.'

'Unless of course we presume that Wally was becoming rather odd. That he enjoyed perpetrating mischief and upsetting people.'

That was entirely possible, Lambert thought grimly. Except that they knew enough now to understand that Wally Keane had kept a very clear eye on the money he was seeking to gain from his malice.

Mary Martindale was with Debbie Keane. It was the first time she had spoken with her since the death of Wally.

'Where are the children?' Mrs Keane wanted to know.

'They're on the golf course. They're getting quite enthusiastic about golf. George was going to go out with them, but young Jamie has taken them out with him. He's thirteen now and my two think that's very grown-up. I suppose it is, when you're eight and six.'

'They're good boys, your two. Well brought up.' For no reason she could divine, Debbie was suddenly back in her girlhood, when she'd been no older than Nicky and Tommy. She could never have imagined then that she'd have been grateful in her sixties for the kindness of a West Indian woman twenty-five years younger than her. The world was a constantly changing place and she wasn't sure that she liked that. But then after what had happened to Wally she wasn't sure of anything. 'What's George doing, then?'

Mary grinned. 'I think his nose was a bit put out when the boys went off to play golf without him. He said he might have a go on the bowling green, if there was no one else about. He's only a beginner at bowls and he doesn't like people around when he's experimenting. He doesn't like to make a fool of himself.'

Debbie managed a wan smile. 'Men are like that.' She sipped the tea which Mary had made for her. 'How's he getting on at work?'

'Very well, I think. The council people must think a lot of him. They've promoted him again. He's in charge of quite a big workforce now. And he'll never be out of work, will he? There are always road works needed somewhere.'

'It must pay well. Your children don't lack for anything. And these places don't come cheap, do they?'

It was a flash of her old inquisitiveness, her desire to learn everything she could about the lives of those around her at Twin Lakes. Generous Mary Martindale didn't resent it. She recognized it as a sign of recovery in a widow who was still genuinely stricken by her husband's sudden death. 'George seems to do all right, yes. He says the overtime pays well. But I leave all financial matters to him.'

But Debbie Keane had voiced one of her own queries. George didn't throw his money around, but he never seemed to be short of it, these days. That was surely good for her and the boys, but some small, persistent part of her mind kept asking where all of this came from. Mary smiled at the older woman and said, 'I wanted to be at home whilst the boys were small. In a year or so, I shall be thinking about going back into nursing.'

Debbie was immediately delighted with this news and diverted from George. She wanted to know all the details of Mary's qualifications and previous experience. They discussed how rusty she would be after the years away, how rapid progress was in medicine, and how some things like the understanding of patients' fears never changed. Mary knew the news that she was a fully qualified state nurse and planning to take it up again soon would fly round the site in the next week, but she wasn't too worried about that. It would be part of the therapy for Debbie Keane, as she fought her way out of her trough of loneliness and despair.

Mary told George about Debbie after the boys had been allowed to leave the table at the end of a noisy lunch. He nodded distractedly: he was plainly preoccupied with some problem of his own. After a few more desultory exchanges he said abruptly, 'I have to go out tonight.'

'But we're on holiday. I thought this week was for us and the children.'

'I know. I'm sorry. I don't have a choice.'

Mary Martindale accepted it, as their relationship said that she must do. But she knew that the council didn't call people out like that. And certainly not at night. Who was it who had this power over George?

'We'd like to see you on your own, Mr Seagrave.'

Richard glanced sideways at Vanessa Norton. 'It's not convenient. We were thinking of going out.'

It was the first Vanessa had heard of it, but she said loyally, 'We were. And in any case, I can't see why you should object to my presence. We are merely good citizens helping you voluntarily with your enquiries.'

Lambert noted her knowledge of the intricacies of the law. 'If you are satisfied that Mr Seagrave has nothing he might wish to remain private, I have no objection to your presence at—'

'It's all right. I'll come with you to your place near the entrance. What you call the murder room, I believe.' Richard Seagrave contrived to invest the simple words with a touch of contempt.

They did not speak on their brisk walk to the unit temporarily allotted to the police for their investigation. Lambert had set up the furthest and smallest bedroom as an interview room. It did not have the constricted feel of an interview room at the station, with its graffitied walls and square scratched table and single high light in the ceiling, but it was small, crowded with equipment and confined, which gave a feeling of claustrophobia to the nervous and the inexperienced.

Richard Seagrave was neither of these. He looked with interest at the photographs and bagged items as he was led through the unit to the room at the rear and his seat opposite the two set out for Lambert and Hook. He watched the DS shut the door carefully behind them before he sat down. He looked hard at Lambert and said, 'This shouldn't take long. I've already told you what I know about Wally Keane and the way he died: about the man, little; about his death, nothing.'

Lambert felt a heavy distaste for this man which he didn't trouble to disguise. He stared into Seagrave's confident, unrevealing face for a moment without speaking. 'That's an interesting observation. It's surprising you should claim to know so little about Keane. He seems to have known quite a lot about you.'

'That doesn't entirely surprise me. His wife was a nosey cow. Still is, I'm sure. I expect she passed things on to her pathetic husband.'

'She did indeed. And then Walter Keane made all sorts of enquiries of his own into the backgrounds of the individuals concerned. Patient and imaginative enquiries. The amount of detail he collected is astonishing.'

Seagrave's broad face showed not a flicker of fear. His brown eyes narrowed a little, but continued to stare steadily back at Lambert. 'That merely confirms my view of the man. I was right not to like him. I didn't trust the little sod as far as I could throw him.'

'I see. You are now declaring hatred for a murder victim. Commendably frank, even if ill-advised. I'm sure your well-paid legal adviser would tell you that.'

'If you're trying to needle me, Detective Chief Superintendent, it won't work.'

'What exactly did Wally Keane discover that he could use against you so effectively?'

The first flicker of alarm. No more than the uncontrolled movement of an eyelid, but it was picked up by two men whose work involved much studying of the human countenance. But Seagrave prided himself on his facility with words. He was, after all, an educated man, he told himself. More than a match for these jumped-up plods. 'You appear to be telling me in your quaint and indirect way that Keane was a blackmailer. The lowest form of life, in my opinion.'

'That is one of the very few things on which you and I might agree, Mr Seagrave. At the moment, our interest in Keane is as a murder victim. As that, he has the same rights as any other citizen.'

'In which case, I should declare that I have no connection with him.'

'Then why did you pay him a large sum of money a month before he died?'

The right eyelid flicked again. The voice remained steady. 'I have no idea what you're talking about.'

'I think you have, Mr Seagrave. I've no doubt you made the payment as indirectly as possible, so as to make it difficult to trace back to you personally. Equally, I've no doubt that we shall be able to provide all the details, by the time the case comes to court. Perhaps this really is the time to start seeking advice from your very expensive lawyers.'

Richard Seagrave folded his arms with extreme deliberation. He wished to confirm for himself as well as these offensive policemen that he remained perfectly calm. 'Defamation of character, Chief Superintendent. Lawyers are good at proving that. The quite gratuitous accusation you are making could cost the police service a lot of money. I think I shall quite enjoy pursuing this. It may well be settled out of court: chief constables don't like bad publicity. But it will be expensive. You will not be a popular man with your superiors.'

Lambert ignored him. 'We shall be interested in due course in what it was you thought it so important to conceal. Something which might well interest us, since it warranted a large payment to a blackmailer. In the meantime, it is my job to arrest the man who killed Walter Keane last Friday night.'

'A time for which I have a watertight alibi. You would be well advised not to offer me further material for a defamation suit.'

Bert Hook said quietly, 'An alibi provided by your present partner. We don't like alibis provided by wives and partners which are otherwise unsubstantiated.'

It was the first time he had spoken. Seagrave looked at him

as if he were something scraped off his expensive shoe. 'I'm sure you don't, Detective Sergeant. Alibis make it difficult for you to frame innocent citizens.'

Lambert had a severe problem with this man. Seagrave and his firm were being investigated by the Serious Crime Squad and very dark things were suspected of him. But that investigation was ongoing and secret and he must not damage it by providing any prior warnings to the man at the centre of it. But he had a murder on his hands here, the most serious crime of all. Seagrave was certainly capable of killing a frail man of sixty and they now knew that he had ample motive. Lambert said tersely, 'Where were you between nine o'clock and eleven o'clock on Friday night?'

'With Vanessa Norton. We told you that on Sunday and it isn't going to change, for the simple reason that it's the truth.'

Richard Seagrave managed to look very complacent. A man could smile and smile and be a villain, as Hamlet said. He liked that comparison. He was, after all, an educated man.

SIXTEEN

Geoffrey Tiler and Michael Norrington were engaged in a serious dispute. That did not happen very often.

It had been inevitable that it would happen, sooner or later, Geoff told himself. It was adolescent romanticism to think that any couple wouldn't have little spats. And he and Mike were well beyond adolescence, he thought ruefully. Sometimes he wondered what might have happened, if they'd met at that age. But this wasn't the moment for that sort of self-indulgence. The death of Wally Keane had changed all sorts of things, far more than he had thought it would. Ironically, it was that death which was now accelerating life, moving it on much more quickly than he would have wished, threatening to take it out of his control. He didn't like that.

Geoffrey Tiler was a man used to exercising control.

He said, 'I think you should tell the police what happened. I think you should give them your real name. They'll find everything out for themselves, if you leave them to it. They have a big team on a murder enquiry. They pry into all kinds of things, just in case they might prove to be relevant.'

'My past isn't relevant.'

'You know that. I know that. But at present those CID men don't seem to know very much, so they're investigating everything. They'll turn up the details you don't want them to have, eventually. And then they'll ask why you needed to conceal them. And what else you might be hiding from them. It will concentrate their attention upon you, in exactly the way you are trying to avoid.'

'You're ashamed of me. You don't want to be associated with—'

'That's rubbish and you know it is! I've known all about it for months, and it hasn't made a blind bit of difference between us. Now has it?'

Michael Norrington looked gloomily out of the window. 'I

wouldn't blame you for being ashamed of me. I was ashamed myself. I wish it had never happened. I wish I could turn the clock back and handle things differently.'

The perennial and impossible desire of the weak, thought Geoff. But he didn't mind this weakness. This weakness was dependent upon him for reassurance and rescue, and he wanted to be the man who offered those things to Mike. 'You can't change a single thing, Mike, and you know it. That's life and we can't make it other than it is. But you were a different person then. We both accept that. I'm sure everyone did things thirty years ago which they wish they could undo now. I think you'd be much better to be honest with the police.'

'Make a clean breast of it, you mean? As we were told to do when we were schoolboys? But I can't go to confession and be absolved of my sins. The police don't work like that.'

'No, they don't,' agreed Geoff grimly. 'They're not in the business of forgiveness. They accept confessions, but they also detect things. They'll find out about your past, whether you like it or not. And when they do, they'll throw it at you. You'd be much better taking the initiative.'

Mike wasn't used to taking the initiative. He hadn't done it many times in his life, and when he had, it had often been disastrous. As it had been in this thing which he wished to consign to oblivion and which Geoff kept bringing up. Sometimes he wished he had never told him. He said sullenly, 'You may be right, I suppose. But I can't bring myself to go parading my sins in front of policemen. It would be inviting the homophobic bastards to laugh at me and persecute me.'

Geoff Tiler came and stood beside him, looking out of the window at the wide, still waters of the lake and the swans and the waterfowl which moved so innocently upon it. His forearm was almost touching the longer and more slender one of the man he intended to marry. He could feel the warmth and it made him wish for physical contact. But something told him that this was not the moment. If Mike shied away from him, that would drive them further apart, accentuate the rift which this stupid dispute had created.

Geoffrey Tiler was a man used to controlling and directing the things and the people within his world. But now he forced himself to say sadly, 'I'll go along with whatever you decide, Mike. Of course I will.'

Jason Ramsbottom came looking for the police. Not many people did that.

He said to DI Rushton in the murder room, 'I understand Mr Lambert wished to speak to me. I can't think why that would be, but I'm here.'

The police had now occupied a second holiday unit, adjacent to the first one which had been designated as the murder room. Lambert had improvised an office in there, with the help of furniture lent to him by Jim Rawlinson. The site manager at Twin Lakes was understandably anxious to keep police activity as invisible as possible.

The chief superintendent sat behind his desk with Bert Hook beside him and regarded Ramsbottom for a few seconds before he spoke. 'Good of you to come here, sir. I expect your wife told you that we'd been looking for you. You didn't fancy doing this alongside her in your own home.'

It was a statement rather than a question. Jason did not know how he should react to it. Perhaps that was what this gaunt, experienced interrogator had intended, he thought. He'd no idea how much the man knew, so he'd need to play this by ear. That wasn't easy, when the CID men seemed to be following his train of thought without apparent effort. Jason said stiffly, 'I thought it best to come to see you as soon as possible, when I heard that you'd been looking for me. Is there something wrong with that thought?'

'Nothing wrong at all, sir. A commendable promptitude, indeed. And I can quite see why you wouldn't want Mrs Ramsbottom to hear this.'

'I don't know what you mean by that, I'm sure. I was hoping that you might have at last discovered who sent us those awful notes, but I suppose that's too much to hope for.'

He was trying to take the initiative, to put them rather than him on the back foot, and he tried to deliver this with a sneer. He stared hard at the impassive Hook, who had been the man invoked by his wife to solve the problem of the notes those many weeks ago. Lambert said, 'We, or rather DS Hook, seem to have solved the problem of the notes, in that they ceased to appear after his visit here two months ago. I understood that because they had ceased you did not wish us to allocate resources to the matter. Am I mistaken in that?'

'No, of course I don't see any point in trying to discover who sent us those notes, since we are no longer being persecuted by them. Naturally I'm still curious about who was cruel enough to threaten us in that way, but I'm sure that your investigation should be abandoned in the face of the much more important matter of a murder investigation.'

'Good. It's always helpful when the public accept that we have finite resources and must allocate them as we see fit. Murder, as you say, has a high priority.' Lambert stared at him evenly. There was the suggestion of a smile on his lips. Jason sensed that the preliminary word-fencing was now concluded. It had not gone his way.

It was Hook who now said unexpectedly, 'We have a very good idea of who sent those horrid notes, but no absolute proof, Jason. We haven't sought out the proof, in view of the fact that they have ceased to be delivered and that we now have a murder on our hands, as you helpfully acknowledged.'

Jason wanted to leave it at that, to tell them that he was well content to let the sleeping dog of the notes lie. But that wouldn't sound natural. Normal curiosity would demand that he responded to what Hook had just said. He heard an annoying tremor in his voice as he spoke as brightly as he could. 'Who do you think sent them, then, Bert?' It took an effort for him to use the sergeant's first name, but he wished to invoke him as a friend and a neighbour, not a policeman.

'I'm sure you have a view on that yourself, Jason.' The weatherbeaten, outdoor face was irritatingly deadpan.

'Well, I suppose I thought it might be Wally Keane. Debbie's a nosey old besom, but not vicious, I'd say. Wally always struck me as darker and more malicious than Debbie. I think he might have been capable of it.'

'Always tempting to blame a dead man, isn't it? We find people do that quite a lot. I suppose that's because the person accused is not able to come back with a robust defence and a threat to sue.'

Jason glared at him, feeling let down. It wasn't the sort of aggressive retort you expected from a friend and neighbour. 'I didn't say it was Wally – not necessarily. I was just speculating. It seems preposterous that it could be anyone around here, and yet it must have been. Wally was secretive and mysterious and perhaps a bit mad. He seemed the likeliest candidate to me.'

'There is one likelier, don't you think?' This was Lambert, his cool voice striking a note which chilled Jason Ramsbottom.

They knew the truth. He was certain of that now. But he had to carry on, as if he was setting up a surprise in some creaking play. 'None likelier that I can think of. Otherwise I wouldn't have suggested Wally.'

'The homes here don't have letter-boxes, I've noticed.'

'No. They're not necessary. Most people's mail goes to their home addresses. We collect any post here from the office near the entrance. Mr Rawlinson says its more secure that way, and certainly no postman would enjoy trying to deliver to identical units without numbers.' He repeated the manager's explanation mechanically, racing through it lest he should be interrupted.

'So how did these messages arrive?'

'They were pushed under the door. It's tight, but it's possible.'

'Maybe. But it's much easier for the home-owner to put them there himself. And in our view that is almost certainly what happened.'

For a wild moment he thought of suggesting that it could have been Lisa. Then he said desperately, 'And why on earth would I want to do that?'

'I can think of a variety of reasons. To alarm your wife, perhaps? You certainly succeeded in doing that – hence her invocation of DS Hook, which you didn't expect. As a diversionary tactic, so that if Wally Keane revealed what he threatened to reveal to your wife, you could discredit him as some sort of unbalanced maniac? You tell us, Mr Ramsbottom.'

The game was up. Jason felt his world collapsing around him. In his head, he could almost hear the sound of walls physically falling. He had known it would come to this. Over the years, he had told himself repeatedly that sooner or later it was bound to happen. For three days, he had thought that with his tormentor dead all might yet be well. He was a fool who couldn't help himself: how many men before him had offered that lame and hopeless explanation of the conduct which had shattered their worlds?

Ramsbottom said in an even, hopeless tone, 'He was threatening me. He'd had money from me. I couldn't afford to go on paying him. But he said he was going to tell Lisa all about my other life if I didn't. He had chapter and verse, he said. I was afraid that he'd speak to her at any moment. I thought if I could convince her that it was Wally bloody Keane who was sending those notes, she wouldn't take him seriously if he talked to her about me.'

Hook said gently, almost therapeutically, 'And what was it that he was going to tell her, Jason?'

Jason stared at the comfortable, persuasive face with his mind racing. Eventually he said dully, 'You know, don't you?'

'We know about Anna Riley, yes. We know her address and we know some of the dates on which you've visited her. Walter Keane had recorded them on his computer.'

'He told me that. He was threatening to tell Lisa. I couldn't allow that.'

'Walter Keane had the names and the addresses of previous women, too.'

Suddenly and without warning, Jason Ramsbottom buried his face in his hands. His shoulders shook and a series of tearless sobs wrenched at his head. His questioners said nothing, offered no words of understanding or consolation. Emotion makes people vulnerable, and extreme emotion makes them most vulnerable of all. This was a murder suspect; the more disturbed and off balance he was, the more he was likely to reveal. They waited silently until he made some sort of recovery and dropped his hands to his lap. 'I've been an utter fool! I know that.'

'You were a blackmail victim. We don't like blackmailers, but Walter Keane has the same rights as other citizens and his death must be investigated just as vigorously.'

'I'm on the road for a lot of the time. My work takes me away from home. There have always been women. Never more than one at a time.' He sounded like a man offering mitigating circumstances in court. 'Wally was demanding more money. I couldn't afford to go on paying him. Not the sums he was demanding. And Lisa would have realized: she'd have wanted to know where the money was going. I'd already given him ten thousand pounds six months ago. I told Lisa that I'd lost my bonus because of the recession and the firm's loss of sales when I paid him that, but I couldn't have explained away any more.'

'So you were anxious not to lose your wife.'

'She means the world to me, does Lisa. She and Ellie. I couldn't bear to lose my daughter.'

Bert Hook said quietly, 'Then why play away? Why leap into bed with a succession of women, if your family means so much to you?'

Ramsbottom shook his head desolately. 'It's a compulsion. I've always had other women. Never more than one at a time, but I've always had them. Monogamy has never seemed a natural human state to me and I've needed the passion.' Now he was reiterating the arguments he'd put to himself many times to this most unlikely of audiences. It was ridiculous, but in his confusion he did not recognize that: he was speaking more to himself than to his hearers. 'And yet still the most important thing in the world to me is my family. The most important people in the world are Lisa and Ellie.'

'And Wally Keane was threatening to destroy that world for you.'

Jason didn't see the implication of that statement. He was far too preoccupied with his own wretchedness. 'Will you have to tell Lisa about this? It will destroy me if you do.'

Lambert didn't answer that. He said instead, 'You said a few moments ago, "He was threatening to tell Lisa. I couldn't allow that." So what steps did you take to prevent it happening?'

Jason Ramsbottom's eyes widened with horror as he confronted the question. 'I didn't kill Wally. I wanted him dead, if that was the only thing that was going to stop his antics. But it wasn't me who strung him up.'

They let the silence stretch, allowed him to hear how lame

his protestation sounded after what had gone before it. It was Hook who eventually said, 'I think you should tell us again where you were last Friday night between the hours of nine and eleven, Jason. It may be that you wish to make adjustments to what you told us on Saturday.'

Jason tried to ignore the air of menace which had somehow descended upon the burly, unremarkable figure of DS Hook. 'I was with Lisa. For those hours and throughout the night. She told you that on Saturday.'

Bert flicked over a page in his notebook, though he knew the facts of the matter perfectly well. 'Correction. You told us that. Lisa did not deny it. The difference may be unimportant; it can also on occasions be significant.'

'Well, that's where I was: in our holiday home with my wife. I didn't kill Wally Keane. I'm not a violent man.'

'Yet you put a man in hospital after a violent brawl. You were lucky he wasn't more seriously hurt. You could easily have been facing a manslaughter charge.'

This felt worse coming from a neighbour and a man with whom he'd had an agreeable round of golf two hundred yards from here, even though it was Lisa and not he who had brought in Hook. Jason said bleakly, 'That was sixteen years ago. I was wilder then. It was before I was married.'

'You were in fact twenty-four. Scarcely a teenager led astray by others.'

'But more stupid and more brutal. I got in with the wrong set.'

Hook gave him a grim smile. 'We never meet anyone who got in with the right set, Jason. We don't accept it as an excuse. If you're into clichés, try the one about the leopard not changing its spots. We find that men who use violence at twenty-four usually still see it as a solution when they're forty.'

Jason said dully, 'I didn't kill Wally Keane. Please don't tell Lisa about Anna Riley and the others.'

It took Jason Ramsbottom a long time to walk back to his home by the lake and the cheerful, unsuspecting wife who awaited him there. His face was grim as he told Lisa, 'You may need to stress to them that I was with you on Friday night.'

*   *   *

Matt and Freda Potts were climbing in the Brecon Beacons.
She'd been surprised when he'd suggested it, but she'd gone
along with the idea readily enough: anything that would take
her away from Twin Lakes and the way Matt was brooding
darkly was fine by her.

The pair didn't speak much as they drove the fifty miles
through the Welsh hills to where they planned to begin their
climb. Freda made occasional remarks about the spectacular
scenery, but most of them met with nothing more than monosyllables from her husband. He was not exactly surly, but he
seemed to be preoccupied with greater concerns than her
nervous prattle. She hoped that the high spaces and clear air
of the Beacons would eventually change his mood.

They were on the lower slopes of the hill, a mile away from
the car, before Matt offered his first conversational gambit of the
day. 'We used to train on these hills, when I was in the army.
The officers used to time us, over the top and down the other
side. We got points for each minute by which we bettered the
target time.'

That was the SAS, she knew, though he never used that
term, even now, unless it was wrung from him. Secrecy had
been bred into him, had become a way of life then. SAS men
hadn't been allowed to talk about their missions, hadn't even
known where they were going nor what they were to do until
the last minute. Action was the keynote: you used as few words
as possible.

Today was a sort of mission, in Matthew Potts's mind.

Freda panted behind him, anxious to make the most of the
nearest thing she would get to a conversational opening. 'This
is a pretty steep climb, isn't it?' She gazed ahead at the steeper
slopes awaiting them. 'You're pretty fit now. You must have
been a really hard man then.'

'We were carrying heavy packs. You should try taking this at
a run with half a hundredweight on your back.' Some unspoken
memory twisted the grim line of his lips into a momentary smile.

He set off ahead of her, moving his compact, powerful frame
forward with rapid strides, his feet seeming to the woman
behind him to race as swiftly as a dancer's away from her. She
was sure that she was a healthy and fit thirty-five-year-old.

She power-walked, whenever she had time for it, and she played tennis every week, being always prepared for a strenuous singles as well as the less demanding and more sociable doubles. And young Wayne Briggs would certainly have said she was athletic . . . She thrust that thought angrily from her mind.

She couldn't catch Matt to extend the conversation. He climbed swiftly and relentlessly ahead of her, moving over the rough stones and steep rises of the path as if he had been jogging on smooth and level ground, leaving her further and further behind him without a backward glance. After each half-mile of strenuous climbing, he paused and waited for her to rejoin him. And after each half-mile she rejoined him breathless and with aching limbs, planting her backside firmly on the nearest flat boulder to recover herself.

When her heart resumed its normal beat and she could summon the breath for conversation, she commented on the view below them and the lonely glory of their day on the hills. His only reaction was to nod briefly or to offer her the monosyllables she had received in the car. She tried challenging him directly with a jocular, 'Who's being moody today? Remembering old times in the Brecons, are we?'

This prompted no reaction beyond a minimal raising of his chin and a sniffing of the cool mountain air. Then, before she could attempt again to dispel his coldness, he was away. All she saw were his strong thighs and powerful back muscles above her on the path, growing ever smaller as his moving figure pressed on and away from her, towards the blue sky and the racing clouds above them. She gave up the effort to keep up with him, even to stay anywhere near him, and concentrated upon the increasingly steep and twisting path beneath her feet, bending low to assist her progress, even using her hands for balance and speed in one or two more tricky spots.

This was the longest stretch Matt had climbed without stopping and waiting for her. She began to wonder whether he had climbed up and over the summit and was now moving swiftly down the other side, as he had done in the days of his SAS training. Was he trying to detach himself from her? Did he wish to leave her alone on the high and lonely slopes of the mountain? She wasn't physically frightened; she was a perfectly competent walker and mountaineer. She would simply return the way she had come, if that was what was most sensible. There was no danger from the weather today, as there often could be in the mountains.

But what was Matt up to? What was upsetting him and making him act so out of character? He had never behaved like this to her before. It was almost as if he wished to punish her. Or perhaps simply to be out of her presence. He hadn't recovered from last night and the brawl after the staff dinner: she was sure of that. She'd known from the start that it was a mistake to take him there. It was Matt who had insisted upon it.

He hadn't abandoned her. He was sitting with his back against the low wall beside the cairn which marked the summit of the mountain. The wall provided minimal shelter against the winds which howled round this peak on over three hundred days of the year. Today there was no need for shelter, but Matt Potts had taken it automatically, after long experience of fighting the elements here and in much harsher places.

Freda studied him for a moment, then moved to sit on the low slab beside him. She felt Matt move minimally to his left. She could not be sure whether he was retreating from the touch of her flesh or merely making room for her to sit. She reached for the small rucksack he had flung five feet away from him and produced the pack of sandwiches and the thermos flask she had prepared what now seemed many hours earlier.

She thought for a moment that he was not going to accept what she offered, but perhaps he was merely preoccupied. He was gazing towards the track far below him, where three tiny, ant-like figures were ascending the route he had covered so rapidly. Eventually he took his sandwiches with a grunt which might have been thanks. He bit into them savagely, as if they had done him some personal injury and he wished them to be swiftly gone from his sight.

They ate the sandwiches and the apple she had put in to follow them. They drank the coffee; it cooled swiftly in the rarefied air of the summit. Freda said nothing, recognizing that the best way to respond to his silence was with one of her own. The tiny figures on the path so far below them were no doubt toiling hard on their ascent, but they looked no closer than when she had first seen them.

Suddenly Matt growled without warning, 'You've fucked me about, Freda!'

He'd never used the word like that before, not to her. No doubt he and the other men used it often on the rigs. Language always deteriorated, when men were shut up with each other. It was Matt who'd told her that – she couldn't remember when. Freda spoke as though she was voicing someone clse's words. 'I don't know what you mean.'

She couldn't think the crisis was going to happen here, in this high and lonely place, with a summer sky above them and mankind and its concerns seeming petty and transient. But she knew now that it was going to happen here, as certainly as if Matt had already voiced his thoughts. He stared out towards the other peaks and towards the invisible Twin Lakes fifty miles beyond them. And then he said, 'You couldn't even choose an ordinary bloke. You had to go and fuck a kid.'

He bludgeoned her with the word. She had welcomed it often enough, in her love-making. Now it had never seemed so coarse and abrasive. It was his own hurt he was voicing She understood that, but she could do nothing to comfort him. She would have given a great deal to be able to deny what he said. Instead, she said lamely, 'I'm so very sorry, Matt. I've been a fool.'

'You'll be drummed out of teaching. And I'll be a laughing stock. Cuckolded by a kid! That's what they call it, isn't it? Cuckolded.' He dwelt on the old, obsolescent word and its harsh consonants, as if he wished to insult her academic pretensions as well as her morals by his use of it.

She said, 'It needn't come to that, surely.' It was the nightmare she had always had, even as she had turned and twisted in her nakedness with the eager young Wayne Briggs.

'Your precious bloody colleagues will be delighted. "That stupid bloody husband of hers who was crazy enough to argue with us at the dinner was a cuckold! Whilst he was away at sea, she was fucking a kid she taught. Ha! Ha! Ha!"'

She reached out and put her hand tentatively upon his, but he flung it away, as she should have known he would. She said, 'I won't be seeing him again. It's over and I wish I'd never done it. I was lonely and I suppose I was looking for something dangerous and daring.'

'Well, you found that all right! Dangerous and daring, was it? So you looked for some bloody kid with pimples and a big dick who would fuck the arse off you!'

His bitterness and frustration poured from his venomous tongue in this isolated place. It was worse because it was so near the truth. She'd enjoyed Wayne's youth and testosterone, enjoyed the reassurance which came from the fact that at thirty-five she could still couple frenziedly with a sixteen-year-old and bring his raw passion to a climax. But she couldn't admit that to Matt. She couldn't even try to explain herself without increasing his pain. She said again in what was scarcely more than a whisper for the breeze to carry away, 'I was lonely.'

'And do you think I'm not lonely? Battered by waves in freezing temperatures with a lot of hairy men who talk nothing but sex and football? Of course I am. Bloody lonely, at times. But I don't grab the nearest under-age floozy and shag her stupid, do I?'

You don't have it to hand, she thought. You're not surrounded by it day after day, with lads getting erections as soon as they look at you and panting to take your knickers off. But she couldn't tell him that. Couldn't tell him anything. She muttered again, 'I'm sorry. I was very, very stupid.'

Matt said nothing, staring unseeingly at the dramatic land-scape and feeling only an increase in his misery.

She roused herself to try to move on, to offer something at least that would mitigate his anguish. 'We can work this out. It's between us. No one else needs to know about it.'

'You little fool!' It was so vicious that it felt like a blow in her face. 'People know already. That chemistry teacher who had the run-in with me last night knew. Debbie and Wally Keane knew. God knows who else knows! The pair of us are probably a laughing stock at Twin Lakes and everywhere else.'

She'd thought he hadn't known about Wally. She'd thought no one at school had known about it, that she'd been discreet. Matt was right: she'd been an utter fool to think that she could get away with it. Probably Wayne Briggs had boasted to his friends about bedding the Head of History, about what that staid lady was like with her clothes off. She'd been blinded by passion – no, not even that. She'd been blinded by sex. She'd thought all might now be well, after Keane had died. But instead it was all worse than she'd ever imagined it could be.

Freda Potts said limply, 'I'll make it up to you, somehow, if you'll give me the chance.'

SEVENTEEN

'We'd prefer to speak to you together, wouldn't we, Mike?' Geoffrey Tiler was uncharacteristically diffident as he ushered in the two CID officers. 'Though what more either of us will be able to tell you, I'm not at all sure.' He glanced at his partner and gave a nervous little laugh.

Michael Norrington tried to take the initiative. It didn't come naturally to him, but he wanted to seem confident. Confidence could mask all sorts of things, he believed. 'Do come in, Chief Superintendent Lambert. You and DS Hook are very welcome to inspect our humble abode, although as Geoffrey says I can't think that we shall be able to enlighten you about anything which bears on Wally Keane's unfortunate death.'

A warning glance from Tiler told him that he was in danger of overdoing things. It was noted by the watchful visitors, but Geoff wasn't certain whether it had registered with his partner. Norrington led them into the living room and indicated the sofa as the place where Lambert and Hook should sit. When they did not immediately speak, it was the nervous Norrington who felt compelled to break the silence. 'Well, I hope you're getting near to an arrest. The site is agog with gossip about your actions, as you'll probably be aware. We're all very sorry about Wally, of course, but I can't deny that it's brought a certain frisson of excitement to the place. We're a pretty staid lot here normally, but murder changes things. But then I expect you're well used to all that. And I'm sure you've been far too busy to take any interest in what people are chattering about here.'

'We're making progress.'

'Oh, good! But isn't that what you always say, when the press claim that you're baffled?'

Lambert gave him the ghost of a smile. 'It is, yes. That or something very similar. It's also the phrase we use when we want to convey that our enquiries are confidential – that we have found out certain things about people but don't wish to make them public property.'

'Yes. I'm sure you have to be discreet, don't you? Especially these days, when people are prepared to sue for defamation of character at the drop of a hat.'

Geoffrey Tiler had been trying to catch his partner's eye to shut him up. The less said the better, he'd asserted beforehand, and he'd thought Mike had agreed with him. He seemed to have forgotten it now. Geoff said, 'Of course anything you discover has to remain confidential. We understand that.'

'Unless of course it proves to have a bearing upon a murder investigation. In which case it may well become evidence in a criminal trial and thus available to anyone who takes an interest in such things.'

'Of course. It passes outside your control at that point, as any sensible person would appreciate. We don't expect to be told anything you've discovered about our neighbours here. We wouldn't even wish to hear it. It's none of our business.' He addressed his words to Lambert, but his tone indicated that they were intended for the man at his side rather more than the police.

'We discover all sorts of things when we concentrate our attention upon the people involved in a murder investigation. Most of it eventually proves irrelevant to the case. But until we know that it is so, it has to be followed up. That is why we are here for a second time.'

Lambert let the words fall into a silence which seemed more significant as it stretched. Norrington had taken the message from his partner that he should shut up and listen carefully rather than talk, but it was costing him an effort. Whereas the thickset Tiler was sitting back in his armchair, his brown eyes keenly observant, Michael Norrington was leaning forward on the edge of his comfortable seat, his very black hair a little tousled and his blue eyes flicking from one to the other of his police visitors in search of enlightenment.

It was Bert Hook, who had not previously spoken, who now said with a deliberate formality, 'Information has come to light which means we need to put certain questions to you, Mr Norrington.'

'How very exciting!' Michael clasped his hands and rocked a little on the edge of his chair. 'If it wasn't for the thought of poor Wally lying dead in the mortuary, I'd really be finding this quite intriguing. Don't you think so, Geoff?' He turned suddenly at right angles so as to speak to his partner, his movement as abrupt as his speech pattern was brittle.

Tiler spoke sternly, almost as if checking an impetuous child, 'I rather think we should concentrate on being helpful rather than excited, Mike.'

Hook moved in quickly on that. 'And you're the one who can help us, Michael. Tell us about Michael Clark, please.'

Norrington's eggshell-thin confidence dropped away from him like a snake's dead skin. He glanced at Tiler with something near to panic on his face, then spoke to him, not Hook. 'You told me this would happen.'

It sounded more like an accusation than an admission. Tiler said softly, 'Tell them, Mike. I'm sure they know everything. You've nothing to lose now.'

Norrington glanced at Lambert, then returned his attention to Hook, as if accepting the easier of two difficult options. 'I changed my name. I used to be Michael Clark, many years ago.'

'Yes. But not officially: not by deed poll. That's why it took our records boys a little while to trace it.'

'I moved to a different place. It seemed a good thing to use a new name in a new town. I never got round to doing the deed poll thing.'

Tiler came in, leaning sideways in his chair so that he was almost touching his partner. 'It's not illegal to call yourself by a different name. And we're going to get married in September, as the law of the land now allows us to do.' It was a declaration of his support rather than a useful piece of information.

Hook did not take his eyes off Norrington's face during Tiler's announcement. He said simply and persuasively, 'Why did you feel the need to change your name, Michael?'

'I was trying to begin again. But you know that.' The man who had opened so expansively was tight-lipped and cornered now.

'I'd rather hear it from you. The bare facts are scarcely flattering. I thought perhaps you'd like to give us your version of how these things happened.'

The man was fifty-three, but he had the tortured, helpless face of an adolescent. Perhaps that was because he was being made to relive his sins, or at least to confront them and account for them once again. 'I was twenty-four at the time. And I suppose I was young for my age. Geoff says I still am.' He gave a sudden violent laugh which showed how near to hysteria he was. 'I got a job teaching in a Catholic seminary in Lancashire. Instructing boys and young men who were training for the priesthood.'

'But you weren't a cleric yourself?'

'No. I had a degree in Theology and Philosophy. The bishop thought it very enlightened to bring in someone from the laity to assist the men of the cloth. I think that they all thought I would take holy orders and become an anointed priest in due course. But I let them down, didn't I?'

'It seems you did, yes.' Hook was trying to be as quiet and neutral as a counsellor collecting the thoughts of a troubled subject. It was a strategy which would have been derided by most of his CID colleagues, who favoured the aggressive approach to interviewing, but it was a characteristic of DS Hook which Lambert found useful when he wanted suspects to talk, rather than retreat behind the blank 'no-comment' tactic. 'Can you tell us how this happened?'

Norrington glanced at Tiler, received the tiniest of nods and said, 'I'd already realized that I was gay. It was legal by then of course, had been for years, but people were much less open about it than they are now. What I hadn't realized until I took the post was that many of the boys who were in the seminary were gay too, though some of them were still in the process of discovering that. I suppose a good proportion of the people who are attracted to the idea of the celibate life of the Roman Catholic priesthood are likely to be gay, or at least uncertain about their sexual orientation. I think even the Church is belatedly beginning to realize that, though it isn't stated openly.'

'And you took advantage of the uncertainties and inexperience of these boys.'

'I didn't see it like that. Now, almost thirty years on, I can see that I was doing just that, though I kidded myself that I was helping young men to find themselves.' He grinned bitterly. 'That was the popular phrase of the day: find themselves. It was the police who said I was taking advantage of kids who knew nothing about life; I think that in that at least they were right.'

'But you avoided criminal charges and a court case. You don't have a criminal record: that is why it has taken us a little time to discover this.'

'I was lucky. Very lucky, in view of how stupid I'd been. I resigned my post and moved on. The clerics were glad to see me go and to avoid a scandal. Those were different times. It wouldn't happen now. The Catholic Church is paying a heavy price for hushing things up and moving people on. I'm not a Catholic any more. I haven't been for twenty years.'

He offered these personal details as if he were revealing himself to a psychiatrist. Hook's low-key and personal approach was teasing out all sorts of facts about a man who remained a murder suspect. The DS prompted softly, 'You took someone else away from the seminary with you, didn't you, Michael?'

Norrington stared at him for a moment as if wondering how he came to be so well informed. But he did not question or dispute his statement. 'Francis Fitzpatrick. You couldn't have a much more Catholic name than that, could you? He always insisted on Francis, not Frank. That was his mother's doing, I think. A lot of the boys in the seminary were very close to their mothers.'

'And you set up house together.'

'Yes. It was Francis who saved me from the police. He was eighteen by the time we were living together and his mother couldn't do a thing about it.' He gave a wan, abstracted smile at the memory. 'He told the police that we hadn't had sex whilst we were in the seminary, even though that wasn't true. I think it was Francis Fitzpatrick who prevented them from bringing charges, in the end. They'd have needed him as a witness.'

'But obviously you didn't stay together.'

Norrington's face twisted a little, with pain, or remorse, or some combination of the two. 'It didn't last six months. Francis was eighteen. I was twenty-five by this time, but scarcely more mature than he was. We weren't suited for a permanent rela-tionship – probably not with anyone, let alone each other.'

In re-living the anguish of those vanished years, Michael Norrington had been conscious only of Hook and Geoffrey

Tiler, listening anxiously beside him to what Michael had confided to him many months ago now. But it was the fourth man in the room, John Lambert, who now struck a different and harsher note. 'We have to ask ourselves as detectives why you chose to conceal your past from us when we spoke to you three days ago, Mr Norrington.'

The man recoiled as if he had been struck a physical blow. 'It was private. I realize that I was lucky not to end up in court and possibly in prison for the abuse of minors. I'm not proud of it.' He glanced sideways at the man beside him and gave him a nervous smile. 'Geoff has been trying to persuade me that I should reveal this to you myself rather than have you fling it in my face. He was right, of course. Geoff's right about most things.'

'Wally Keane knew all about this, didn't he? He was planning to make use of it.'

'He'd already made use of it.' These words came grimly from Tiler, not Norrington. 'He'd already had money from me. He was threatening to contact some of those boys from the seminary, who must now be in their middle forties, and invite them to sue Michael for sexual abuse. He said that in the present climate they'd have an excellent chance of success, and he was probably right. Especially as Mike is too honest for his own good and would have admitted things.'

He did not look at his partner, but his hand stole to the edge of his armchair as if he wished to touch him. Lambert said, 'You're saying that Keane's death was highly convenient for both of you.'

'Highly convenient. I fancy that not many people mourn a blackmailer, apart perhaps from his wife. We're both glad to have his nasty mind and his even nastier actions removed from the world. However, neither of us killed him.'

'You obviously recognize that you are murder suspects. Can you do anything now to change that?'

'Neither of us can add to or modify the statements we have already given to you about our movements on Friday night. We were together throughout the evening and the night, until Michael rose early and shortly afterwards accompanied George Martindale in the discovery of the corpse.'

He spoke the words like a formal declaration, as if he was reminding Michael Norrington of the form of words they'd agreed earlier.

George Martindale didn't like the long bright evenings of summer. Not for this other life of his. Winter was better, when the nights concealed you, once you hid yourself away from the street lights. The July daylight seemed to be lingering. And he wasn't on familiar ground here, with people he knew around him and his escape routes already clear in his mind.

He was growing more uneasy with each passing day. He needed the money and the paymasters he never saw were offering more of it. But he detested what he was doing. He was horrified at the thought of Mary and the boys discovering what he was up to when he went out in the evenings to these mysterious assignments. Drinking with his mates, he told Mary. But she was too shrewd to swallow that. She knew that he was up to something, but as yet she'd chosen not to question him about it. It could only be a matter of time. And she surely must suspect drugs.

His work for the council was a doddle compared with this. Repairing roads could be hard graft at times and the conditions unpleasant, with traffic roaring within a few feet of you. But it was honest toil. He'd laughed at that simple phrase when his teacher had used it in their last year at school, but now he appreciated what it meant and what it implied about your satisfaction with life. He liked most of the men he worked with in Kidderminster. Rough diamonds, his manager called them, but there were some real gems beneath the dirt. And now that he was a foreman, he was able to foster the good men and control the more dubious ones. He was surprised how much he enjoyed the responsibility, how ready he had found himself for it.

George had ample time to revolve these things in his racing mind as he drove south towards Bristol. He had a bad feeling about the extra assignment he had been allotted by the Barbadian in the sunglasses he had met three days earlier. He shuddered as he drove past the lay-by near Hope Under Dinmore where the Mondeo Graphite had pulled up behind him on Saturday. He wondered if he would see that man this evening. He hoped not.

Martindale didn't know Bristol and he didn't like big cities. His apprehension increased as he left the fields behind and drove first through suburbia and then through the higher buildings and busier streets of the conurbation. He was glad of his satnav. And yet he resented it, as it guided him inexorably towards the meeting he did not want.

He was near the old docks now. This had been the centre of the slave trade. This is where the fate of his ancestors had been decided, as they were transported like animals to the sugar plantations in the West Indies and the tender mercies of the white men making their fortunes there. He wished he hadn't had that thought: it seemed an ill omen for an evening that was already full of menace. A menace he could neither define nor envisage, but which he felt more strongly than much more tangible threats. He could handle personal violence, could defend himself with his fists in any fair fight. But this business was not fair, and you wouldn't be able to solve anything with your fists.

He'd set the satnav for St Teresa's church, as he had been instructed to do. The steeple rose against the night sky above him, its height accentuated by the increasing gloom around him and the single bright star which was visible above it. The church was deserted, locked and barred against intruders, shutting out men like him from the forgiveness of the Lord.

George could hear his long-dead mother's voice in his ear. He was being far too imaginative.

He found the place he needed easily enough, a hundred yards further on. It was a failed garage, its petrol pumps long defunct on its forecourt. Two of the windows were broken on the frontage which had once revealed highly polished second-hand cars. 'Awaiting development' the sign by the road said. A block of flats, probably, delayed by this recession which seemed to be affecting everyone's life.

He drove round the back of the derelict building and parked close to its rear wall. It was almost dark now, but the bright red Focus still seemed much too conspicuous. He had thought at first that the former garage was deserted, but as his eyes grew accustomed to the gloom he detected a faint light behind the closely curtained windows of the only room he could see on the upper storey.

He had been told to wait and he sat very still, feeling his body grow tauter with the suspense, yet still wishing that no one would come to the car to thrust him on into the next scene in this baleful drama. He wished heartily that he'd never got involved with drugs at all. It had seemed so easy, a rapid way of raising money to give himself and his family a better life. That is the way he had sold it to himself at the time. And for a while, it had seemed just that. He had even enjoyed the sense of danger, the act of outwitting the law. And the rewards were substantial. What they hadn't told him was that he wouldn't be able to get out of this trade when he'd had enough. It wasn't like overtime or an extra job on the side, where you could pocket extra funds and have them tax-free if you cared to take the risk. The men who ran this lucrative industry, the drug barons whom everyone whispered about but no one ever saw, didn't let you give in your notice. Once you were in, you were there for as long as they cared to retain your services.

The returns were good, but you couldn't resign. A lot of the dealers were users who had taken to selling to feed their habit: they used their gains to meet their own addictions. Once they became real junkies and thus unreliable, they were discarded. Those who knew nothing were left to suffer and often to die. Those who knew anything which might endanger the men in the chain above them received a bullet in the back of the head or drowned mysteriously. In most sectors of a man's life, knowledge meant power. Here, knowledge too often meant death.

All this passed for the umpteenth time through George Martindale's too-active mind as he waited to receive his allotment of drugs for this mysterious extra assignment. He lifted his arm so as to see his watch, unable to believe the evidence of the clock in the Focus, which told him that only seventeen minutes had passed since he had switched off the engine and settled down to wait. It seemed much longer and it was very quiet here. If it hadn't been for that faint orange light behind the curtains above him, he would have hoped that no one would come and that he would be able to drive away after a decent interval.

Strange adjective to use: decent. There was nothing decent about this.

The man came with soft footfalls, but George's hypersensitive ears heard every one of them. He still jumped when his driver's door was flung open abruptly. A voice as dark as the night now was said, 'Come in, Mr Martindale.'

It was the Barbadian, and he contrived to make the four simple words of the invitation sound sinister. He led George in through the back door of the building and gestured towards a chair at the bottom of a narrow staircase. He wasn't wearing the sunglasses as he had at their meeting in the lay-by, but George could see no more of his eyes now than then. He hesitated, then sat and said, 'Give me the drugs and tell me where I'm to go to sell them. And give me everything you can about the place. I don't know Bristol at all.'

It sounded from his voice as if the big man was smiling as he spoke, but George couldn't see enough to be certain of that. 'Relax, Martindale! You're in luck, tonight. You might be in line for promotion, if you play your cards right. Lucky old George!'

Martindale opened his mouth, then shut it again quickly. He'd almost said that he didn't want promotion, not in this industry. But you didn't argue with the monkey. You waited for the organ-grinder. And with the organ-grinder, he realized fearfully as he sat and squirmed, you might not be able to argue.

Sixty seconds was all the time that George had to wonder what the Barbadian's words might mean for him. It was no more than a minute before an unseen door at the top of the stairs opened and a voice called softly, 'Send him up now.'

Martindale climbed the flight of narrow stairs softly, almost silently, as big men almost always do, treading as if afraid that their weight might disturb others if they move clumsily. He had an overwhelming sense that his life was about to change.

He had thought he was prepared for almost anything, but he was still surprised. Two men sitting behind a desk, beneath an unshaded light bulb which could not have been more than sixty watts. He could scarcely see their faces, but the little he saw told him they were Asians. He'd never expected that. They both had beards and they both had dark and deep-set eyes. One had a broader face than the other, but both were muffled to the chin.

It was the one with the thinner face who said, 'You're lucky, Mr Martindale. We have watched your efforts and we like what we have seen. You sell well and you sell quickly. And you know how to keep your mouth firmly shut. You realize the importance of silence in our work. If the police of this land ever question you, you will have the sense to keep completely silent.'

It was an injunction as well as a compliment. The man spoke good English, but with the light lilt and soft consonants which betrayed his origin. George said, 'I'm happy where I am. I'm happy to take what I get and to ask no questions. I don't need more money and I don't think I can handle promotion. I'm not good at authority.'

It was the best excuse he could offer at short notice. He'd tried to deliver it with a smile, but had signally failed in that. There was no smile from the stony faces opposite him. The thin face said coldly, 'You do not have a choice. You would be very unwise to refuse this splendid offer. The man who controls us and who controls you will not be pleased if you refuse.' He picked the words and spoke them carefully, as if he wished to be precise in a second language.

Martindale looked at him steadily, striving to reveal nothing of the fear he felt. He tried to pick his words as carefully as the Asian had. 'I have a full-time job with the council. I have just been promoted in that. It is important that I carry on with this legitimate work, if the police are not to suspect what I do when I am away from it.'

'I expect that is so. Legitimate work is important. But the other work you do is so much more lucrative, eh?' The narrow features smiled a mirthless smile, denoting that he had made a kind of joke.

'I thought I'd been doing all right. I'm shifting the stuff. I could do more coke, if you want me to. And Rohypnol. I could—'

'Ah, Rohypnol, yes. The sex drug is always in demand, is it not?' The man behind the desk laughed outright at the thought, but it was not a happy sound. His voice hardened. 'You have done well with the drugs. Now the master has in mind a more ambitious role for you. You would be most unwise to refuse it.'

George said desperately, 'I don't know Bristol. I wouldn't be anything like as effective operating here as on the patch I know. I really—'

'You will not be operating in Bristol, Mr Martindale. You have been brought here solely to be briefed on this new and exciting assignment. The people you select and groom for us will be operating in the Oxford area. But you do not need to know that area, either. You would be a supplier. You would recruit in your own area.'

'Recruit?' An even deeper shadow fell across George's mind. 'I don't want to bring in other people to sell drugs. I wouldn't—'

'Not drugs, Mr Martindale.' There was both impatience and contempt in the man's tone. 'There is one industry which all British men and some British women find more irresistible than drugs. Sex, George. They can't get enough of it. So it's up to us to supply the goods, don't you think? We're businessmen, aren't we, and we must meet the demand.'

'I don't know anything about the sex industry. And I'd be no good working in it. I—'

'We supply what is needed, George.' It was as if Martindale had not spoken. 'We give people what they want. And what they want is girls. The younger the better. They have to be prepared, of course. Grooming, it's called. But we do most of that. You supply the goods and we'll present them to the customers. The younger the better, George. We have more control of the young ones. We find that they do whatever we ask them to do without too many complaints.' He looked at the broader-faced man beside him and they exchanged knowing smiles. 'Kamar here has groomed a few in his time. Thoroughly enjoyed the process, I believe.' This time the smiles became sniggers.

'But I simply wouldn't be any good at this. I've never—'

'You black blokes have a great reputation, haven't you? Big dongers, everyone says. But we haven't time now for you to demonstrate that, George. We're here on business. And business says we need black girls in our sexual portfolio. There's a demand for them, see? It's a niche market, black girls. But a lucrative one: you'd be surprised how many white and brown men want to try a black girl. Maybe lots of times, or maybe just once, to see if they really do go like steam engines! No offence intended, and none taken, I'm sure. But you're being offered a great opportunity here, George. You'll be in on the ground floor. You'll supply us with, say, half a dozen black girls, to start with, and then there's no knowing where you might go. We'll give you guidance, to get you started. There must be black girls in a care home somewhere near you: that's always a good place to start. A dozen next year, then maybe twenty or thirty. You could eventually have other people working for you. The sky's the limit. We aim to supply all tastes.'

Martindale tried not to show the revulsion which was rising within him. Any sign of weakness would be a mistake with these men. He was sure of that, but of nothing else in this nightmare scenario. He fought down his nausea and said, 'I haven't the contacts. I wouldn't be any use to you in this sort of—'

There was a sudden tremendous noise on the stairs he had recently climbed so carefully. Then the door was kicked open, so violently that it crashed against the wall beside it, and a voice yelled, 'Don't move. Stay exactly where you are!' The light which now suddenly blazed into the dimly lit room was blinding. Yet Martindale was conscious only of the black muzzles of the two weapons in the doorway: he could see nothing of the men behind them. The voice said, 'You are under arrest. Lie flat on the ground on your bellies. Move slowly. Any attempt at resistance could result in your being shot.'

They were handcuffed and frisked. The plump Asian was relieved of a pistol, the thin one of a wicked-looking knife. George Martindale was flung with them into the police van.

His arrest brought to him a strange feeling of relief.

EIGHTEEN

John Lambert gave the murder team their assignments for the day, then called DI Rushton and DS Hook into his improvised office at Twin Lakes.

'New developments overnight. George Martindale was arrested in Bristol last night. It's part of the investigation into a sex-crimes ring based in Oxford. They think it has connections with the gangs already exposed in Rochdale and Telford and Derby. Vulnerable teenage girls being taken from other places and touted around the back streets of Oxford, as well as subjected to all kinds of other abuse. It's well organized: men are travelling by prior arrangement from considerable distances and paying big sums for their pleasures.'

'And Martindale was involved in this?' Bert Hook could not keep the surprise out of his voice.

'He was arrested with two of the Asians who've been directing operations and have been watched now for many months.' He glanced at Rushton. 'Mark Patmore was working undercover and was instrumental in exposing all this. He's now been withdrawn and sent to a safe house well away from his scene of operations.'

Chris Rushton said curtly, 'He's a good man, Mark Patmore. I couldn't do the things he's done.'

He had trained with Patmore many years earlier. They had been companions in distress during the rigours of cadetship, had compared notes on the problems presented to them and the ridiculous expectations of the powers that be. They had kept in touch for a while after they had become full-time officers, united by the common experience of training and their early-career steps in the police service. But they had been very different personalities. Rushton's determination to play by the rules and take the logical route to an inspector's job had contrasted with Patmore's more maverick and unpredictable approach to authority and to the whole ethos of police work.

Lambert grinned. 'Not many people could do the things Patmore's done, Chris. Under-cover work demands a special kind of personality. You have to be brave and resourceful. You could manage that. You also have to be unscrupulous at times, and it helps if you're not quite sane. You and I wouldn't be much good at that.'

Chris felt consoled by the great man's words. He had always envied the initiative, resourcefulness and naked courage of men like Patmore. They made him feel very puny. Chris was intelligent, very thorough, and he had an absolute integrity which Lambert recognized and valued but never mentioned. Rushton was dimly conscious of his own strengths, but they seemed very humdrum against those of his erstwhile colleague. It takes all sorts, he told himself unconvincingly.

He addressed himself determinedly to his own problems. 'So we now know that Martindale's a villain. Can we add murder here to what he's been up to elsewhere?' There was satisfaction in his voice: he hadn't taken to the popular George Martindale, the family man who was so extrovert and approachable as to be almost the opposite of how Chris saw himself.

'We shall keep an open mind on that. We don't know exactly what he's going to be charged with yet. He's admitted to being a small-time drugs dealer, but nothing more as yet. Apparently Mark Patmore, who's been getting nearer and nearer to this sex-grooming ring over the last six months, knows nothing about Martindale and has never come across him before. He thinks the men involved might have been trying to recruit him, but that's still to be established. I've had a long conversation with the Serious Crime Investigation superintendent down in Bristol and explained exactly where we are up to in a murder investigation here. He's agreed to release Martindale on bail and send him back here. He was a little reluctant, but I think he's far more interested in the two Asians who were arrested with him.'

Rushton reflected that there were advantages after all in having a celebrity detective in charge of your team, however reluctant John Lambert might be to accept that role. 'Last night's arrest and questioning should have softened the bugger up for you. You might get a confession out of him today.'

'Only if he did it. We shall keep the open mind I mentioned.' Lambert felt very priggish with his iteration of that principle. 'The Serious Crime Unit superintendent gave me some much more interesting information. They think that Richard Seagrave is one of the big men behind this sex-grooming business, which has been going on in northern and midland towns as well as Oxford. There's big money in it, but there's also big money needed to set it up. It sounds like the most evil and despicable business you could envisage and the network is extensive and efficient. It's needed brains to set the whole thing up and money to finance it. Seagrave has both. He also strikes me as completely amoral. Does that sound like a better candidate for murder than Martindale?'

'Definitely. But of course we must keep an open mind.' Rushton didn't make many jokes. He wasn't even sure that this repetition of Lambert's injunction qualified as a joke, but he'd enjoyed it. 'We've checked the alibis of everyone else on site. Unless we care to assume a mass conspiracy, your suspects are confined to the ones you've been concentrating on. Which means the people that Walter Keane was trying to blackmail. Have you managed to eliminate any of them?'

Lambert looked at the silent Hook, then shook his head. 'We plan to see Martindale and Seagrave again today. Wally seems to have known as much about Seagrave as the Serious Crime Squad. Of course, they have to prove things, whereas Wally could operate on mere suspicion. It looks as if he succeeded in taking Seagrave for a very large sum of money.'

'Which would also be highly dangerous, from Wally's point of view. Seagrave isn't the sort who'd meekly accept paying out money to a blackmailer.' Bert Hook spoke up for the first time. He knew whom he favoured for the killer, whatever John Lambert said about open minds.

Lambert nodded. 'Seagrave says he spent all the key hours of Friday night with his partner, Vanessa Norton. Whatever we think about alibis provided by spouses and partners, they're very difficult to break.'

Bert frowned. 'A man like Seagrave doesn't do his own dirty work. He has people to do it for him.'

'True enough. But this death doesn't on the surface look

like one perpetrated by a contract killer or professional muscle. This looks like something improvised on the spot – perhaps whoever met Keane on Friday night didn't initially intend to kill him. The victim was hit over the head and strung up on a rope, which was almost certainly already on site. The bullet through the back of the head is more the method of the man or men hired to kill.'

Rushton said thoughtfully, 'You're right about that. The MO in this death looks like the work of an amateur.'

Lambert nodded thoughtfully. 'We're almost all of us amateurs when it comes to killing, Chris. It's possible that even Seagrave, whom we now know as a vicious criminal, has never killed a man himself before. He has other people to do his dirty work.'

Rushton frowned. 'What do you think of the idea that this killing could be a joint effort? Most of the people you've been interviewing are paired. Most of them had a joint interest in seeing Keane off the face of the earth.'

'That's true. The pairs who are providing each other with alibis are also possible joint murderers.'

'And with most of the pairings, at least one of them seems capable of violence. Martindale and Seagrave we already know about. Jason Ramsbottom almost killed a man when he was much younger and is clearly desperate that he shouldn't lose his wife and family. Freda Potts has her marriage and her career at stake after sleeping with one of her pupils, and her husband is SAS trained, which means he has been taught how to kill. Tiler and Norrington don't have a history of violence, but they are very concerned to conceal Norrington's past abuses under another name. If we accept the idea that whoever met Keane on Friday night didn't initially intend murder, one or both of these two might be the likeliest candidates.'

Rushton was unusually pessimistic. 'There are too many candidates. And with all these pairs supporting each other, too many dodgy alibis that we'll find it impossible to break.'

The three senior men had an unexpected visitor waiting for them with the female detective constable in the murder room.

Lisa Ramsbottom rose and said nervously, 'I'd like to speak to Detective Sergeant Hook, please. Alone, if that's possible.'

Bert looked at Lambert, who nodded his assent. He took Lisa into the improvised interview room at the end of the mobile home they had commandeered. She looked round it curiously and said, 'This is an exact replica of the second bedroom in our unit. It seems odd to be talking to a policeman in here.'

It was no more than a diversion, a means of putting off what she had come here to say, and they both knew it. Bert said gently, 'I don't want to hurry you, but I have to ask you to be as brief as possible. We have other people to see today.'

'Of course. I'm sorry and it's probably nothing.' But it wasn't. It was highly important. Important for her alone, she hoped. If not, the consequences were too awful for her to contemplate. She took a deep breath and said, 'I need to know what Jason said when he came to see you yesterday.'

'I'm afraid I can't tell you that, Lisa. All our exchanges with the public are confidential. Sometimes we have to talk to other people as a result of what they reveal to us. This is not one of those occasions.'

'But I'm his wife. He doesn't have secrets from me.'

How often had he heard that, and how often had it been absurdly wide of the mark? 'I'm sorry. Perhaps you should ask him about it yourself.'

'I've done that and he won't tell me. That's why I'm here. We're neighbours when we're in our real homes in Tewkesbury, Bert.'

'And in this case that makes no difference. I'm sorry.'

She stared out of the window for a moment, watching a wagtail hopping away from them over the close-cut turf. 'What did you make of my suggestion that it might have been Wally Keane who sent us those ridiculous threatening notes?'

Bert had a problem. He couldn't reveal confidential information, but he sensed that Lisa Ramsbottom had something to tell him. Something which for all he knew might have a vital bearing on the case. He wanted to offer her something, so as to encourage her to keep talking, but he had precious little available to him. He said rather stolidly, 'It was an interesting

suggestion. We haven't ignored it. But I can now tell you that
we don't think that those letters came from Wally Keane.'

'It was Jason who made up those messages, wasn't it?'

'I can't tell you about that. Perhaps you should talk about
it with Jason, if that's what you think.'

'Jason was appalled when I brought you here to talk about
those notes back in May. He tried to pretend he wasn't, but I
know him too well.'

Too well and not well enough, Bert thought. He said stiffly,
'If you think that, you should discuss it with your husband.
I'm sorry we can't help, but I'm sure you understand.'

She nodded absently and continued to look out of the
window, staring without reaction towards the spot a hundred
yards away where a young spaniel leapt high in the air after
the ball with which a ten-year-old boy was teasing it. Bert
said softly, 'I think you came here to tell me something.
Something you feel is important. I think you should tell me
that now.'

She glanced fiercely at him for a moment, then resumed
her gaze through the window. She was looking beyond the
boy and his dog, towards the hill which rose gently away
behind them as she said dully, 'Jason went out on Friday night.
I can't be sure of the time. It was on the edge of darkness.'

Bert's tone altered not an iota. He remained as low key as
ever as he said calmly, 'And how long was he out for, Lisa?'

'About half an hour, I should think. Maybe a little longer.
It was quite dark when he came in.'

'We need to speak to you on your own, Mr Seagrave.'

The powerful figure stood above them in the door of his
holiday home and showed no inclination to relinquish that
dominant position. 'I think I'd like Vanessa to hear this. Just to
make sure you don't twist anything I choose to say to you.' He
looked down on Lambert and Hook and made his derision quite
clear in the smile which he allowed to twist his broad features.

Vanessa Norton appeared suddenly beside him in the doorway.
'It's all right, Richard. The officers might have things to say
to you in private, and I understand that. I can busy myself on
the golf course. I'll probably have more frustrations there than

you will endure here.' She slipped past him, descended the three steps, then lifted the lid on the storage bin beside the wall. She lifted out a bag of golf clubs, as if providing evidence of her honesty. She slung the bag over her shoulder and departed without another glance at the trio behind her, an attractive figure in yellow shirt and green slacks. On this bright summer morning, her tall, willowy figure seemed a personification of innocent activity in that outdoor world which was so alien to the man she had left behind her.

Hook, staring after her, wondered if this was her declaration of non-involvement.

Seagrave said heavily, 'I suppose you'd better come inside and sit down.'

He motioned to the sofa in the living room, then sat down heavily in the armchair opposite them. Its seat was two inches higher than theirs; his superiority was preserved. It wasn't important or significant, but the idea of it pleased him.

The CID men waited, stretching the silence to see if it would unsettle him. He was too wily a bird for that. He'd played these games before, he told himself. He was an educated man, wasn't he, and far too intelligent for these jumped-up plods?

Lambert said, 'We've been examining again the full details of what Walter Keane had recorded upon his computer. He had collected some interesting and highly damaging facts abut you, hadn't he?'

'Mere speculation. I treated Keane with contempt. I'm not going to pretend I'm sorry he's dead. I don't go in for that sort of mealy-mouthed sentimentality.'

'No. The Serious Crime Squad is well aware that you are not a man who shows sentiment. Grooming helpless young girls for sex with callous and perverted older men shows a complete absence of sentiment.'

Lambert detected the first flash of fear in the narrowed brown eyes. Seagrave said, 'I've no idea what you're talking about, Chief Superintendent Lambert.' He invested his enunciation of the rank with a sneer of contempt.

'Oh, but I think you have. The whole network is about to be exposed. It covers many cities and towns, as you are well aware.'

Seagrave made himself take his time. There was never anything to be gained by being too hasty. They had to be bluffing. No doubt they were trying to get him to give them facts they needed but were never going to have. 'I've read a little about these sex rings. Quite interesting stuff. Little sluts being introduced to the game early. Apprentice tarts being taught their trade, as far as I can gather. It's an alien world to me, of course, as a respectable businessman.'

'Yes, it would be.' This time it was Lambert who did not care to conceal his contempt. 'These activities have been financed by businessmen like you. A lot of money's gone into this. You must have been anticipating rich rewards.'

'What a vivid imagination you have, Lambert! Unusual in a policeman, I'd say. And likely to get you into a whole lot of trouble, when I sue for defamation. "Who steals my purse steals trash. But he that filches from me my good name makes me poor indeed." Othello says that, Chief Superintendent.' Let the bastards know they're dealing with an educated man here, not some thug with pretensions, Richard thought.

The riposte came from the man he hadn't even deigned to consider. Bert Hook regarded his adversary steadily as he said, 'That's not an exact quotation, but near enough. And it comes from Iago, the villain of the piece, not Othello. The greatest of all villains, most people think. The kind of man who might set up innocent kids to provide for the sexual tastes of rich villains.'

It was ridiculous, but Richard Seagrave was more shaken by this than by their previous assertions about his involvement in the Oxford set-up. If you couldn't rely on plods to be thick and ignorant, what on earth could you rely upon? He said with as much conviction as he could muster, 'I've no idea what you're talking about, but I'm taking notice of your accusations and your attitude. In due course, you will suffer for what you are saying.'

Lambert said crisply, 'Other people will substantiate what we've been saying about the grooming of minors for illicit sex. DS Hook and I are concerned with something much more local. What involvement did you have in the death of the man who was blackmailing you here?'

'I had nothing to do with the death of Wally Keane. He was a snivelling little toad and I'm glad he's gone. I didn't kill him.'

'You have muscle at your disposal. Some of the men you employ are being questioned this morning, probably at this very moment, about the tasks you have given them in the pursuit of your criminal activities. Did you instruct them to dispose of the troublesome Mr Keane for you?'

He was shaken by the news of how close the police were getting to his machine. Quotations sprang into his head when he least needed them. 'Now does he feel his title hang loose about him, like a giant's robe upon a dwarfish thief.' Macbeth, he thought, in his final hours. Not a good model: he wished that he hadn't got this talent for recall of those school days now so far away. He said evenly, 'I'm telling you for the last time: I had no involvement in the murder of Wally Keane.'

Lambert regarded him without comment, allowing the seconds to stretch. 'We may need to speak to Ms Norton about your movements on Friday night.'

NINETEEN

There are large teams attached to any murder enquiry. They collect a lot of information, most of which proves to be totally irrelevant to the case in question. Occasionally and unpredictably, someone on the edge of the investigation turns up a fact which seems highly significant.

Detective Constable Tessa Jones had only been in CID for two months and this was her first murder case. More senior officers told her that the case at Twin Lakes would be routine and boring, that she would spend hours on repetitive questioning of innocent people who had nothing to do with the crime, that she was learning her trade. She would need to become accustomed to being at once bored and meticulous.

They weren't very far wrong. But the excitement carried her along. Murder had its own dark glamour; her mother and her younger siblings asked her about the progress of the investigation every night. For almost the first time since she had joined the police service, Tessa felt very important.

And on her fourth day of involvement, Tessa turned up something quite important. Something which she felt might even be a gem.

The setting was most unpromising. At ten in the morning, before the place was open, she was interviewing the landlord of a village pub. He was overweight, he looked jaded, and he was anxious to be rid of DC Jones and get on with the rest of his day. He'd seen her yesterday and told her everything he had to say. But now here she was again, bright and youthful and distressingly enthusiastic.

The White Hart was in Chardon, the nearest village to Twin Lakes. It was exactly half a mile from the gates of the leisure park, the zealous Tessa Jones had calculated, and thus no more than a brisk stroll for anyone who fancied moving off the site for a drink. The landlord had mentioned one such person yesterday. 'Definitely not a local,' he'd said. 'Very likely from up there.' The gesture with his head had been in the direction of Twin Lakes.

This morning DC Jones was back with a photograph, thrusting it under his nose before he was properly prepared for his working day. 'Is this the man?'

The landlord peered at the picture, then produced a pair of spectacles from beneath the bar. He was obscurely conscious that this might be important. He might just have a part to play in the drama which had been the talk of the pub since last Saturday. He said with an unexpected touch of excitement, 'That's him. That's the man. He was in here last Friday night.'

'You're sure of that?'

'Of course I am. That's why I got my glasses out.' But he looked again, just to check.

'What time did he come in?' Tessa had her notebook out and was looking suitably official.

'About half past eight. I told you that yesterday.'

'And how long was he here?'

'It couldn't have been more than half an hour. He had a pint, but just the one. He didn't join in the conversation with my regulars.'

'Thank you, sir. You've been most helpful.'

Tessa Jones couldn't wait to deliver her news to that handsome and serious DI Rushton, who collected and collated all their findings. Matthew Potts had made no mention of leaving the site in his written statement. He'd said that he'd been with his wife in their mobile home throughout the evening.

Black men couldn't look pale and distressed. Bert Hook had decided that many years ago. But George Martindale certainly looked distressed.

He'd exuded an air of confidence when they had seen him earlier, especially when he had been with his family. Without any detailed evidence to support the view, Hook had no doubt that the Jamaican was a good husband and a devoted father. But he reminded himself sternly that many vicious criminals had been good family men.

Lambert's concern was to put Martindale on the back foot, to render him least able to defend himself and most likely to reveal things about himself and others which would help the enquiry. John Lambert had taught himself long ago to be professionally blinkered in the pursuit of his goals.

He said severely, 'You've landed yourself in a lot of trouble, Mr Martindale.'

'I'm not guilty of what they've charged me with. I'm not guilty of procuring. I'm nothing to do with this sex ring. I know nothing about it. They were trying to involve me in it last night, when your lot turned up. I was trying to tell them I wanted nothing to do with it.'

He stopped abruptly. They weren't going to believe that. These were coppers: it was their job to think the worst of you and then try to find the evidence to prove they were right. A sense of hopelessness settled on top of his misery and his broad shoulders drooped.

Lambert studied him as if he were a specimen under a micro-scope. He felt no compunction in extracting all he could from this distress. The man was a criminal, whether or not he was involved in grooming kids for sex. He might yet be a murderer. The more vulnerable he became, the more frank he was likely to be. 'You were dealing in drugs. Have been for the last two years.'

'Yes. I've already admitted that.'

'Walter Keane knew that.'

Martindale started, even in his wretchedness. It was as if someone had jabbed a pin into his powerful frame. 'I'd almost forgotten about Wally.'

It was DS Hook who now said, 'You shouldn't do that, George. Wally's a murder victim and you are a suspect. A greater suspect, in view of last night's happenings.'

'I didn't kill Wally.' He said it hopelessly. He was a man who no longer expected to be believed.

'Wally knew about the drugs, didn't he? He'd had money from you on account of that.'

'And he wanted more. More than I could afford to give him. He'd had thousands and he wanted more. I tried to tell him that Mary was going to find out if I gave him more, but he didn't care about that. He said that wasn't his concern.'

'Unpleasant men, blackmailers. They always come back for

more, even when they've promised that they won't. It's too easy for them. And they're almost invariably greedy men. Too greedy for their own good. That makes people desperate. They become desperate enough to kill, when they can't see any other way of shutting the man up.'

George looked down for so long at his broad and powerful hands that they wondered if he was contemplating what they had done on that fateful Friday night. He said in his low, rich voice, 'I'd like to have killed him. I so wanted him to shut up and leave me and my family alone.'

'And did you do that, George? Did you hit him over the head and then string him up from the tree? It must have been easy for you. He didn't weigh much more than a child. Not a lot more than your Nicky, I should think.'

Now, at last, Martindale was animated. He was almost shouting as he said, 'I didn't kill Wally Keane! I would have done, if he'd done anything to threaten my boys!'

'But he was threatening them, wasn't he, George? He wanted more money, which you couldn't provide for him. He was threatening to tell Mary and the children, as well as the police, wasn't he?'

He nodded miserably and thrust his head briefly into those powerful hands. He said, 'I'll plead guilty to the drug-dealing. I wanted out, but I don't expect you'll believe that. But I had nothing to do with grooming black kids for that sex ring. And I didn't kill Wally Keane.'

There was a curious contrast between the immense physical strength of his body and the abject state of his spirit. George Martindale was a man who no longer expected to be believed.

The dinghy moved very slowly across the lake. There was so little breeze that it seemed at first not to be moving at all, but Michael Norrington realized after a few minutes that the far bank now definitely seemed nearer to them. Geoffrey Tiler had been an expert sailor in his youth. He had sailed dinghies round the tricky waters of the Menai Straits and won prizes for it. His expertise was one of the many surprising things Michael had discovered about the man with whom he was to share the rest of his life. He enjoyed the process of discovery.

A lover should be full of surprises, so long as they were pleasant ones.

Geoff made the tiniest adjustment to the rudder, then watched the swans and their cygnets pass within ten yards of the hull of the little boat. The cygnets were growing surprisingly quickly, but they retained their brownish plumage, making the whiteness of their parents seem even more dramatic and immaculate. Michael Norrington watched them pass, then dipped his right hand into the water, enjoying its coolness as it flowed gently between his fingers.

'I'm glad Wally Keane's gone.' The words surprised even Mike. The thought had been in his head, but he hadn't known he was going to voice it. Perhaps the serenity of the lake and the isolation it was affording them had prompted him to lay bare his innermost thought to his companion. Or perhaps it was merely an impulse which he hadn't resisted. He tried to be honest with himself. He didn't want any sort of pretension, when he was alone with Geoff in such a perfect setting.

Tiler now said, 'He'd had money from me. He wanted more. Blackmailers always come back for more: everyone says so.' Geoffrey spoke as if pronouncing some sort of epitaph. He looked over the calm water to the spot where Keane had died. The police had this morning removed the scene-of-crime tapes which had cordoned it off, but no one was at present treading the path through the tall trees. Did the police action mean that they felt the case was concluded and that they were near to an arrest? Or only that they'd discovered all that they could possibly find after their minute examination of the site?

Mike said with as much finality as he could muster, 'It's good to be rid of him.' He turned his back resolutely on the place where Keane had died and directed his gaze towards the other shore of the lake and the golf course beyond it. As he looked, the athletic figure of Vanessa Norton appeared on the highest point of the course and he watched her swing a club easily and elegantly at an invisible ball. Then she smiled and spoke to someone else, but he couldn't see who was her companion on the course. Her yellow-shirted torso disappeared again, and Norrington's too-vivid imagination suggested to him that she was a significant vision that had been offered to him, rather than a random sighting.

Geoffrey Tiler hadn't turned with Norrington, hadn't seen the fleeting view of the supple Ms Norton. He moved the tiller again and looked up towards the Welsh hills above Twin Lakes. 'Life's much better with Wally out of the way. I couldn't have endured what he was going to do to us.'

Freda Potts looked down from the door of her mobile home on Lambert and Hook and felt an immense foreboding.

'Matt isn't here. He's out. I don't know where.' The two of them hadn't been together much in the twenty hours or so since they'd come back from the Brecon Beacons. Matt hadn't slept with her last night. He'd hardly spoken to her this morning. She didn't know what was going to happen; couldn't even think a day ahead, let alone to next week and next month. And now the police were here again, looking as bright and alert as she felt jaded and defeated.

John Lambert smiled up at her. 'That's all right. We'd like a few words with you on your own, Mrs Potts.'

She led them with a feeling of inevitability into the sitting room, conjured up a wan smile for them as she sat down opposite the tall man with the lined face and the clear, unblinking grey eyes.

Lambert watched her closely, unwaveringly, as if the slightest movement of her features would offer him new and valuable insights. He seemed almost apologetic for the familiar phrases when he eventually said, 'Certain information has come to light which needs to be followed up, Mrs Potts. It casts doubt on the statements which you and your husband gave to us concerning your movements on Friday night.'

'And what is the source of this information?'

'I am not at liberty to disclose that.' The police jargon was useful, when you wished to give nothing away. 'It appears that your husband was not with you for the whole of the evening, as both of you claimed in your statements.'

'Oh?' The monosyllable was ridiculous, and she felt it so as it dropped on to the rug between them. But she had nowhere to go and all three of them knew it.

'We have a witness who is quite certain that your husband was in the White Hart public house in Chardon at eight thirty last Friday night. He stayed there for around half an hour and then left.'

'He didn't kill Wally Keane.'

'He hasn't been accused of that. Not yet. But if both of you have lied to us, we need to know why.'

Freda flicked her black hair back from her forehead and her dark eyes glittered. She looked for a moment as if she might fly into a rage. Then, with an effort, she spoke very calmly. 'I should have thought that was obvious. Matt needed an alibi for when Wally was killed. I knew he hadn't done it, so I was quite prepared to say that he'd been with me.'

'Why did you think you would be suspected, Freda?'

The question came very quietly from Bert Hook. It was as unexpected as the use of her first name. Both factors disconcerted her. 'We – we didn't ask each other that. You were questioning us along with everyone else who'd been around at the time, so we had to account for ourselves. And Matt has worked in some violent places and with some violent people. He's seen people killed. He was in the SAS for four years. And life on the oil rigs in the North Sea is no picnic. Lots of tough men living together can lead to incidents. Matt doesn't talk about it much, but I know that happens. We knew you'd find all this in his background. So when we knew he'd been out at the time of the killing, it seemed best that I said he was with me. Surely you can understand that?'

Bert smiled at her. 'And why would Matt want to kill Wally Keane, Freda? What would be his motive?'

The dark eyes looked at him blankly for a moment. Then she glanced at Lambert and said, 'That's right. He had no motive. I rather liked Wally and Matt hardly knew him.'

Hook was quiet but insistent: his tone seemed to emphasize the logic of his argument. 'Wally knew about you, didn't he, Freda?'

Her eyes were a very dark blue as they widened. 'About me? Knew what? I don't understand.'

'Oh, but I think you do, Freda. Wally knew all about you and Wayne Briggs, didn't he?'

'What do you mean? He knew about my nephew, yes. Everybody here knew about my nephew. Wayne had been here with me a couple of times, so the people who were here regularly all knew about him. He enjoyed it here.'

She stopped abruptly, realizing how banal this must sound to these experienced men, knowing that she was in danger of speaking too much and merely underlining the lameness of her case.

'You should have expected gossip, Freda. But people who are normally realistic become very naïve, once sex is involved. We see that quite often.'

She said dully, 'Debbie Keane chatted to me about Wayne. She tried to pry and I shook her off. I thought she was just being her normal gossipy self. But Wally followed it up. He spoke to Wayne himself. I think he even contacted people at my school in Bristol, but I'm not sure of that.'

'And he was pressing you for money.'

She stared at him for a long moment, as if estimating the possibilities of further denial. Then she said, 'He'd had money. All I had, in my own bank account. He was demanding more. He said that my whole career was at stake, that I'd be banned from teaching for life if he revealed what he knew. He said that he'd ruin me and make Matt a laughing stock – the tabloids would love it, he said.' She looked at them wildly, reliving that moment and pleading for them to relive it with her. 'I know that Matt didn't string Wally up, but I could understand it if he had done. I'm very grateful to whoever it was who shut his rotten mouth for good.'

Bert stared at her for a moment, then nodded. 'I think you now realize how unwise it would be to tell us more lies, Freda. What time did Matt come back in on Friday night?'

'I couldn't be precise. But it was round about eleven o'clock.'

Vanessa Norton returned to their unit whilst Richard Seagrave was still making phone calls. She couldn't hear the words, but she listened to his low, urgent tones behind the door which he had shut upon her. She stared at the places on the sofa where the CID men had sat an hour ago and wondered what had passed between them and Richard. Then he came back into the room and she uttered the well-worn phrase she had sworn to herself she would never use. 'We need to talk.'

He looked hard at her, then nodded. He looked round the familiar room. His eyes dwelt for a moment on the sofa she had stared at. Then he said, 'Not here. I need to get out for a little while.'

She looked at him and assessed him. 'We'll walk through the woods and round the lakes. It will be quiet enough there at this time of day.'

He looked longingly at the dark blue Jaguar as they left their home. He'd rather have driven out of here and many miles away, with her beside him. He felt at home in the leather seats of the sleek luxury car, more confident of himself and his words when he was there. He needed her; he felt he might be able to convince her of his need, if they were in the car.

Instead, they walked around the perimeter of Twin Lakes, as if affording themselves a tour of its many attractions. They passed the spot where last Friday's murder had taken place, each of them with an eye upon the other, each of them trying to behave as if the place had no significance. He took her hand as he moved on, gave it a squeeze, but received no answering pressure.

He said, trying to recall lost innocence, 'This reminds me of my first girlfriend, walking through the woods in broad daylight and holding hands like this.'

Her voice seemed to come from a long way away as she said, 'It's too late for that,' and detached her fingers gently from his.

'It's never too late, Vanessa.' But he knew even as he said the words that it was. It was a long time since he had needed to plead, and the words came awkwardly to him. 'I need you to help me in the next few days. I need you to say that you were with me at certain times. We can work out together what we were doing and what we're going to say.'

'That isn't going to happen, Richard. It's not that I can't lie – I've done plenty of that in my time. It's that I don't want to. You're not worth saving.'

He sought hard for a quotation, something which would remind both of them that he was an educated man. Nothing came. He said abjectly, 'You know how to kick a man when he's down.'

'I'm not kicking, Richard. The law will do that eventually, despite all your money and all your contacts. I'm merely refusing to help you.'

They walked on. He looked across to the far side of the lake, where Geoff Tiler and Mike Norrington were drifting with only minimal rudder guidance from Tiler. Richard wished heartily that he'd remained the centre-pin of a small and successful business, like Tiler. He should never have struck out into the waters of the criminal unknown and the dark leviathans which lurked there. This was no more than self-indulgent nostalgia, and he knew it. He said, 'You knew I was no angel when you took up with me. Don't come the school head girl with me now. The moral high ground isn't available.'

Vanessa was suddenly glad that she was out in the open, that a cry for help would be heard here. It was a long time since she had been frightened of a man. She said, 'I'm no angel either, Richard. But what you've done is unspeakable. I won't shop you, but I want no part in defending you.'

'We could still be close.'

'No. We could have been, once. That was before I knew about what you've done with these girls. The things you've set up with innocent kids, to gratify the sexual tastes of evil men. And all for money.' She despised herself as much as him with the contempt she poured into that last phrase. She could be clear-sighted about herself and him now, when it was much too late. She'd been brought to him by a sense of danger, by the sense that he could outwit the forces of law and order. And yes, by his money. She'd kidded herself that it wasn't so at the time, but she had accepted too easily the things he had lavished upon her. She thought the very worst of herself for that at this moment, but she knew that she was still worth more than this.

They had almost completed the circuit now. Vanessa was wondering what she would do when they got back to their unit. She wanted to pack her bag and leave. She'd hire a taxi, get it to take her all the way back home, if necessary. Home: she'd thought for a few crazy weeks that home might have been with this man. Now she was afraid even to go into this holiday home with him, fearful of what he might do to her when he finally accepted that she was not going to help him.

It was then that the police cars came. Three of them. Not with blaring sirens, nor the flashing lights which would announce their presence to all. They came almost silently between the units and their grassy surrounds, observing the ten-mile-an-hour limits of the site, creeping as inexorably as crocodiles towards their prey in shallow water. Or like Birnam Wood coming to Macbeth and Dunsinane, thought the horrified Richard Seagrave.

He was, after all, an educated villain.

TWENTY

John Lambert watched the procession of police cars drive out of Twin Lakes. Richard Seagrave was in the back seat of the middle one of the three, handcuffed to a uniformed constable and staring grimly ahead of him. Lambert didn't think that he'd ever been more satisfied to see a man arrested, even though the capture by the Serious Crime Unit had had nothing to do with him. Was there a crime worse than murder? Certainly, in his experienced view, and Seagrave by his callous disregard of human suffering was the man who had been guilty of it.

Now it was time to arrest the murderer of Walter Keane, control freak turned blackmailer. He turned with a sigh into the murder room and called, 'Bert, are you ready?'

They'd agreed tactics beforehand. He knew he could prove this, if he had to, but a confession would certainly ease the process.

From their vantage point near the entrance to the leisure park, Chris Rushton and Bert Hook had seen Matthew Potts drive back grim-faced on to the site thirty minutes earlier. They'd agreed with the chief that they would allow him time to talk to his wife and have a snack, but they'd have stopped him if he had attempted to leave Twin Lakes again. Chris Rushton filed the details of Tessa Jones' report on Potts's Friday-night excursion with some satisfaction. It looked to Chris as if he'd have a clear weekend, with the case concluded and the killer in custody. He said to Hook as they munched their sandwiches, 'Allowing the condemned man to eat a hearty lunch rather than a hearty breakfast, are we?'

Hook gave him no more than a patient smile by way of reply. He was wondering what sort of exchanges were taking place between the Potts in their home with the view over the largest lake and the neatly cut grass around it. The mower had worked its way carefully around this section of the site during the morning, and the smell of new-mown grass, one of the most evocative scents for a countryman like Bert, wafted pleasantly into their nostrils as they walked back to the place where they had so recently spoken with Freda Potts.

She had obviously been awaiting their arrival, as was to be expected after their earlier exchanges, and she had the door open and was looking down at them whilst they were passing her bright blue Peugeot and still ten yards from the steps of the unit. 'Matt's back. I've told him that I had to tell you the truth about Friday night this morning. He's quite willing to talk to you.'

He doesn't have a choice about that, thought Bert Hook grimly. And Matthew Potts when they saw him looked exactly like a man who didn't have a choice. He sat with a stony face in an armchair. Like many powerful men, Potts didn't sit easily. His hands were clenched tightly upon the arms of his chair and he looked as if he might spring out of it at any moment.

Lambert said, 'I think you know why we want to talk to you.'

'Friday night. I understand that. I should have told you the truth at first.'

'You should indeed. We might have arrived at the solution to this crime earlier if you'd done so.'

Hook didn't bother with his notebook. There was no need for notes now; no need to use the silent intimidation of making exact records of times and places. He said only, 'You'd better give us your account of exactly where you went and what you did last Friday night.'

Matt Potts noted that 'your account' with a grim smile. It was an indication that he could no longer expect to have what he said accepted, that his earlier deceit meant that he had forfeited any right to have what he said believed without it being checked. He wasn't used to that. He was a straight-talking man who had gained respect in the harsh world of the oil rigs. He had grown used to any facts he delivered being instantly accepted. He was surprised how diminished he felt with the realization that this was not so here. Matt was accustomed to being a strong man in a man's world. Perhaps that was his natural metier, however those poncey schoolteacher colleagues of Freda's might mock it as sexist.

He looked at the carpet. He found it easier to concentrate upon his words when he was not looking into the attentive

faces of these men who had caught him out in his lying. 'I
went to the White Hart in Chardon. I had a pint there. I don't
think I spoke with anyone, except the man who served me at
the bar. I didn't go there for conversation.'

'How long were you there?'

'I don't know. I was thinking.' Matt was an intelligent man,
but he made thinking sound a difficult process. As indeed it had
been for him, on that fatal Friday night. 'I drank slowly and
stared at the wall. I remember feeling surprised when I saw that
my glass was empty. I left when the pub was getting noisier,
when the seats round me were filling up. I suppose I was there
for about half an hour – certainly not for a full hour.'

'So that you left at about nine o'clock?'

'It must have been about that time, yes. There was still
daylight, but the sun was well gone.' Sunsets at sea flashed
before him. He had watched many times as the sun sank
beneath the waves in the west, sometimes with icicles forming
on the metalwork of the ship above him. That fierce and
isolated world seemed now much cleaner and less complicated
than this green and pleasant one.

'And what time did you return here?'

Freda willed him to look at her. He surely must do that now,
in recognition of what she had said to them before he came.
She had told him exactly what she had said to the CID visitors;
he had sat like a statue and accepted it, sat so still that she had
not been certain how much he had comprehended. Surely Matt
must look at her now, as a confirmation that he remembered
what she had said. But he did not. It seemed that he had shut
her out of his world and had no plans to re-admit her. Matt
stared at the carpet as he said, 'It was about eleven o'clock
when I got back here. I believe Freda has already told you that.'

Hook said with surprising gentleness, as if teasing out the
truth from a child who had lied rather than from this toughest
of men, 'And what did you do during those two hours, Matt?'

Now at last he looked up, not at Lambert but at Hook. 'I
walked around and thought. First in the village and then around
Twin Lakes. I walked all round the golf course. There was a
moon, and it was quite easy to see where you were going, so
long as you kept to the middle of the fairways.'

'Do you do this sort of thing often?'

'No, not often. It's the first time I've done it here.' He paused, waiting for the question he felt was obvious. It did not come because Hook sensed that it was not needed. 'I was thinking about Freda and what Wally Keane had said to me.'

There was a start from the woman sitting in the armchair beside him. Freda was perhaps three feet away from him. She reached out a hand towards him, then let her arm collapse hopelessly beside her when she realized he was not going to take it.

Hook said quietly, relentlessly, 'Did you take the path through the woods? Did you pass the spot where Keane died?'

'I went there at first. There was still daylight then, but it was pretty dark among the trees. I didn't see anyone. And I didn't go back there. I spent the rest of the time on the golf course and around the small lake at the other end of the site. I didn't see anyone, apart from a few shadowy figures leaving the bar and the restaurant. I didn't talk to anyone.' Matt Potts spoke as if he did not much care whether they believed him or not.

'So there's no one who can vouch for your whereabouts at the time Walter Keane was killed.'

The powerful shoulders lifted a fraction, then fell. It wasn't a large enough movement to be called a shrug. 'No. I'm telling you the truth, but I can't expect you to believe it, when I lied to you in my original statement.'

'Matt didn't kill Wally Keane!'

It was insistent, with the tone rising towards hysteria. It came from Freda Potts.

Lambert's voice cut through the silence which followed like a freshly sharpened blade. 'And you can prove that, can't you, Mrs Potts?'

It sounded more accusation than question, and that indeed is what it was. She said, 'Matt was back here by eleven, as I told you this morning. He didn't know anything about what had happened to Wally. He didn't know until the next day, when everyone found out about it.'

'But you knew, didn't you, Freda?' Where Hook had spoken to Matthew Potts almost like a therapist, allowing him to voice facts which it felt a relief to deliver, Lambert was now aggressive and challenging. He made his quarry feel that he knew exactly what had happened, so that further prevarication would be useless.

She said evenly, 'I hadn't been back here long myself when Matt came in.'

Matt looked at her at last, for the first time since they had sat down for this final scene, and his dark eyes widened with a dawning horror. He felt now that he had known this for the last five days, but refused to acknowledge it to himself. He said dully, 'Don't, Freda. You shouldn't do this.'

But the woman who had been willing him to speak to her through most of those five days now ignored his words. 'I didn't mean to kill him when I went there. Even when I hit him, I don't think I meant to kill him.'

Lambert nodded and spoke as calmly as if she were giving an account of a shopping expedition. 'Tell us how it happened, please.'

'He'd said he wanted to see me. Edge of dark, he said. I went up there at about half past nine. It was already pretty dark under the trees. Wally was already there. He said he wanted more money. I said I couldn't give him any more. I tried to brazen it out. I told him I hadn't the money to buy him off and that I was going to take the same attitude as the Duke of Wellington: "Publish and be damned!"'

'And what did he say to that?'

He laughed in my face. He said I wasn't in the same position as the Iron Duke, who was the most powerful man in England. He said he wished to remind me that I was Head of History in a comprehensive school, with a whole career at stake. He said if he went to the tabloids with what he knew about me and Wayne Briggs I'd never teach again and I might well be sent to prison for the rape of a minor. He had a bottle of wine and he'd been drinking from it. He was laughing at me, enjoying my misery. I'd never seen him like that before.'

'And how long did all this take?'

'I've no idea. Longer than it's taken me to describe it to you. Much longer, I suppose, because it was quite dark eventually and he was still flinging his filth at me. He said I'd better tell Matt about it and get the money from him, because he must be making plenty on the rigs. All I could see of Wally by this time was his mouth and his teeth. He kept laughing. I'd never seen him drink before and I'd never seen him really laugh before. It was horrible.'

'So tell us what you did about it.'

She spoke quickly, almost eagerly, as if she wished to make them understand this. 'He said he was sure Matt would be pleased to hear all the details of how I'd opened my legs to an eager young stallion who'd delighted in fucking the arse off me.' She stopped wonderingly; it was important to her to get the recital of the man's obscenities exactly right. 'I think it was a sexual thing with him: I think talking about what I'd done and painting the pictures of it excited him. He said I was a strong young woman and I must have enjoyed girls on top.'

There was a long pause. Lambert and Hook both knew that there was no need to hurry now. It was Hook who eventually prompted her. 'Do you think Wally spied on you, when you were here with Wayne?'

She glanced for the first time in many minutes at her husband, but Matt Potts sat as if turned to stone, staring steadily through the window at the innocent world outside. 'I think he must have done. He kept telling me how much he would enjoy telling Matt about what he called my "sexual athleticism" and how fast I could get my pants off, unless I came up with the money he wanted. And each time he taunted me, he laughed and took another drink.'

'So eventually you stopped him doing that.'

'Yes. I'd no intention of killing him, none at all. I just wanted to shut his filthy mouth and stop him laughing at me and taunting me about Matt. Eventually he said I could have a drink with him. He'd give me a glass and we would drink a toast to my future. When he turned away from me I grabbed the bottle and hit him on the back of the head with it. I hit him as hard as I possibly could. I only wanted to hit him the once. I just wanted to shut that filthy mouth of his. He didn't even shout or grunt. He fell on his face on the ground in front of me.'

She stopped again, staring out of the window alongside her husband, watching the Martindale boys, Nicky and Tommy, going past with their golf clubs in small bags on their shoulders, the epitome of excited childish innocence. She said like one in a trance, 'I like children, you know. I'm quite good with them: I get them to enjoy history. I don't know what I'd do if I couldn't teach.'

'Did you think he was dead?'

'I thought he might be, yes. I didn't want to touch him. I know that you should check the carotid artery, but I couldn't bring myself to touch him. Matt would have known what to do, but I didn't.' This time she didn't look at her husband, but spoke as if he wasn't there.

It was left to Hook to prod her forward. 'But you knew where there was some rope.'

'Yes. In the boatshed which was almost beside us. I think that it was because Wally had talked about Wayne and me in there that I got the idea. I thought if I could throw the rope over the branch of the oak tree and make a noose, people might think he'd hanged himself. I can see now that that was never going to work, but I couldn't think straight then. I just kept staring down at the blood seeping from the back of his head. Matt would have done something much better, but I didn't want him involved. I put the noose I'd made round Wally's neck as he lay on the ground, then hauled him up and fastened the rope around the tree. It was easy. He didn't weigh more than a child. And I'm a strong, fit woman – an athlete, as Wally had said.'

She gave a strange sound which was almost a giggle, then sat straight-backed, composing herself like a self-conscious schoolgirl. 'I managed to do the whole thing without looking at his face. I didn't want to see Wally's face ever again. I had the crazy idea that he might still be laughing at me.'

They put her in the back of the waiting police car, handcuffed to a female officer in uniform. She turned to Lambert and Hook as soon as she was seated and repeated her words: 'It wasn't Matt. He would have done something much better, you know.'

Then she looked straight ahead and sat fiercely upright as she was driven away.